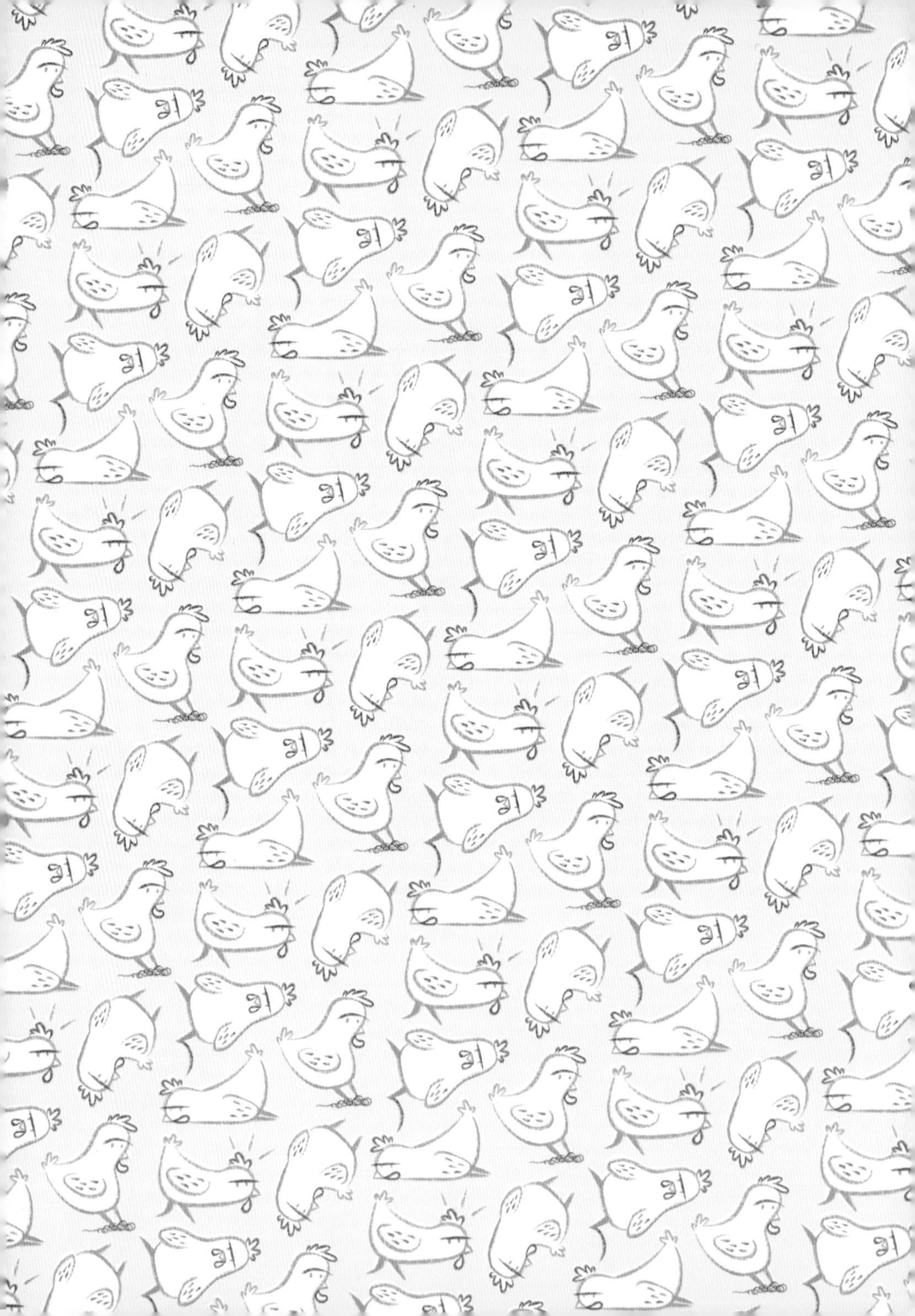

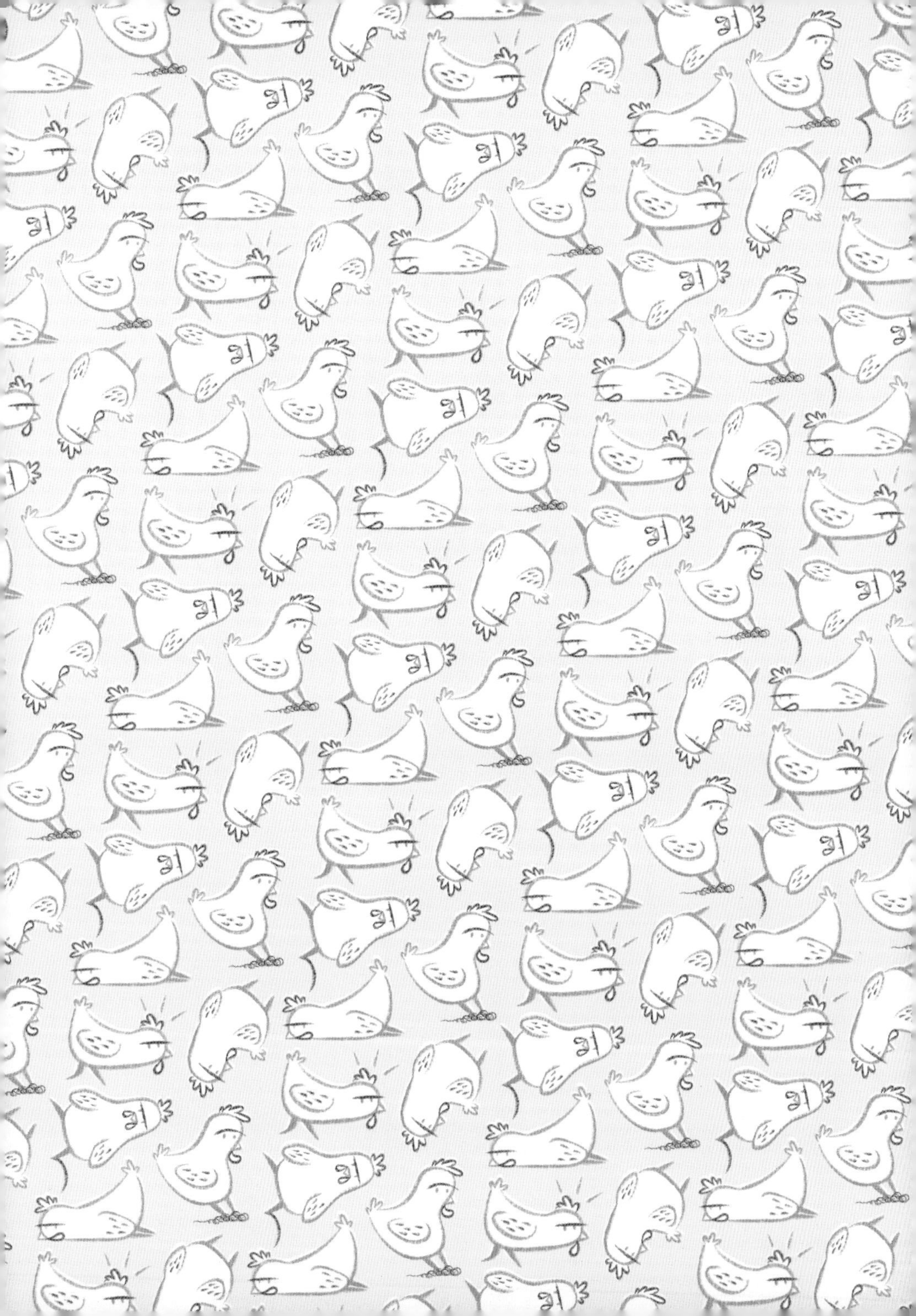

CRANKY CHICKEN

QUEEN
OF
CRANK

KATHERINE BATTERSBY

MARGARET K. McELDERRY BOOKS

NEW YORK   LONDON   TORONTO   SYDNEY   NEW DELHI

For Niamh and Scott,
siblings who both inspired
and weathered my crankiness

V50

MARGARET K. McELDERRY BOOKS
An imprint of Simon & Schuster Children's Publishing Division
1230 Avenue of the Americas, New York, New York 10020
© 2021 by Katherine Battersby
Book design by Rebecca Syracuse © 2021 by Simon & Schuster, Inc.
For information about special discounts for bulk purchases, please contact Simon & Schuster Special
Sales at 1-866-506-1949 or business@simonandschuster.com.
The Simon & Schuster Speakers Bureau can bring authors to your live event. For more
information or to book an event, contact the Simon & Schuster Speakers Bureau at
1-866-248-3049 or visit our website at www.simonspeakers.com.
The illustrations in this book were rendered digitally using
custom chalk, pastel, and watercolor brushes.
Manufactured in China
0422 SCP
First Margaret K. McElderry Books paperback edition
1 2 3 4 5 6 7 8 9 10
Library of Congress Cataloging-in-Publication Data
Names: Battersby, Katherine, author, illustrator.
Title: Cranky Chicken / Katherine Battersby.
Description: First edition. |
New York : Margaret K. McElderry Books, [2021] | Audience: Ages
6–9. | Audience: Grades 2–3. |
Summary: Cranky Chicken inadvertently saves the life of Speedy, a
very optimistic worm that is looking for a friend.
Identifiers: LCCN 2020051768 (print) | LCCN 2020051769 (ebook) |
ISBN 9781534469884 (hardcover) | ISBN 9781534469907 (ebook) | ISBN
9781534469891 (paperback)
Subjects: CYAC: Chickens—Fiction. | Worms—Fiction. | Friendship—Fiction. | Mood (Psychology)—Fiction.
Classification: LCC PZ7.B324376 Cr 2021 (print) | LCC PZ7.B324376 (ebook) | DDC [E]—dc23
LC record available at https://lccn.loc.gov/2020051768
LC ebook record available at https://lccn.loc.gov/2020051769

We acknowledge the support of the Canada Council for the Arts.

Conseil des arts   Canada Council
du Canada   for the Arts

CONTENTS

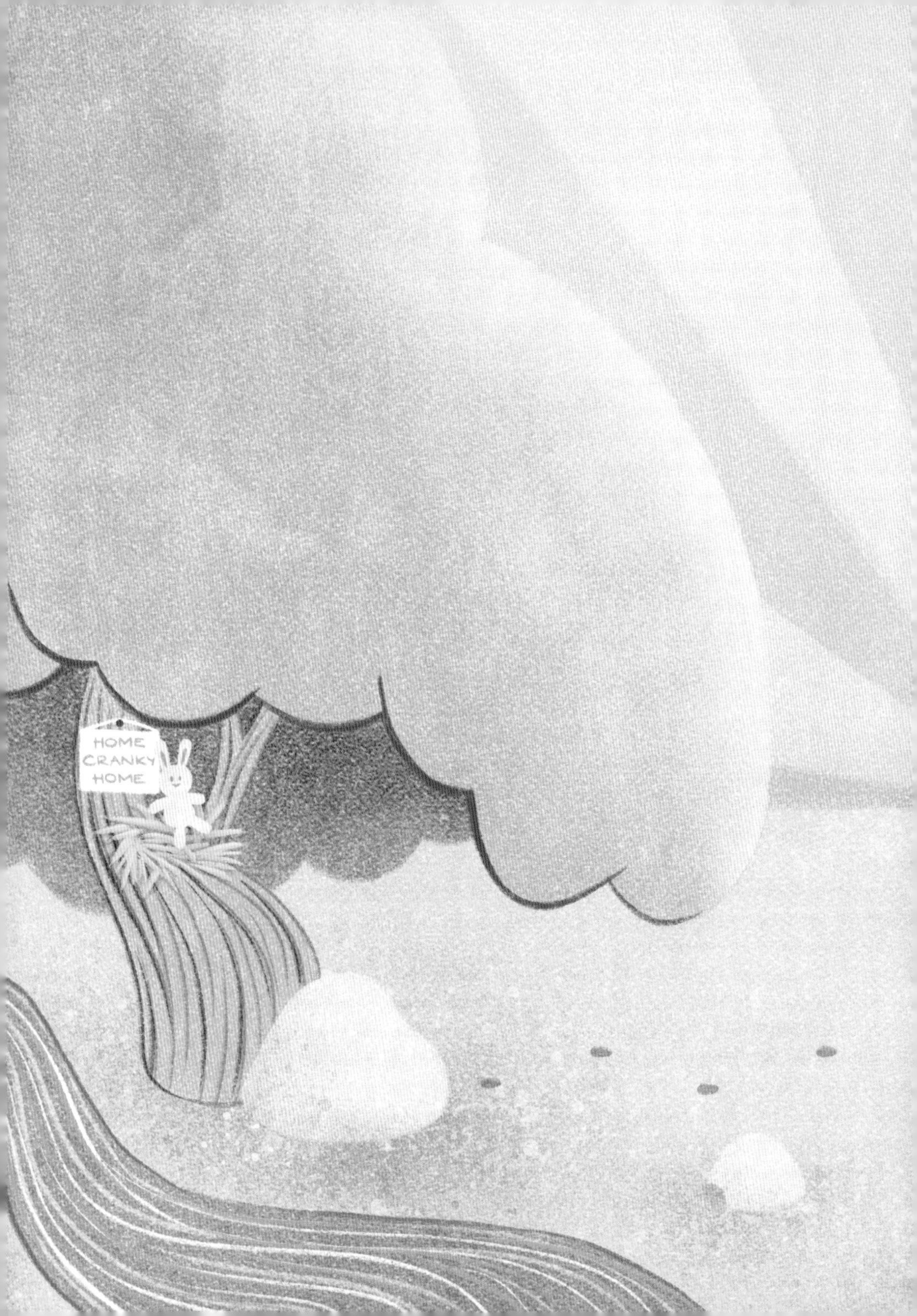
HOME
CRANKY
HOME

① SUPER CRANKY CHICKEN

Look at that.

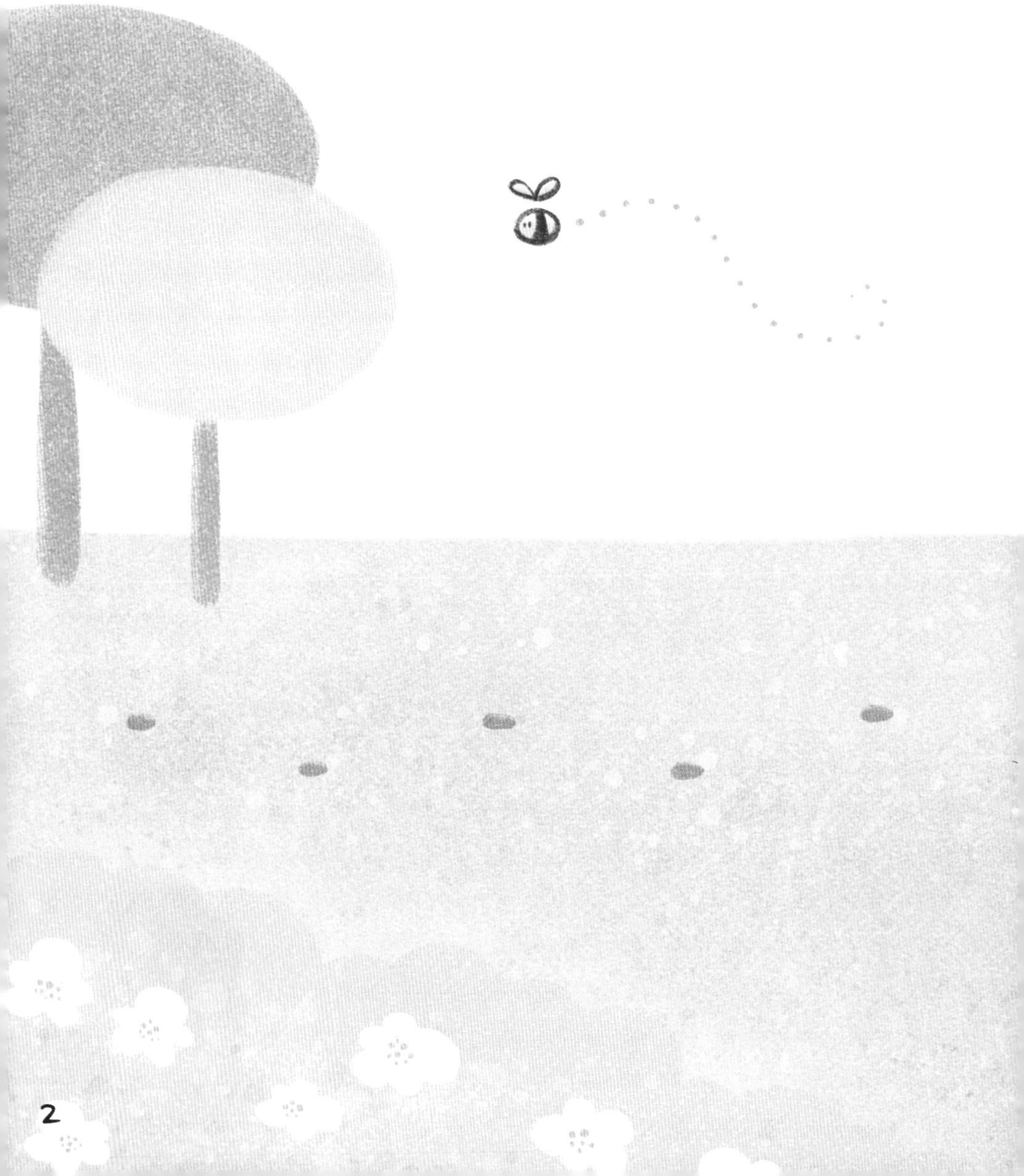

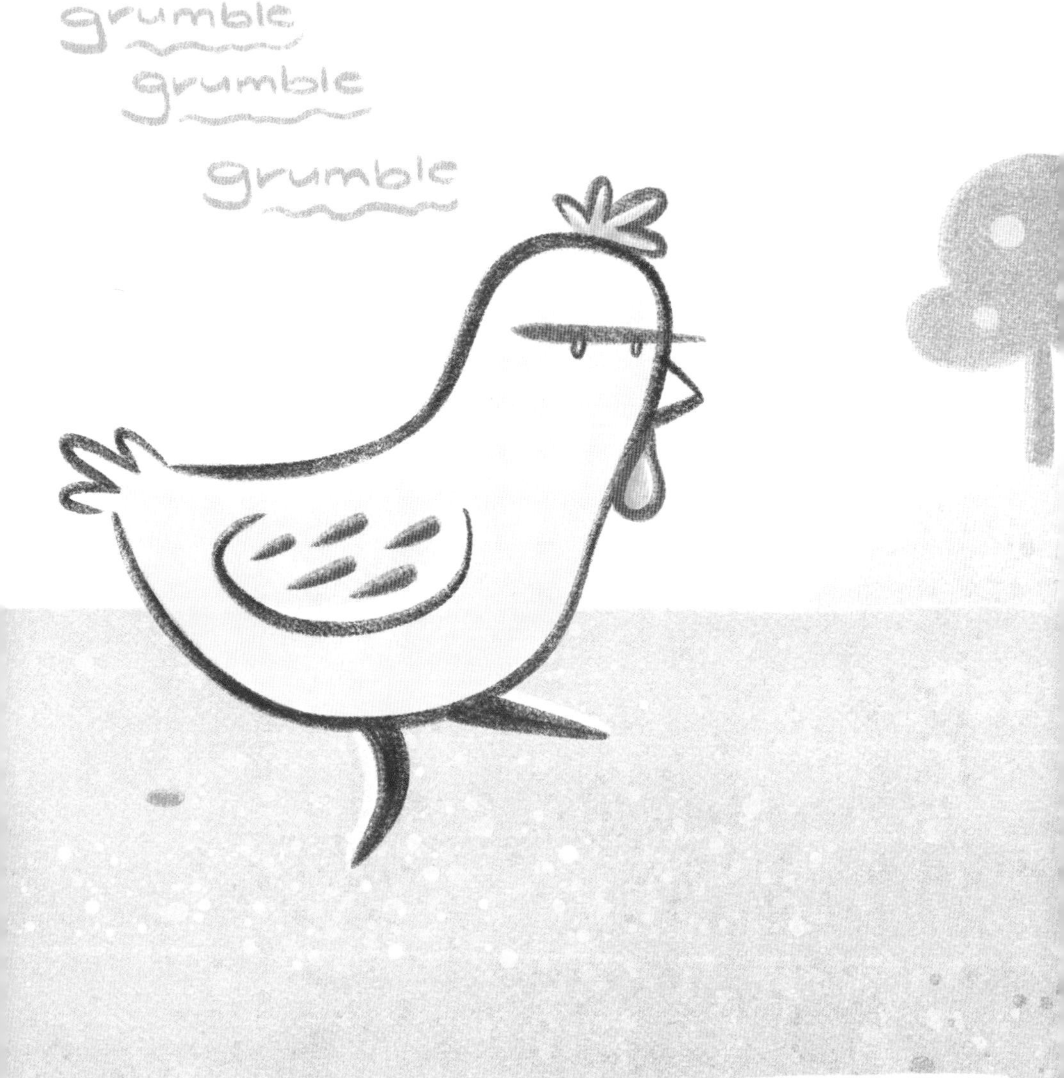
grumble
grumble
grumble

That is one cranky chicken.

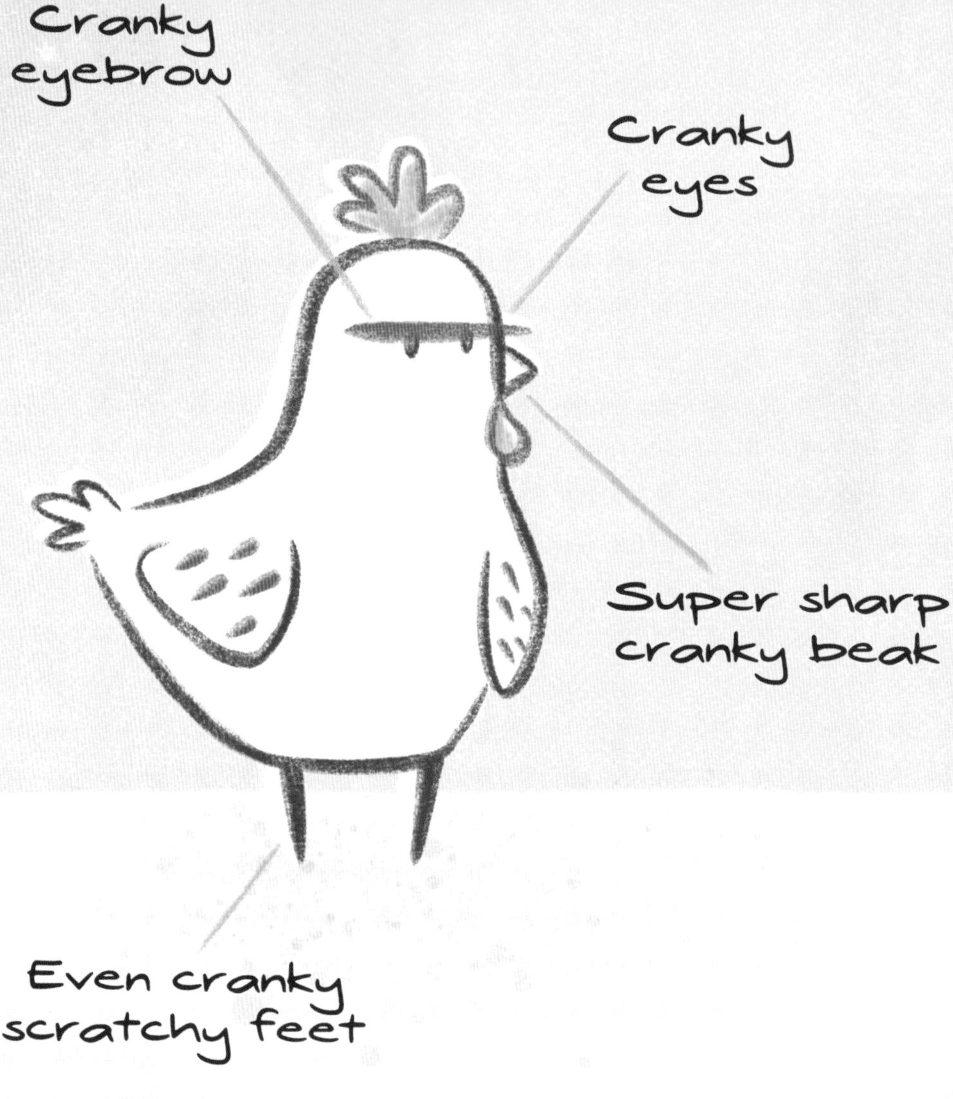
Cranky eyebrow
Cranky eyes
Super sharp cranky beak
Even cranky scratchy feet

That's a lot of crank
for one small bird.

What could make this chicken so cranky?

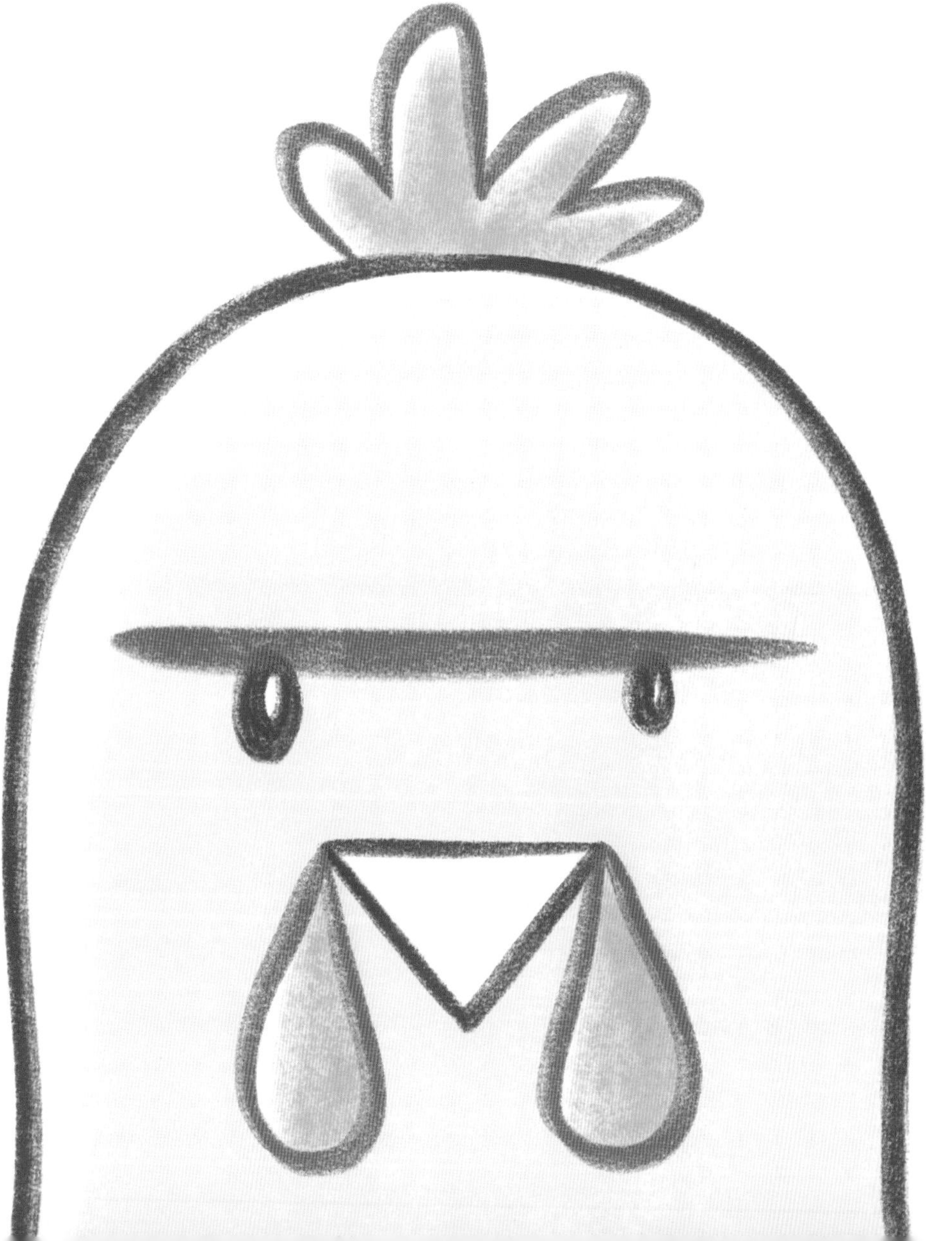

EVERYTHING.

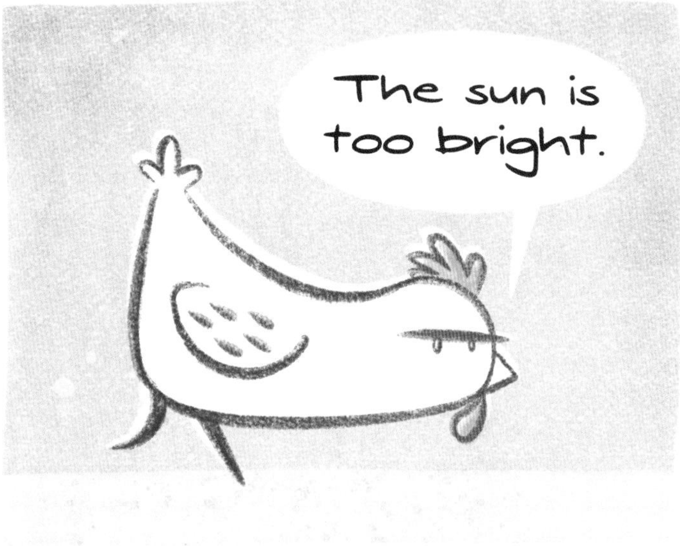
The sun is too bright.

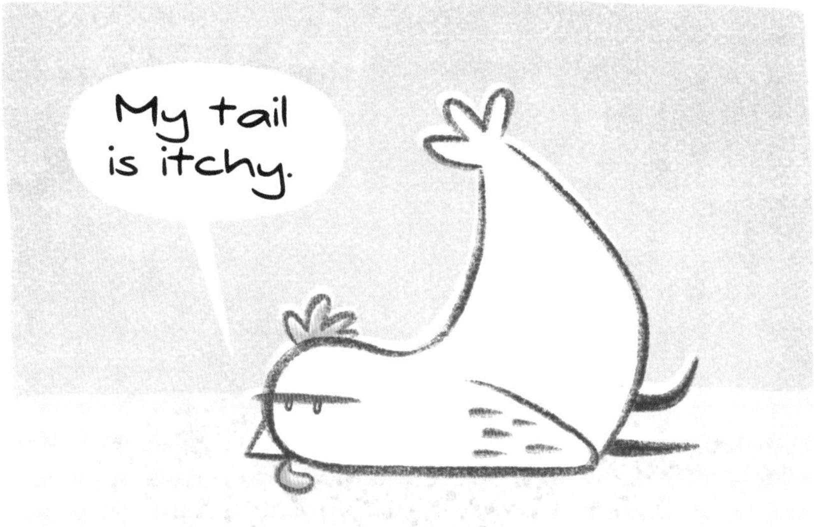
My tail is itchy.

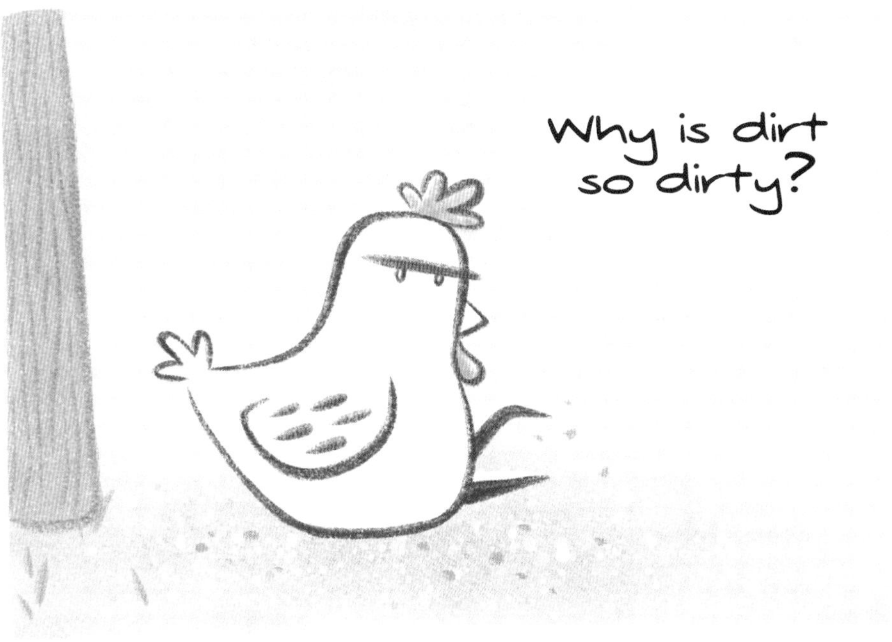
Why is dirt
so dirty?

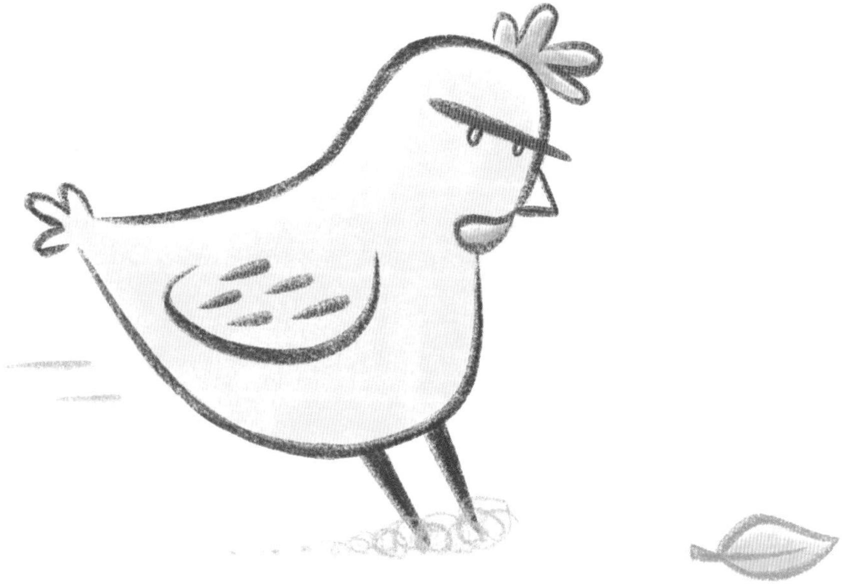

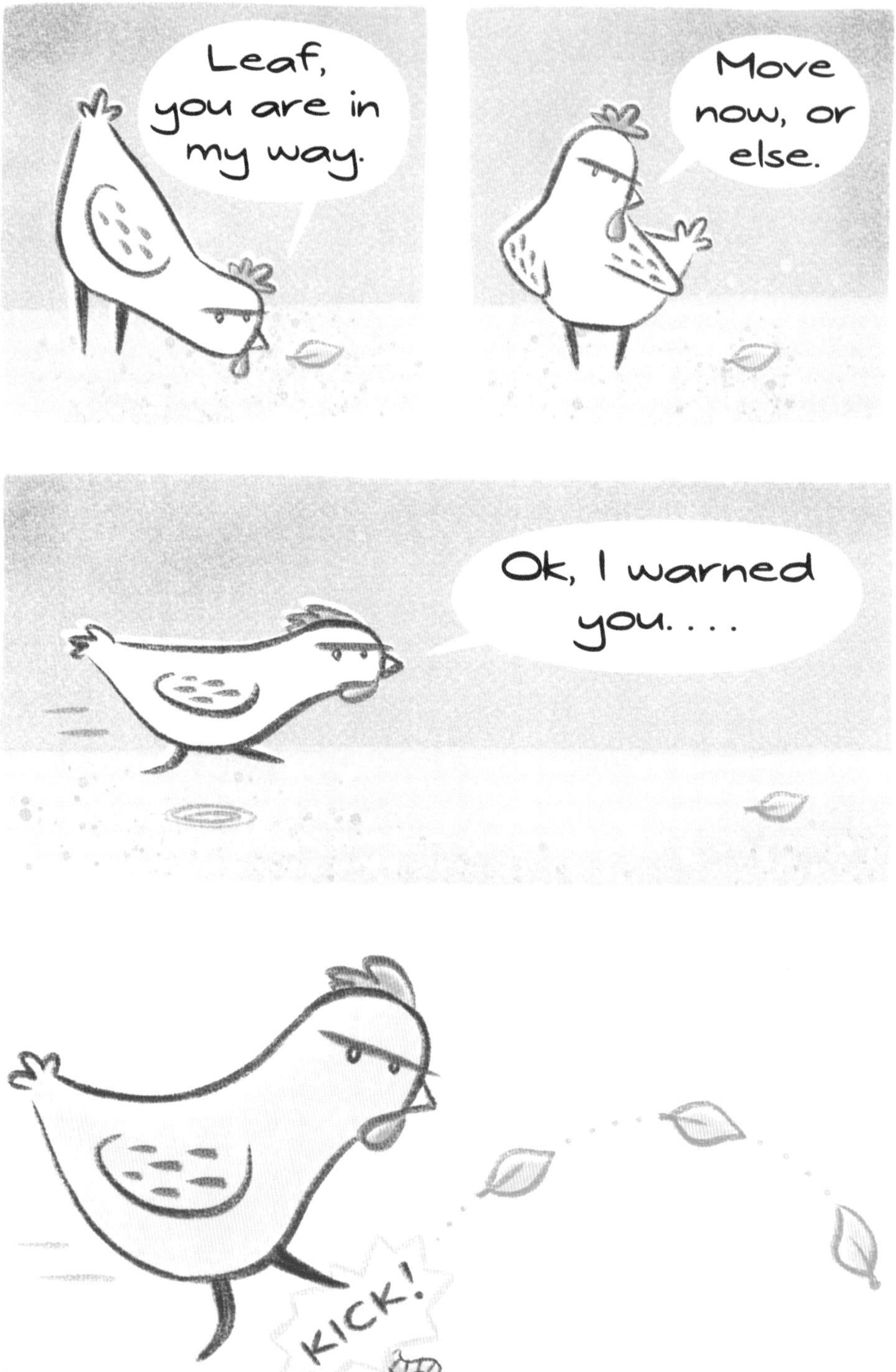
Leaf, you are in my way.
Move now, or else.
Ok, I warned you. . . .
KICK!

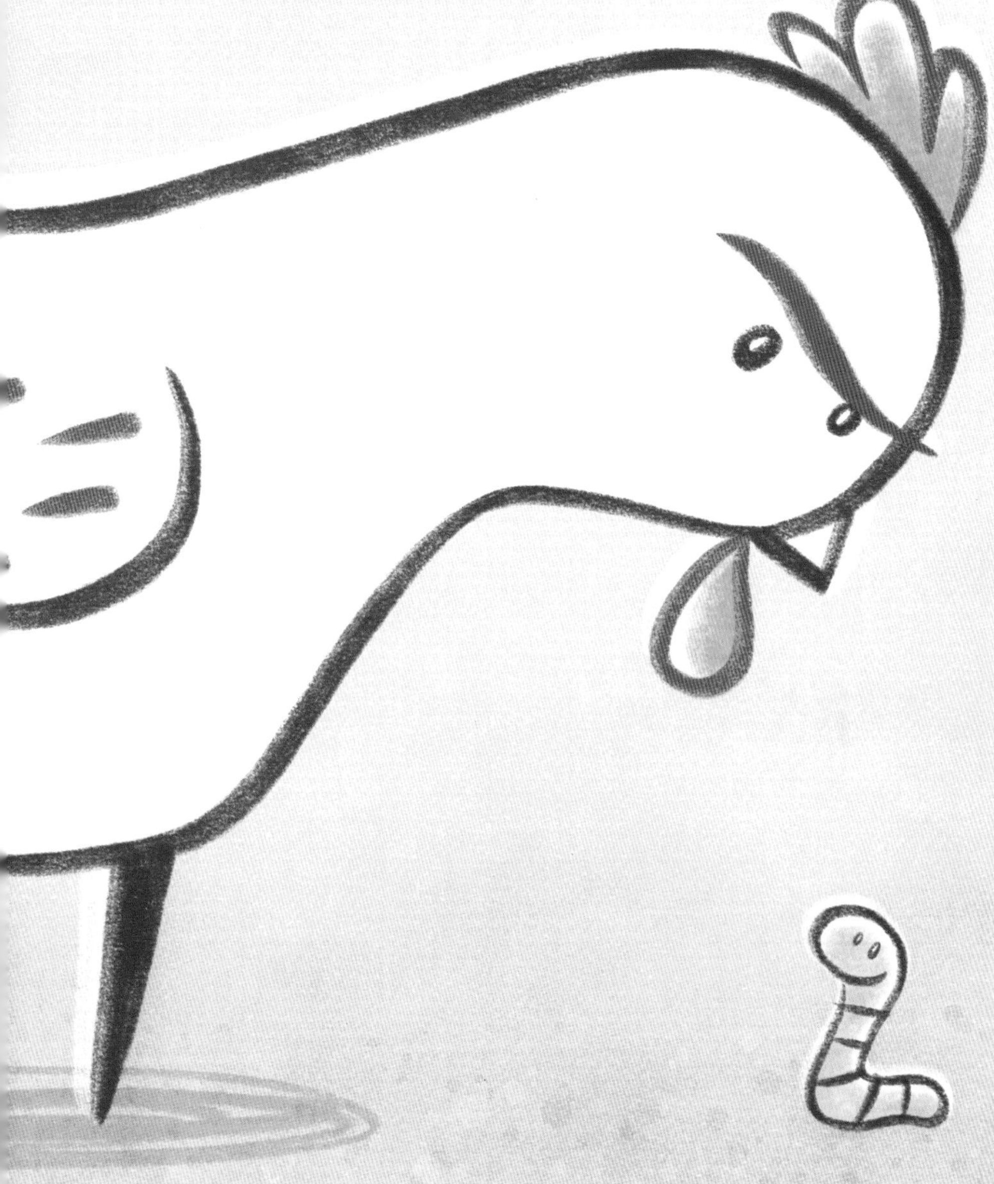

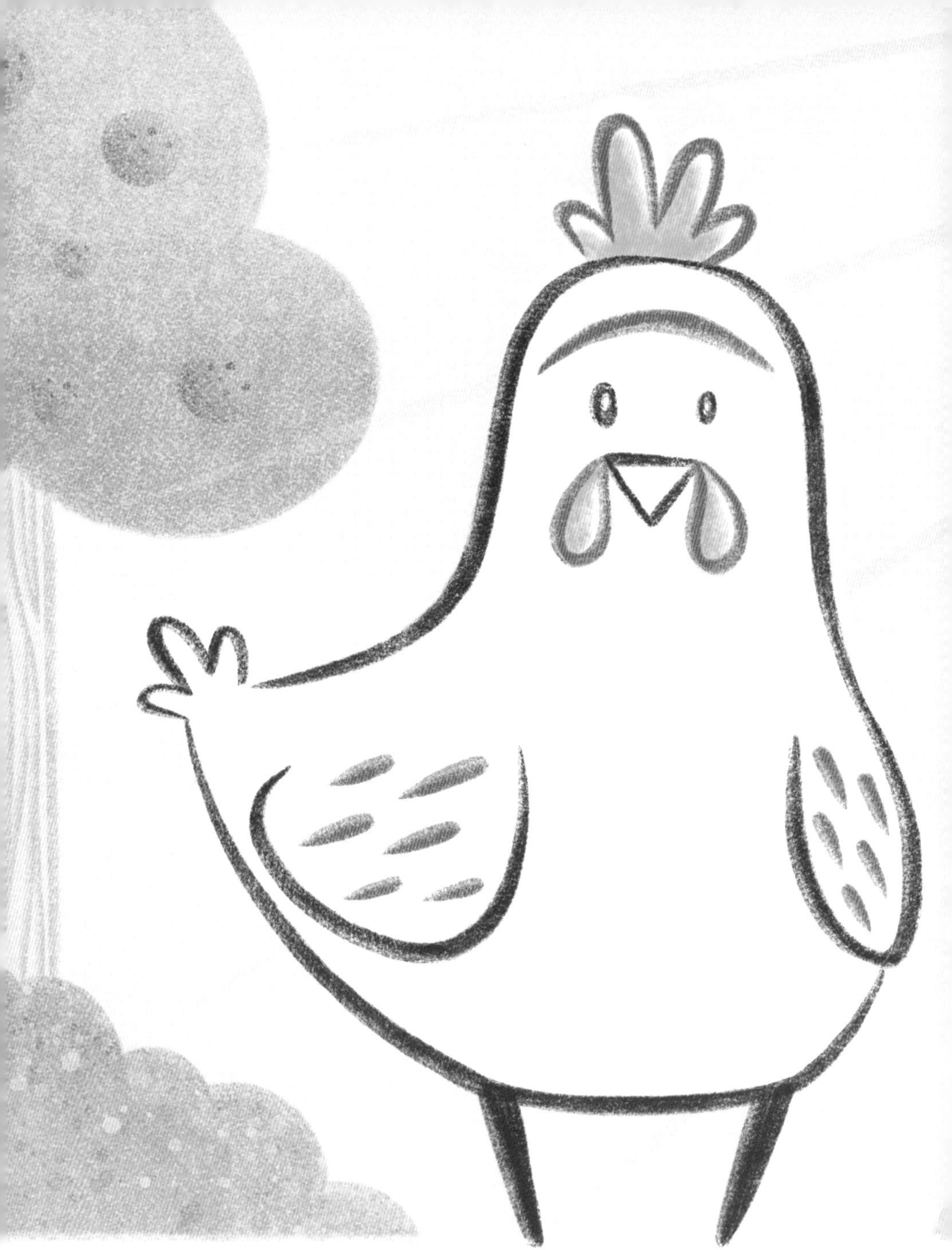

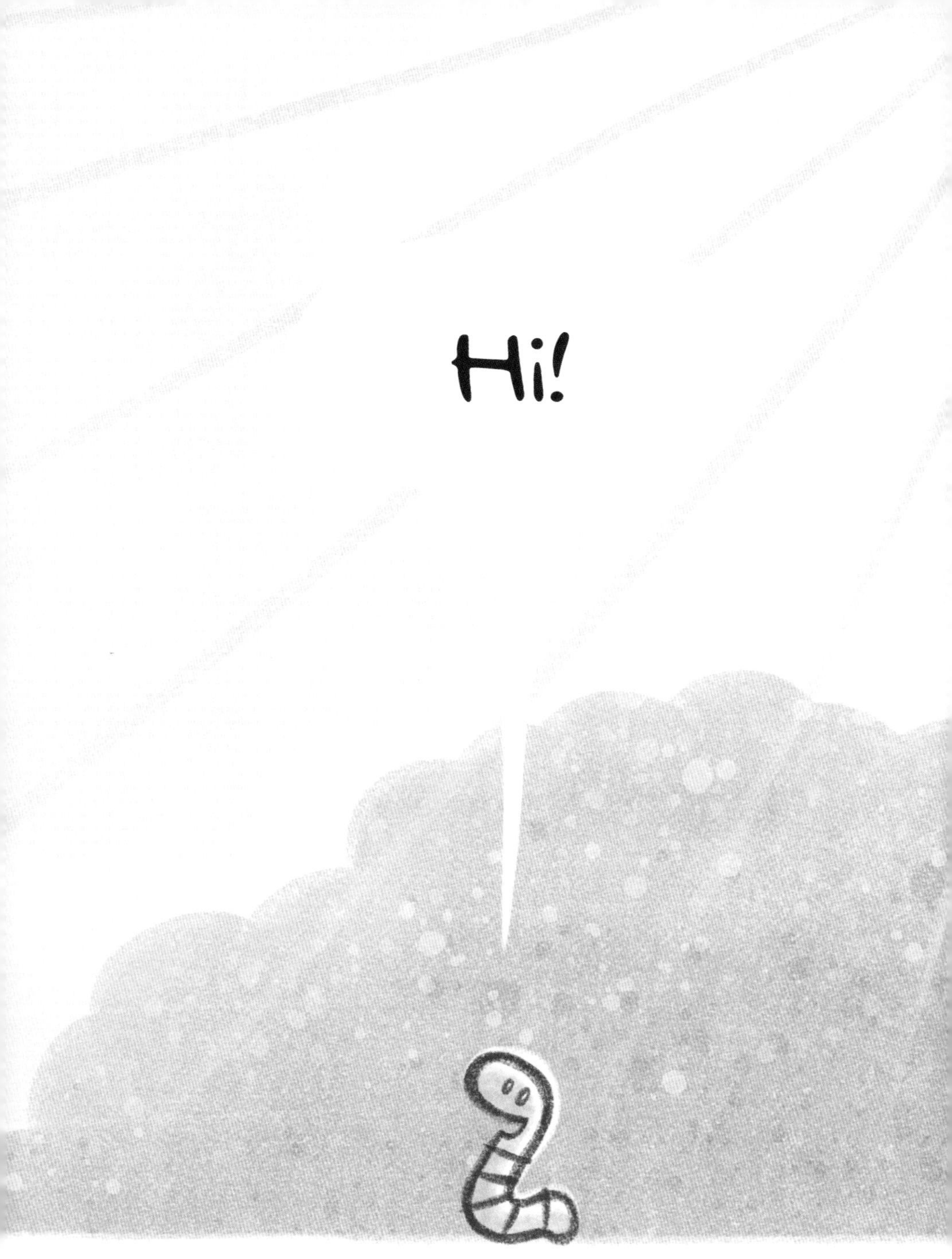
Hi!

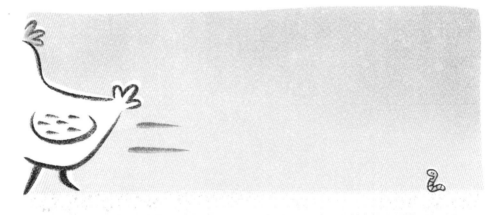

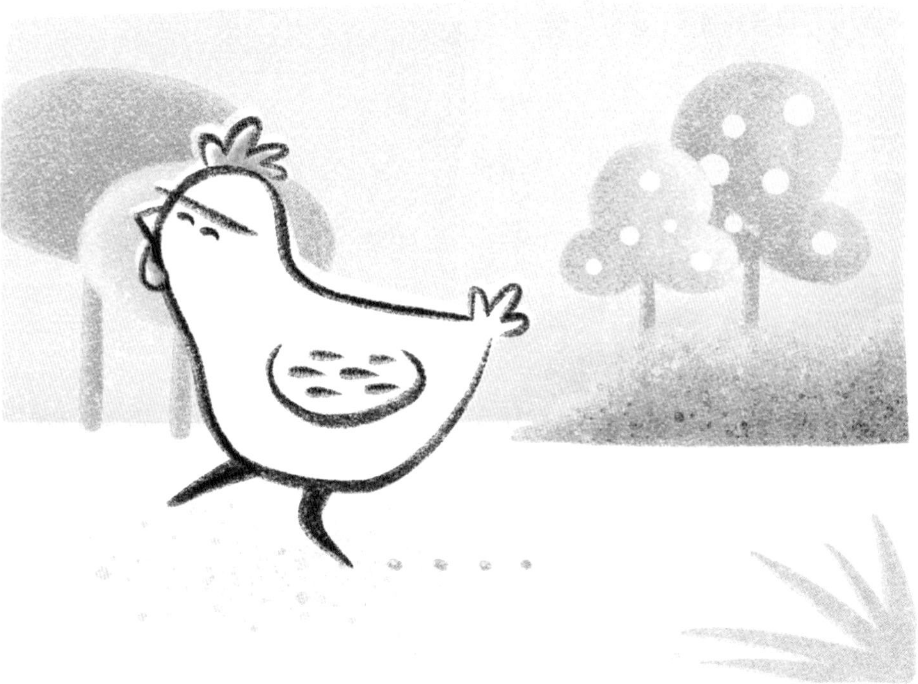

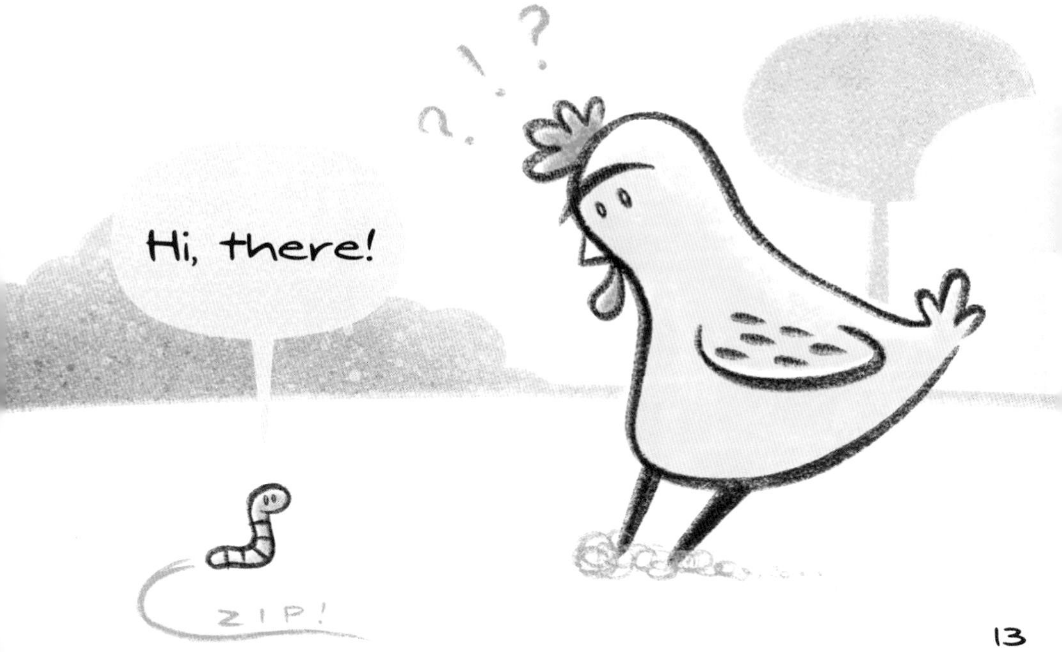
Hi, there!
ZIP!

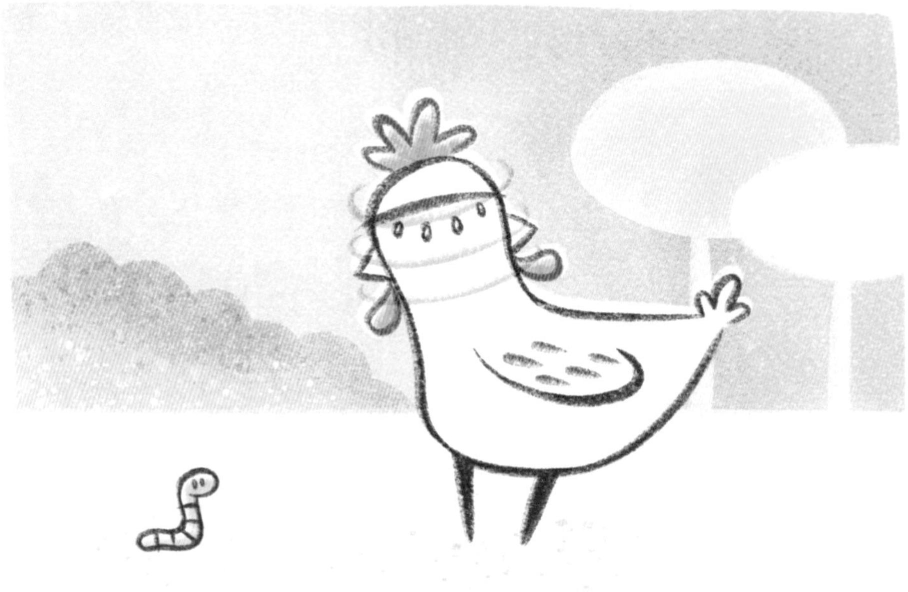

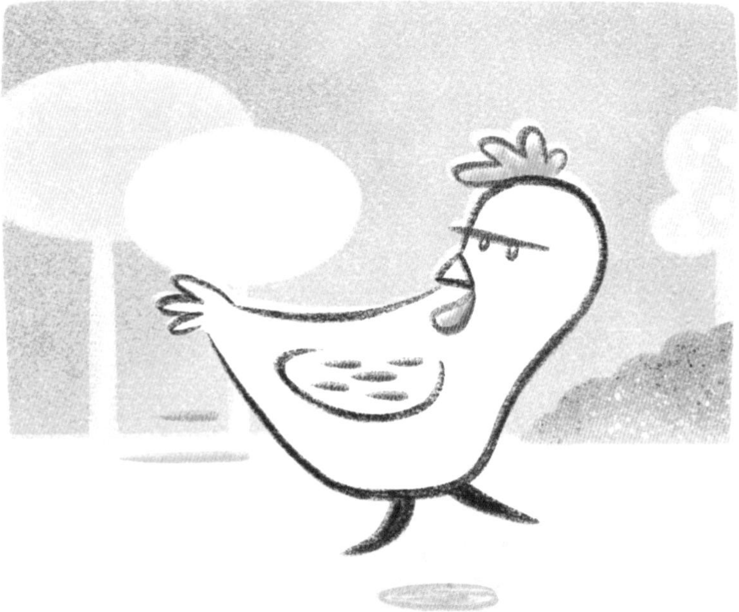

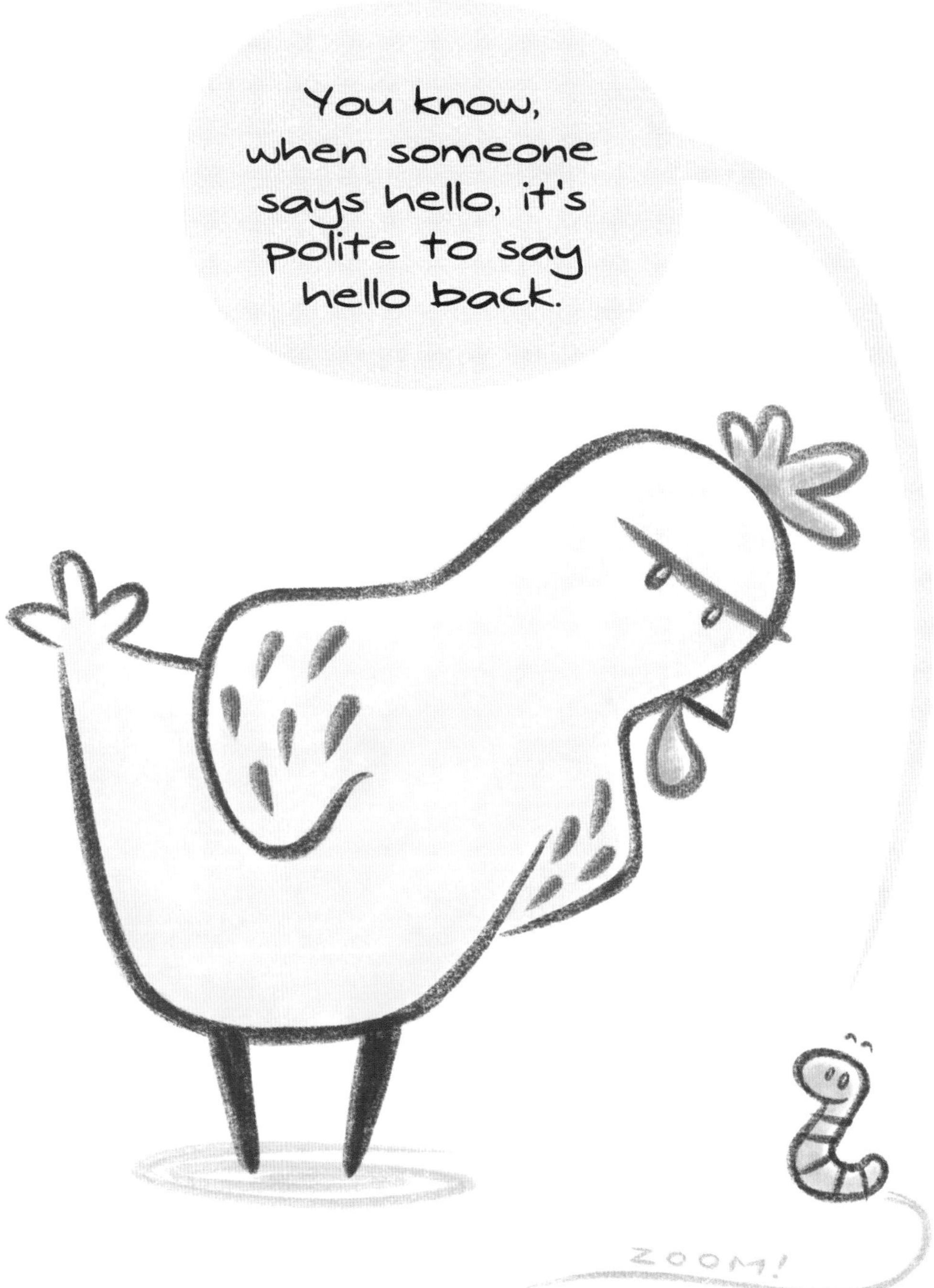
You know, when someone says hello, it's polite to say hello back.
ZOOM!

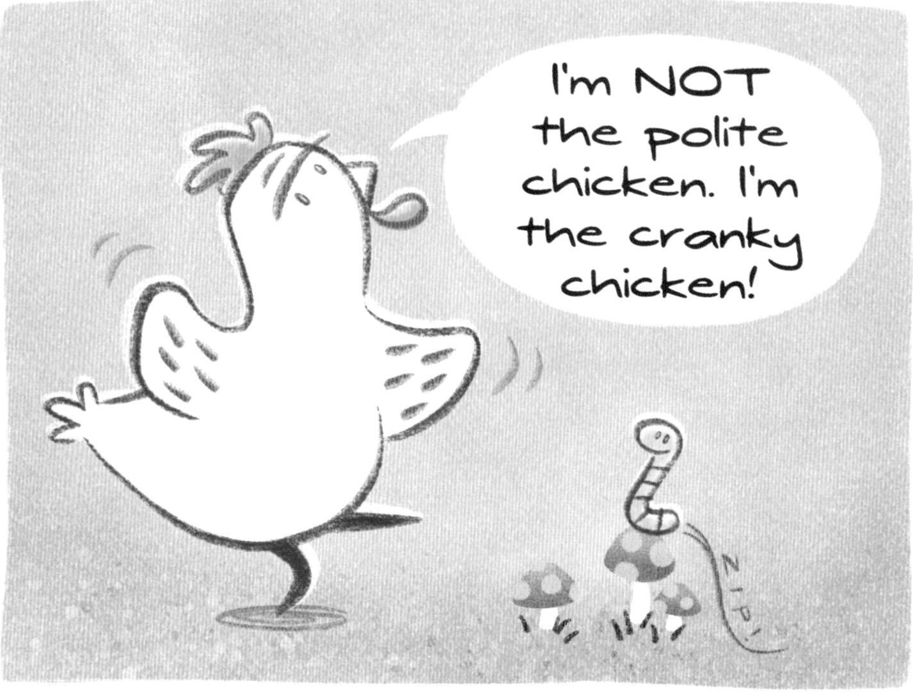
I'm NOT the polite chicken. I'm the cranky chicken!
ZIP!

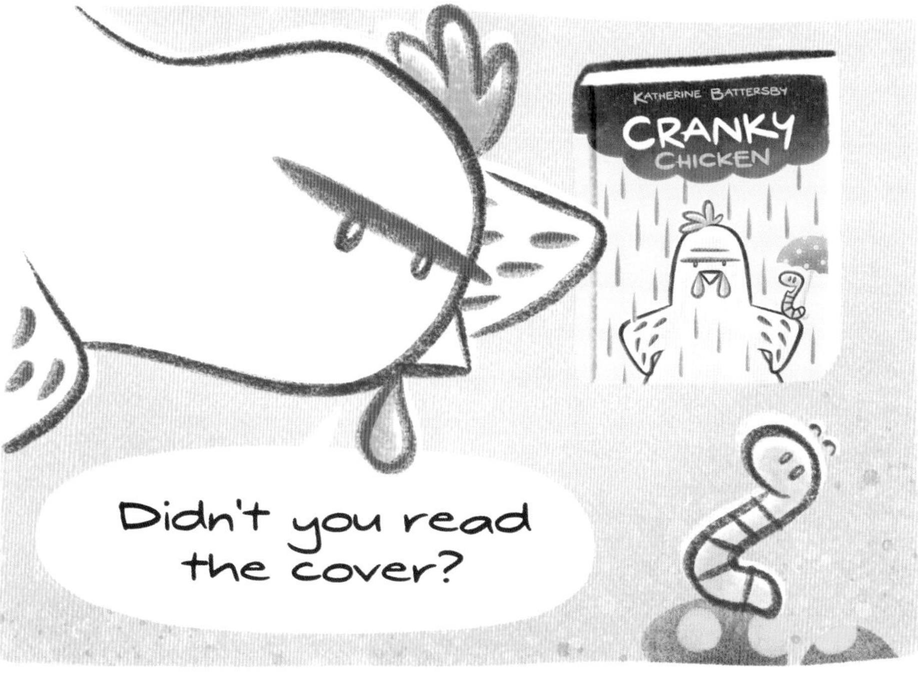
KATHERINE BATTERSBY
CRANKY CHICKEN
Didn't you read the cover?

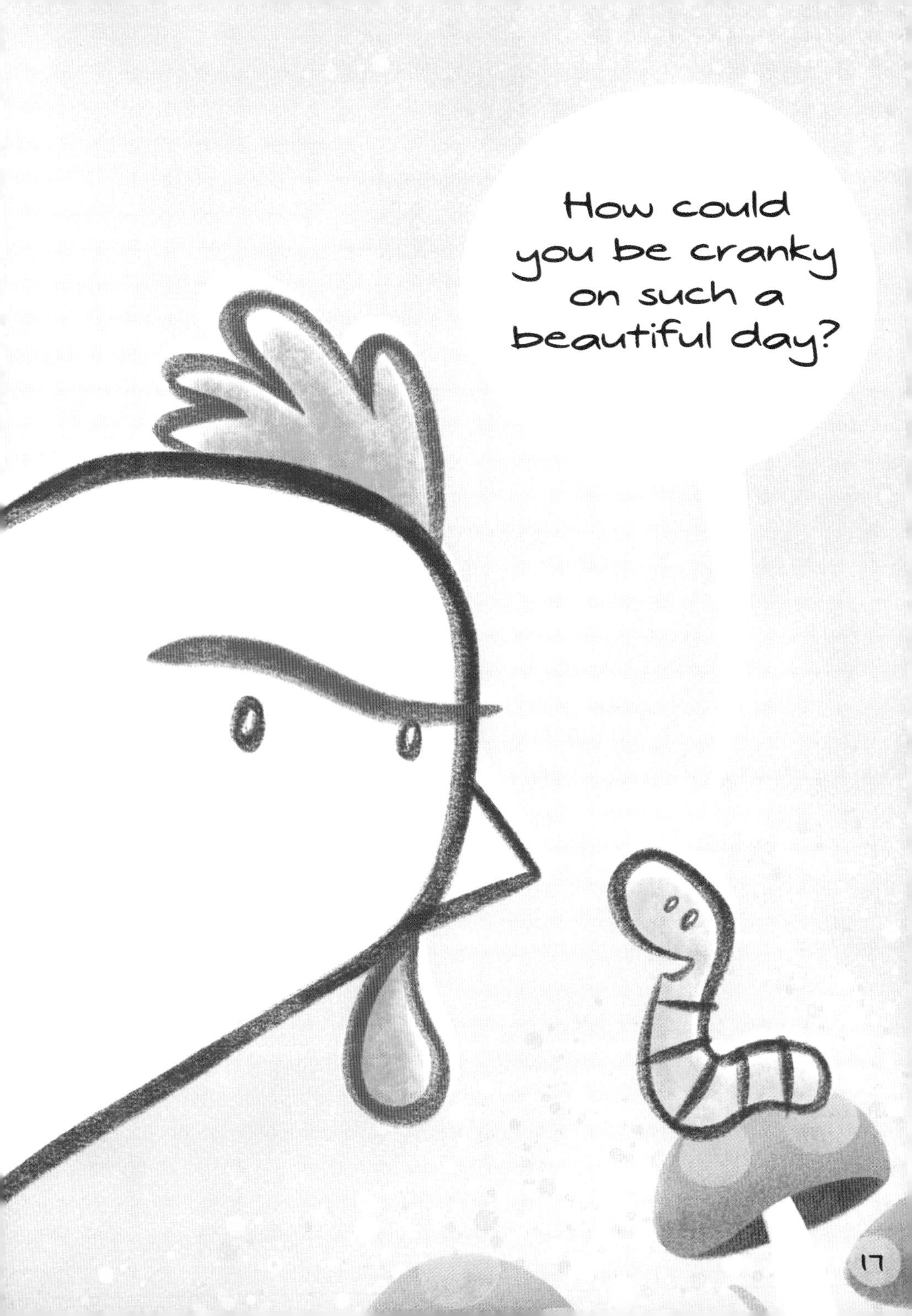
How could you be cranky on such a beautiful day?

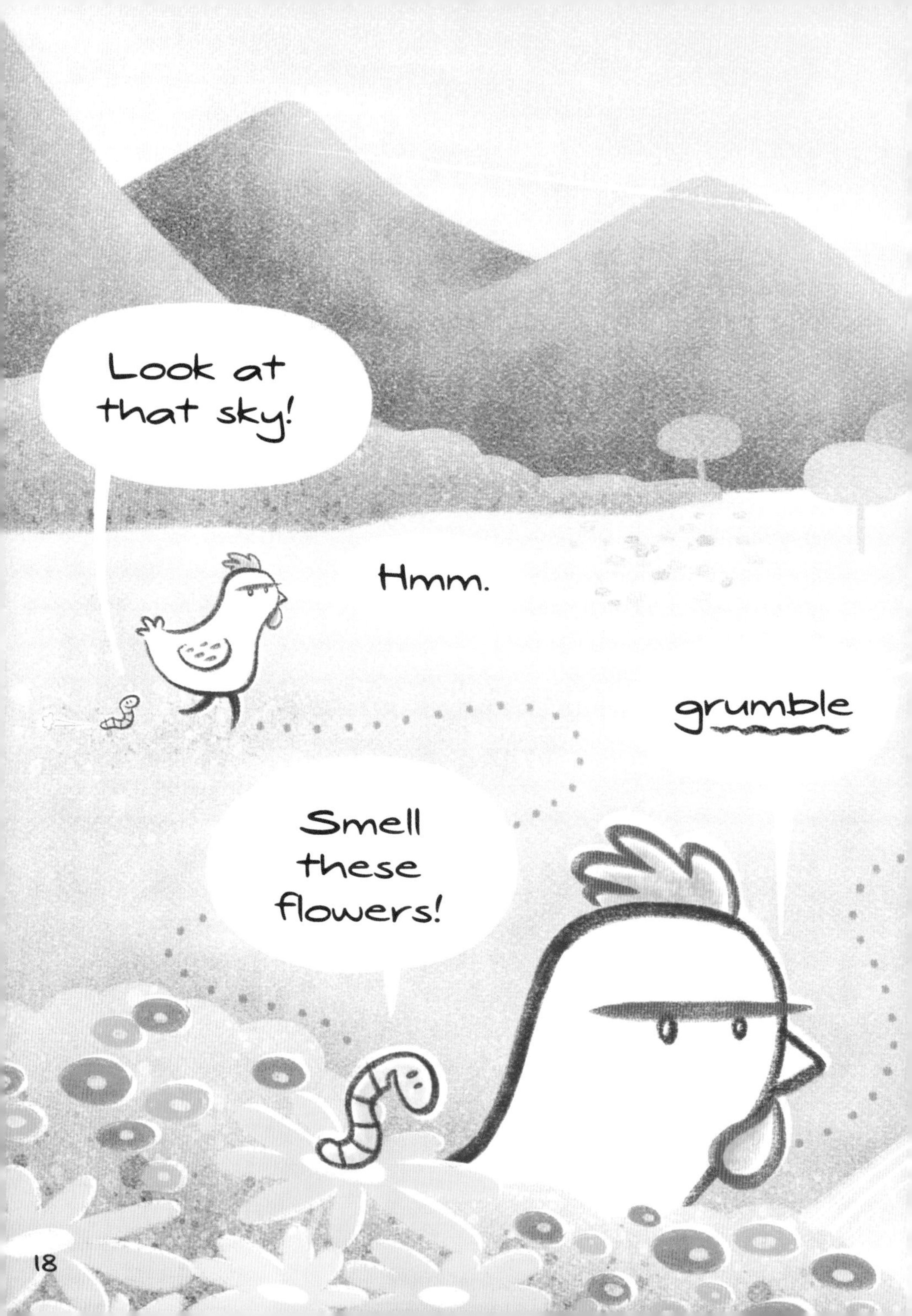
Look at that sky!
Hmm.
grumble
Smell these flowers!

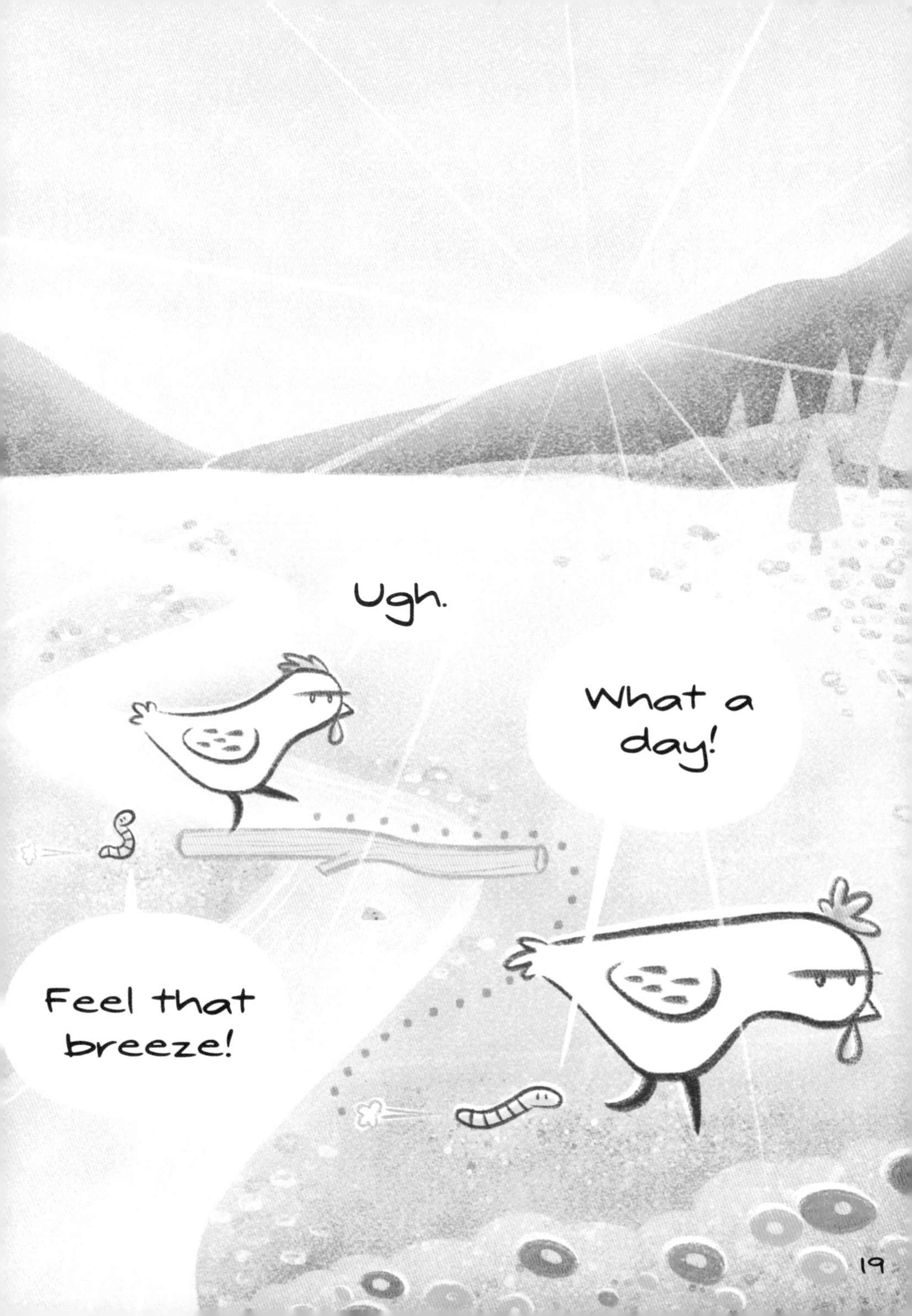
Ugh.
What a day!
Feel that breeze!

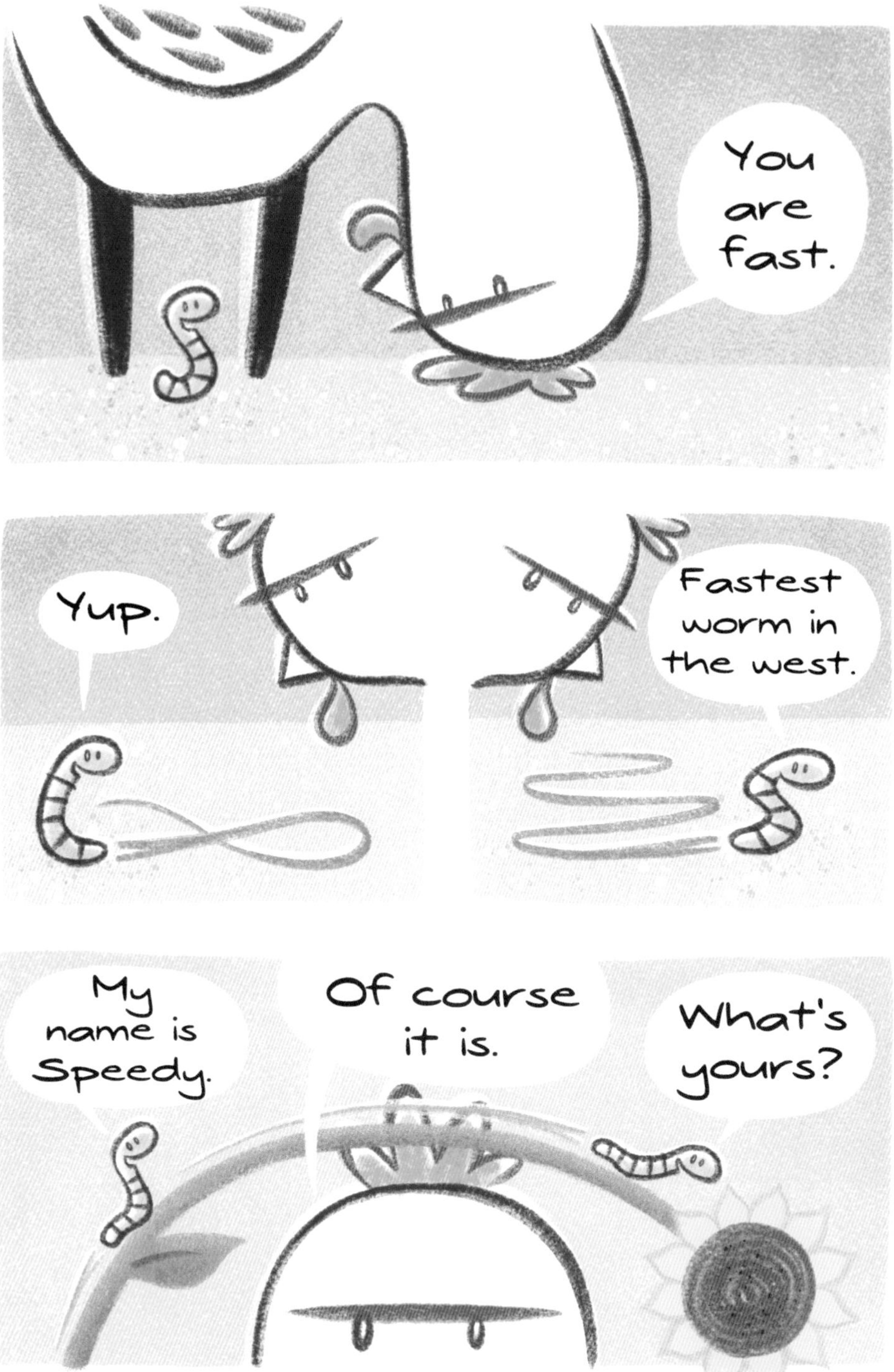
You are fast.
Yup.
Fastest worm in the west.
My name is Speedy.
Of course it is.
What's yours?

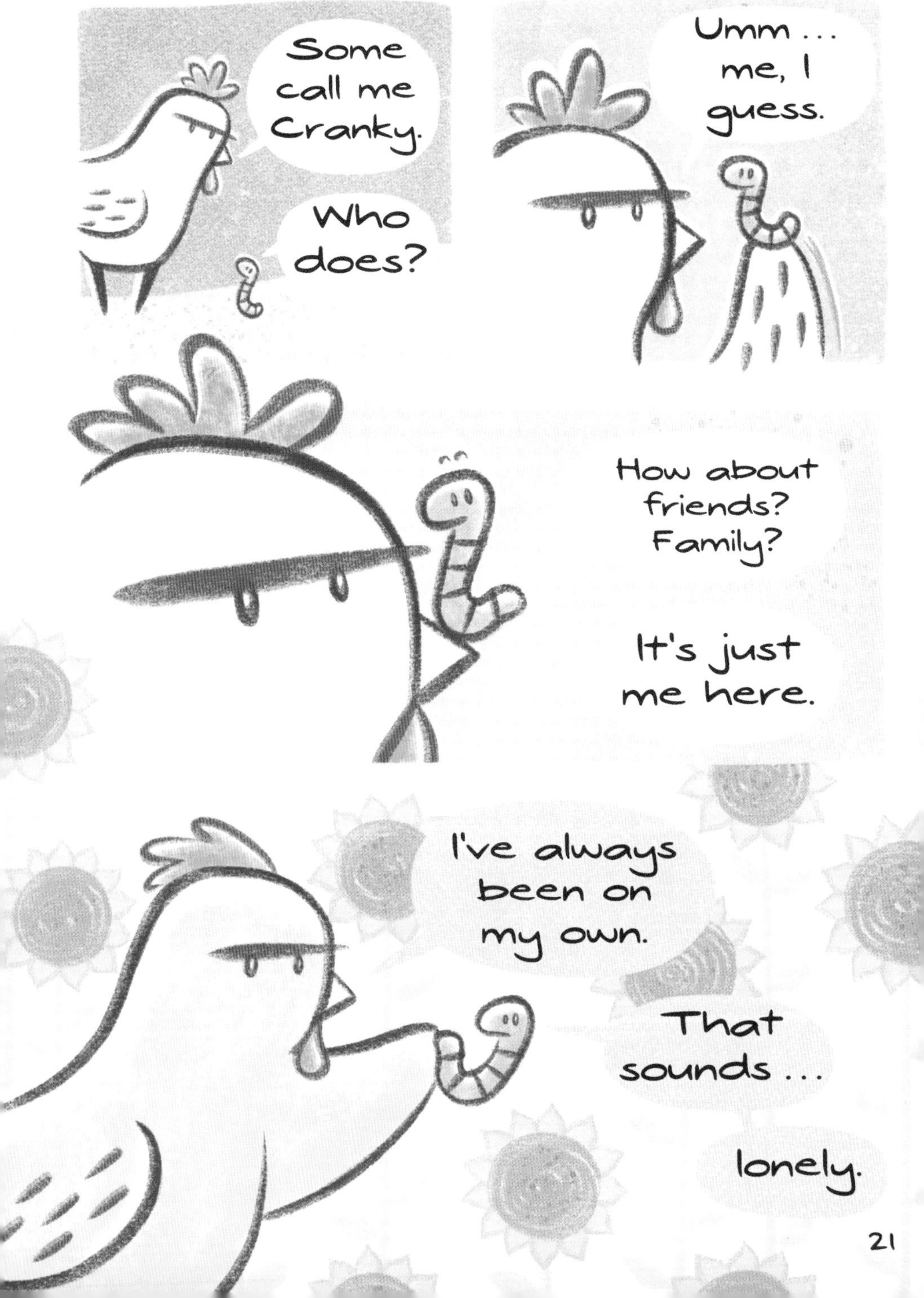
Some call me Cranky.
Who does?
Umm . . . me, I guess.
How about friends? Family?
It's just me here.
I've always been on my own.
That sounds . . .
lonely.

LONELY?

Do I <u>look</u> lonely!?

Would a lonely chicken be so well adjusted??

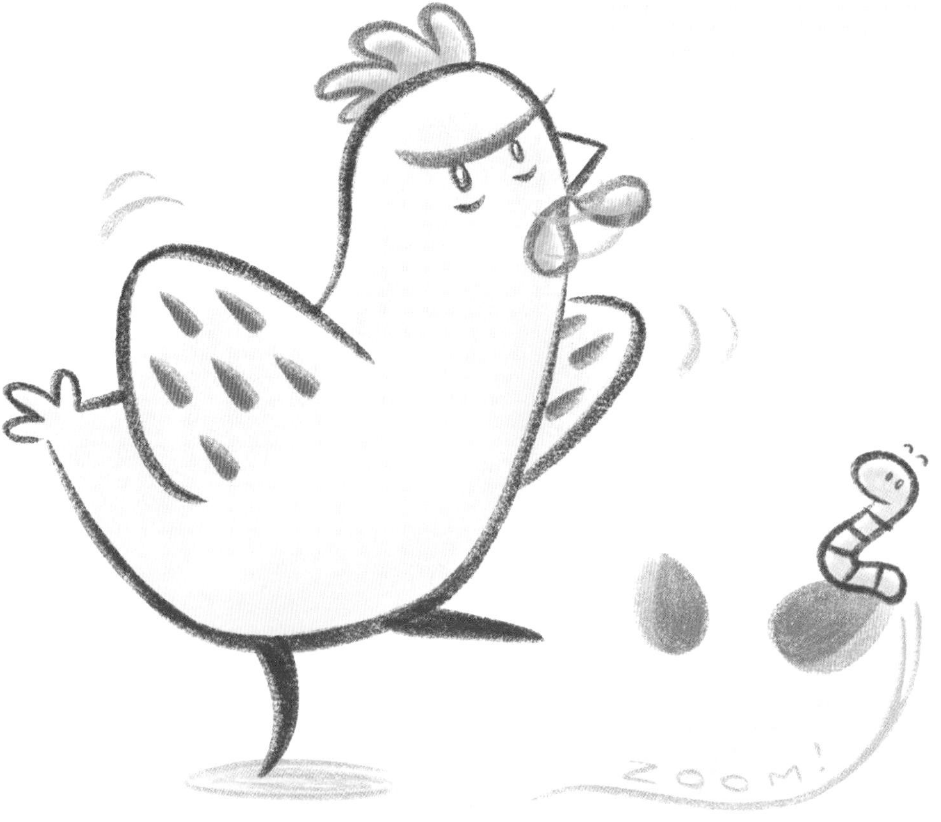
ZOOM!

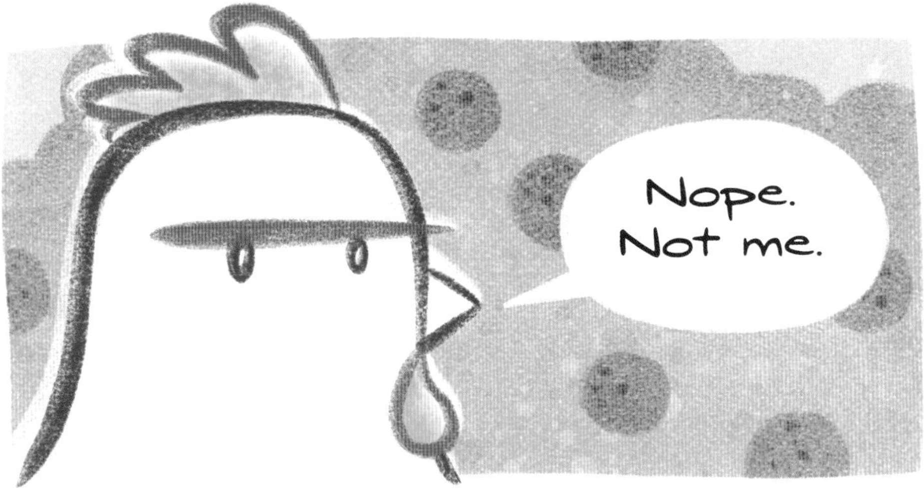
Nope.
Not me.

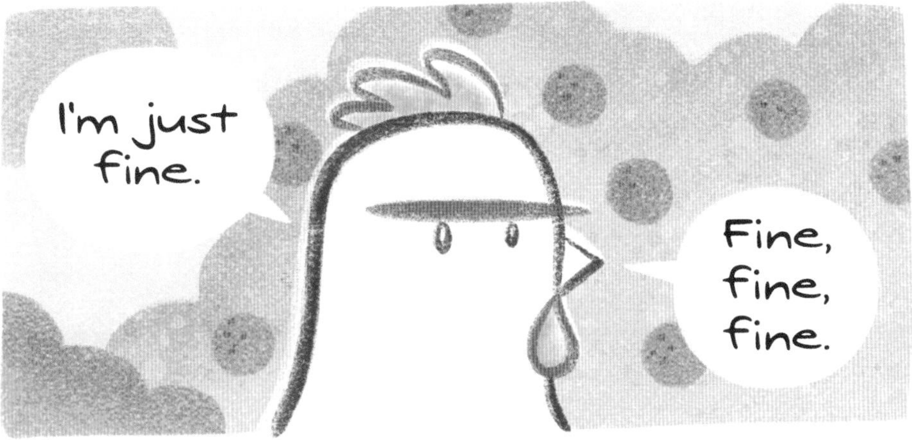
I'm just
fine.
Fine,
fine,
fine.

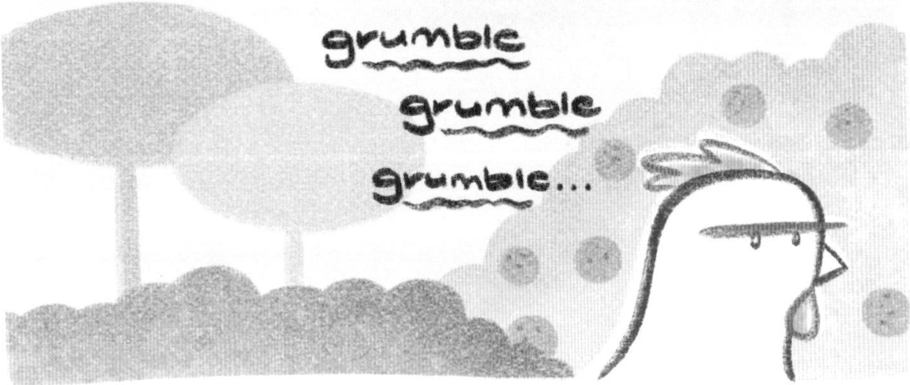
grumble
grumble
grumble...

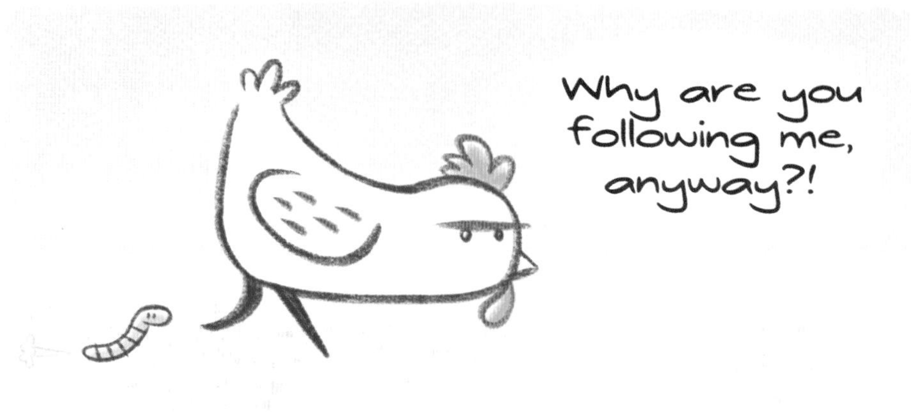
Why are you following me, anyway?!

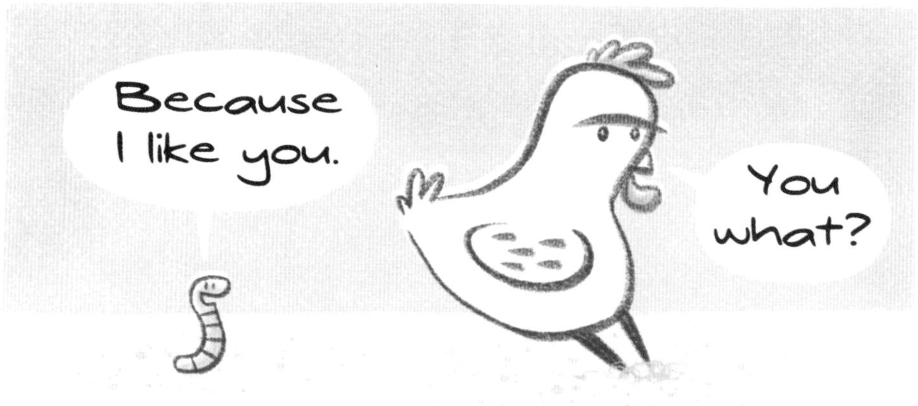
Because I like you.
You what?

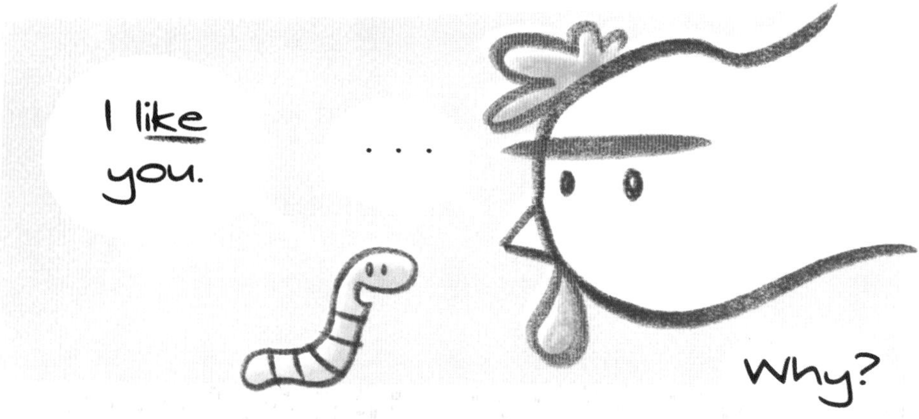
I like you.
. . .
Why?

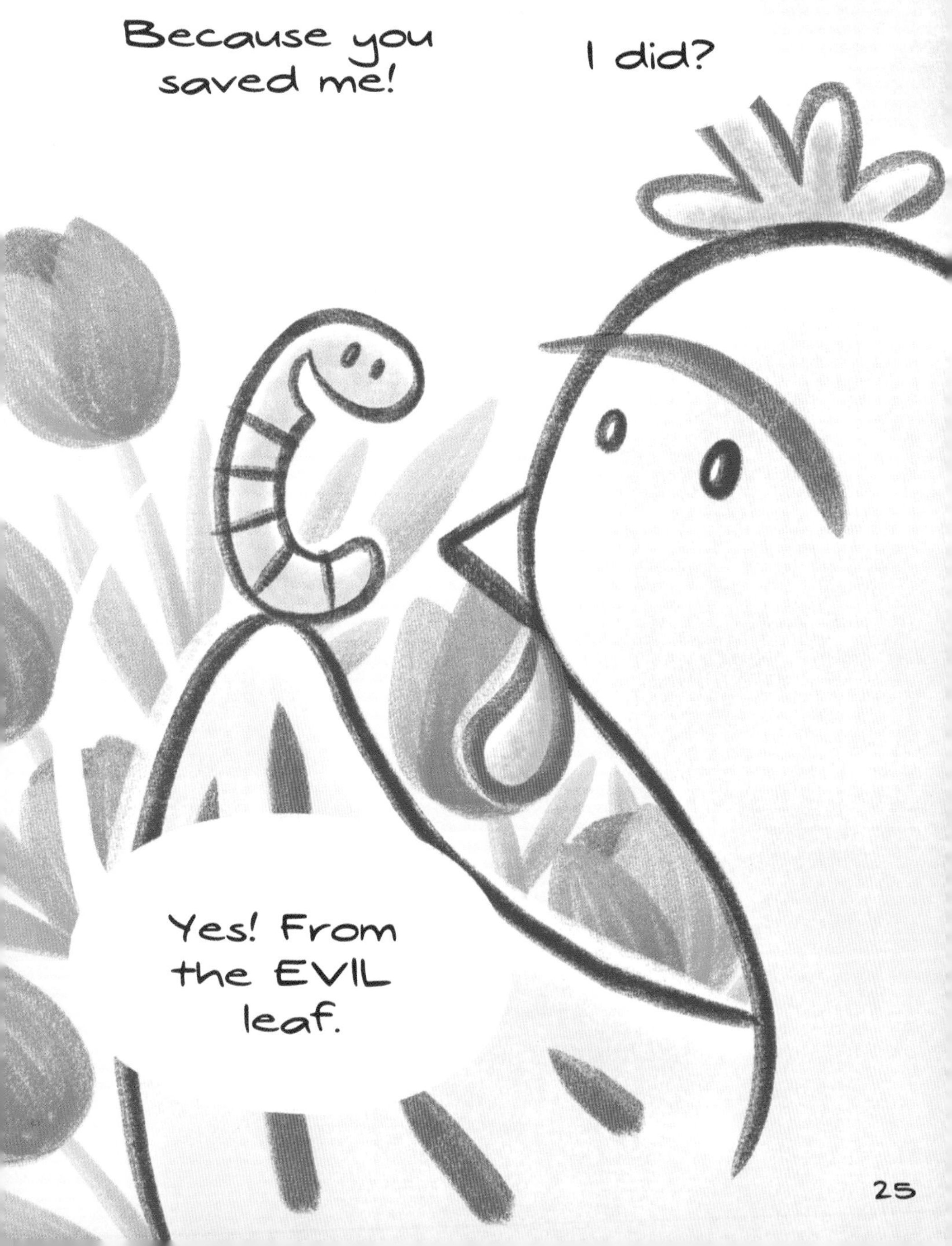
Because you saved me!
I did?
Yes! From the EVIL leaf.

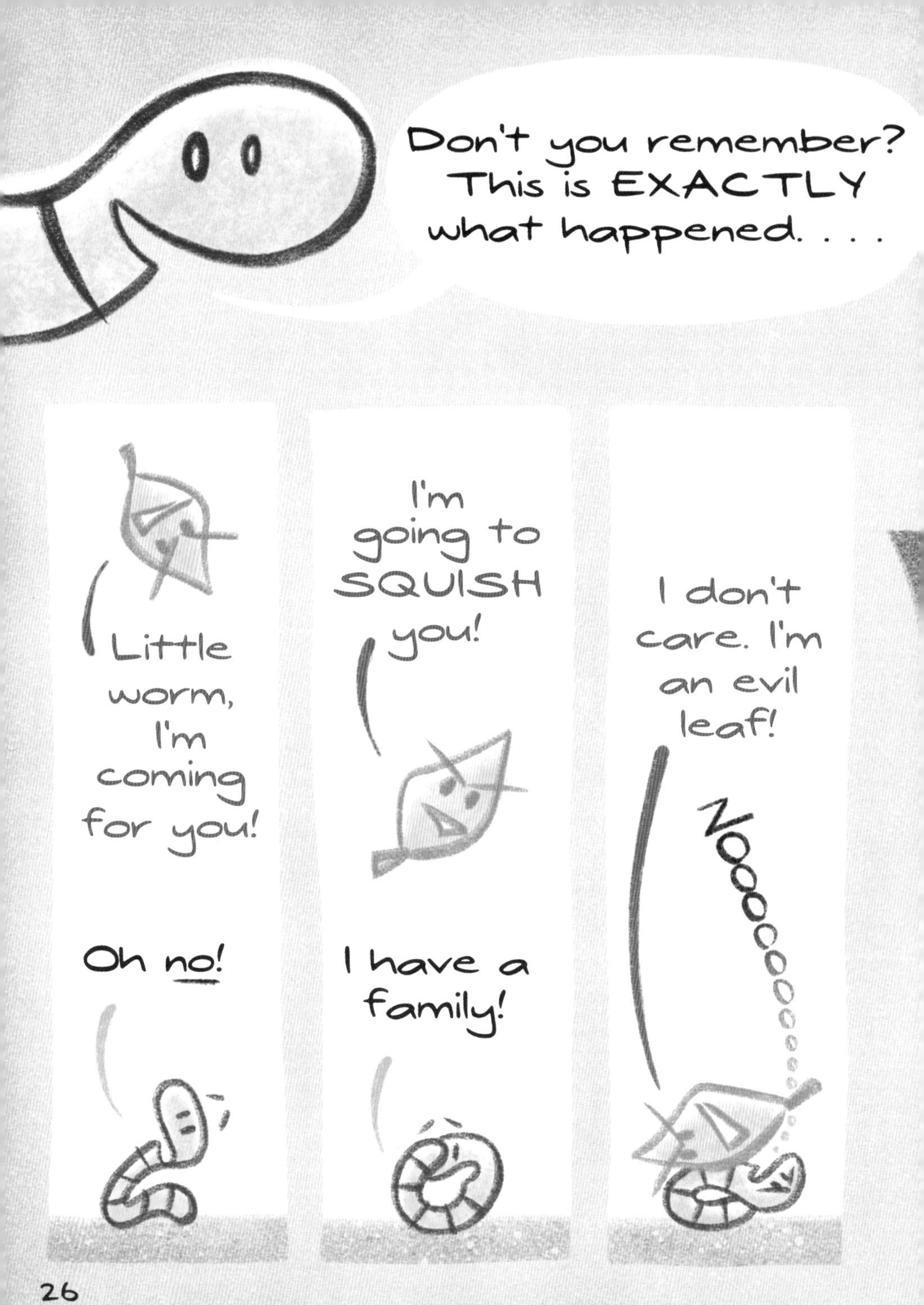
Don't you remember? This is EXACTLY what happened. . .
Little worm, I'm coming for you!
Oh no!
I'm going to SQUISH you!
I have a family!
I don't care. I'm an evil leaf!
NOOOOOOOOOOO

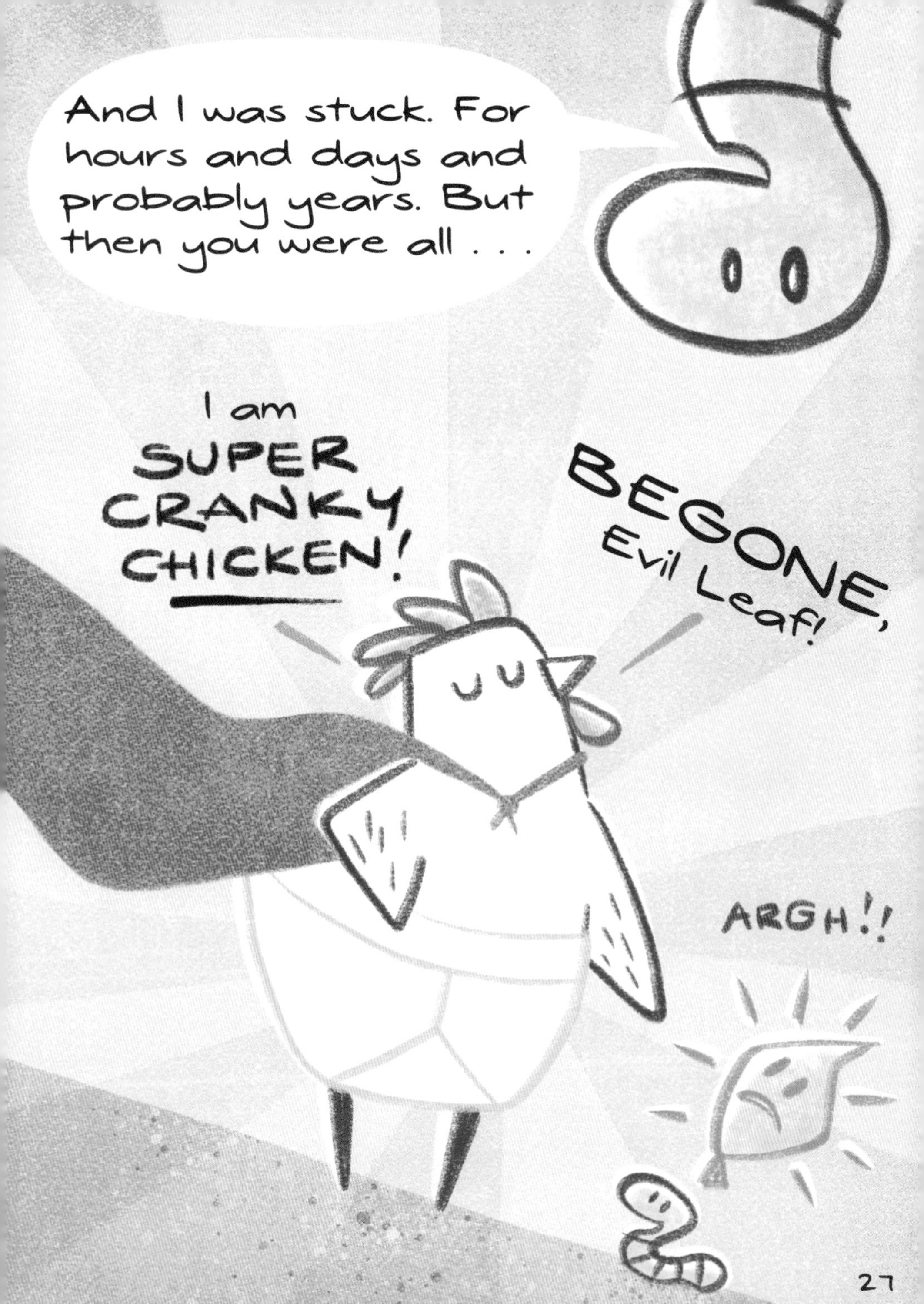

And I was stuck. For hours and days and probably years. But then you were all . . .
I am SUPER CRANKY CHICKEN!
BEGONE, Evil Leaf!
ARGH!!

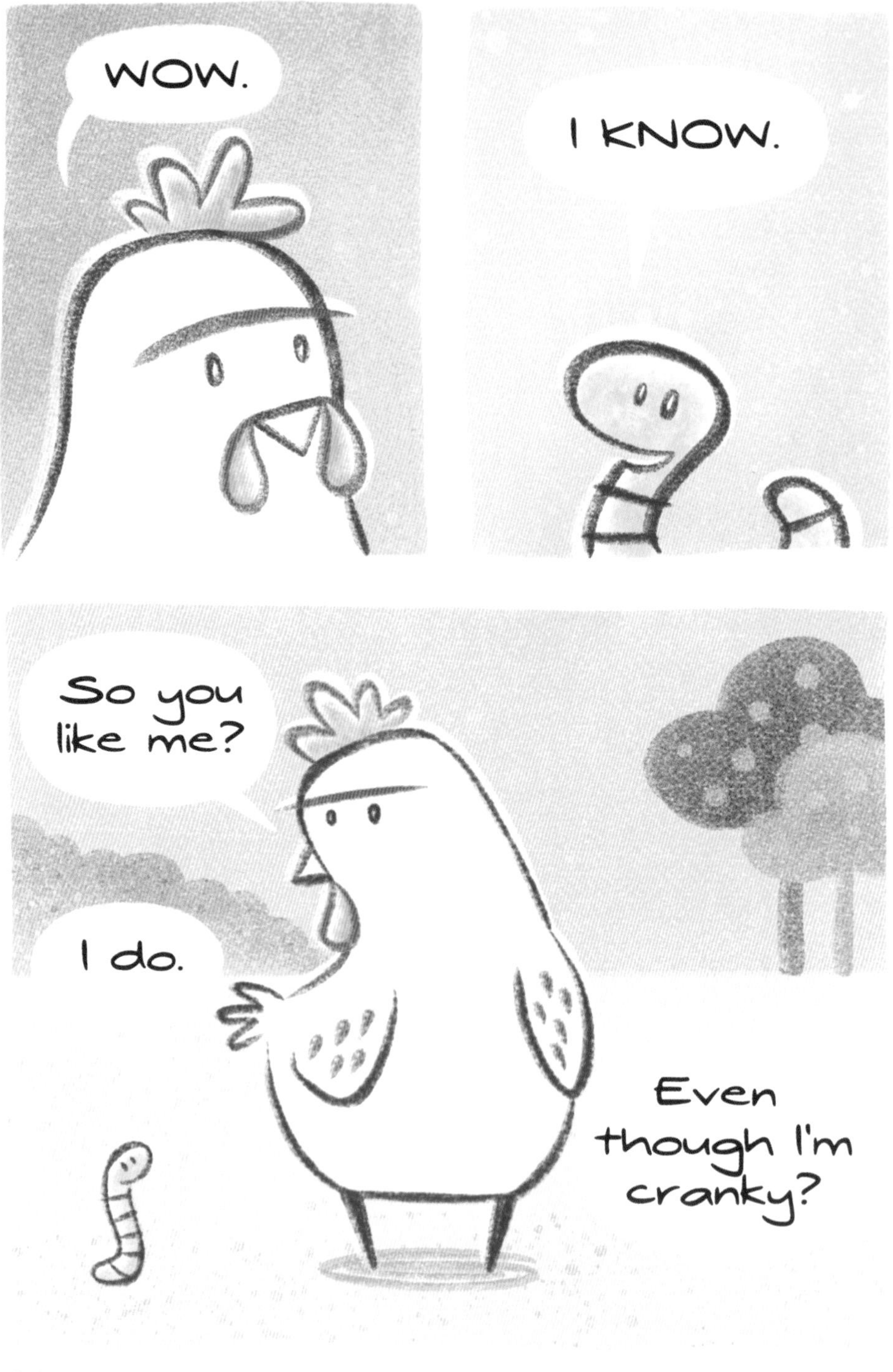
WOW.
I KNOW.
So you like me?
I do.
Even though I'm cranky?

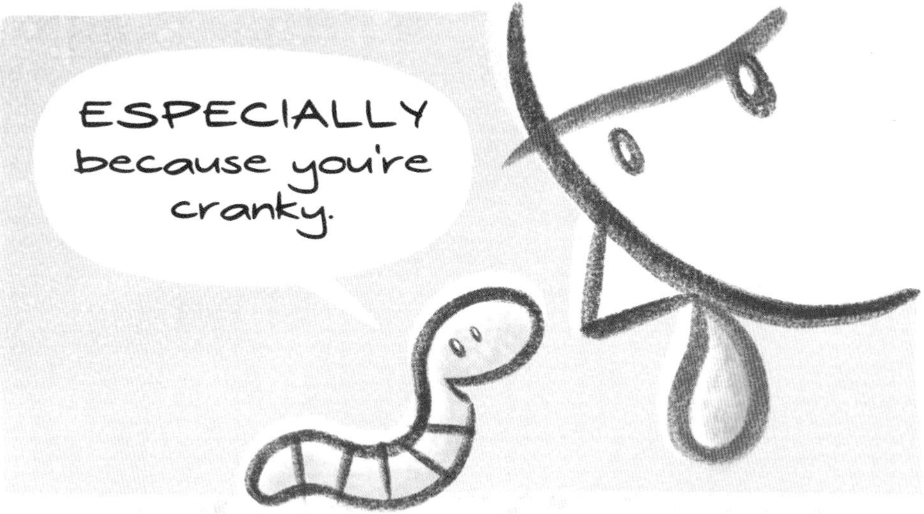
ESPECIALLY because you're cranky.

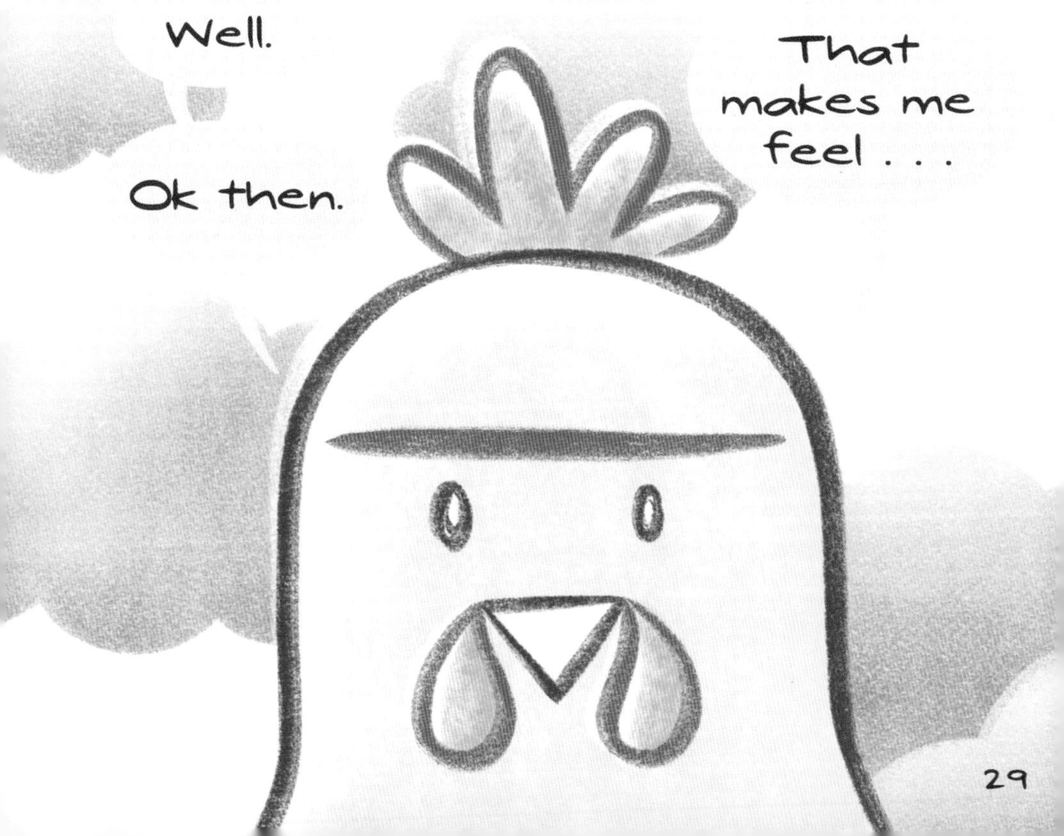
Well.
Ok then.
That makes me feel . . .

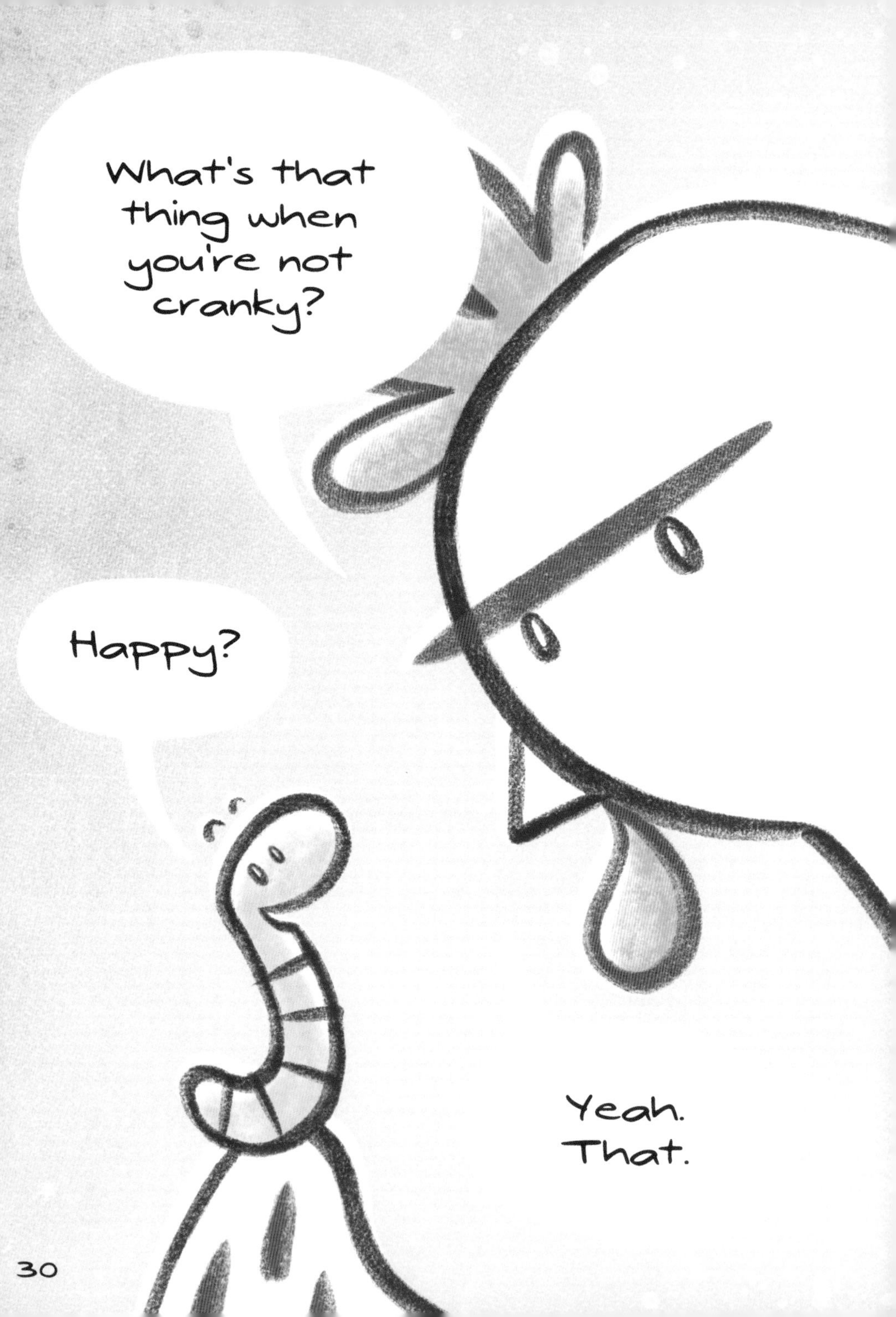
What's that thing when you're not cranky?
Happy?
Yeah. That.

You sure
look happy,
friend.

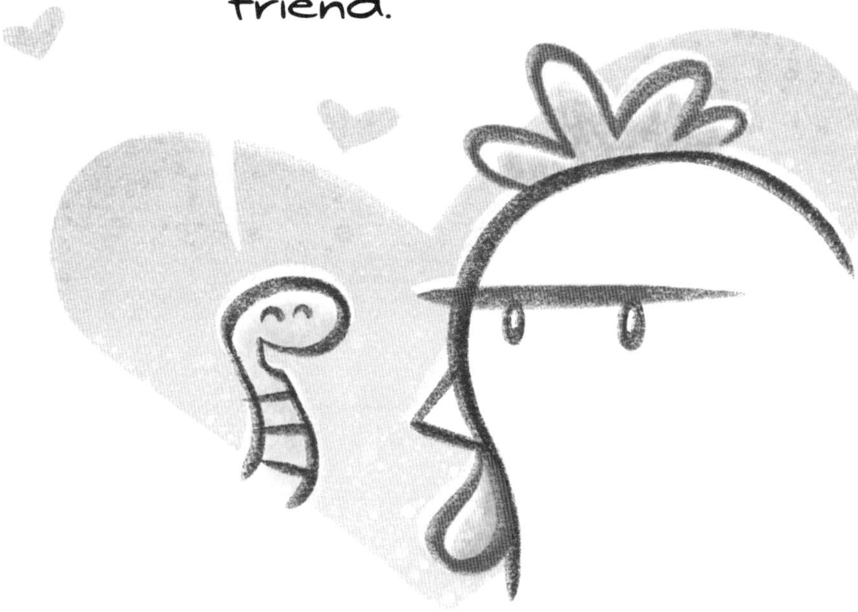

Find Out
More About
CHICKEN

Chicken's Cranky Pants

Biking cranky pants

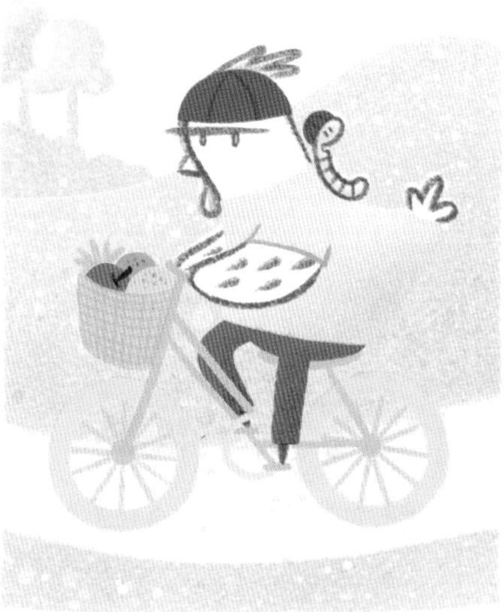

Fancy cranky pants

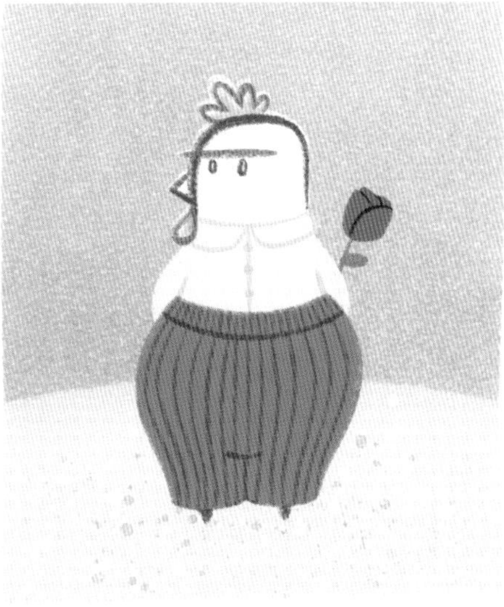

Pajama cranky pants

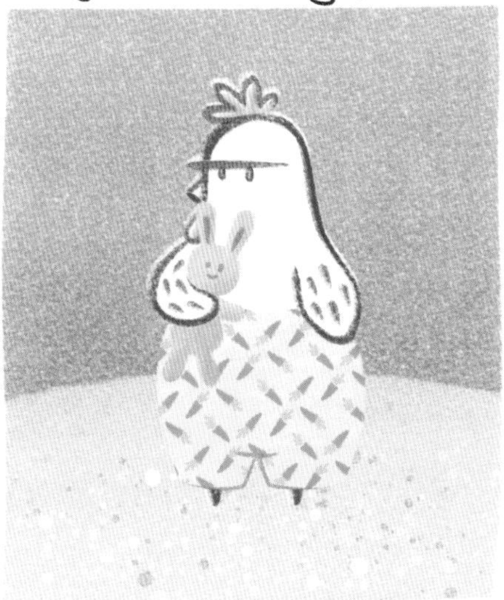

Holiday cranky pants

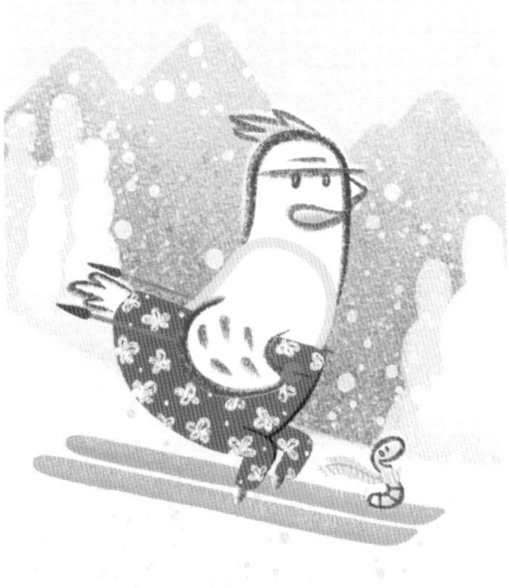

Things That Make Chicken Cranky

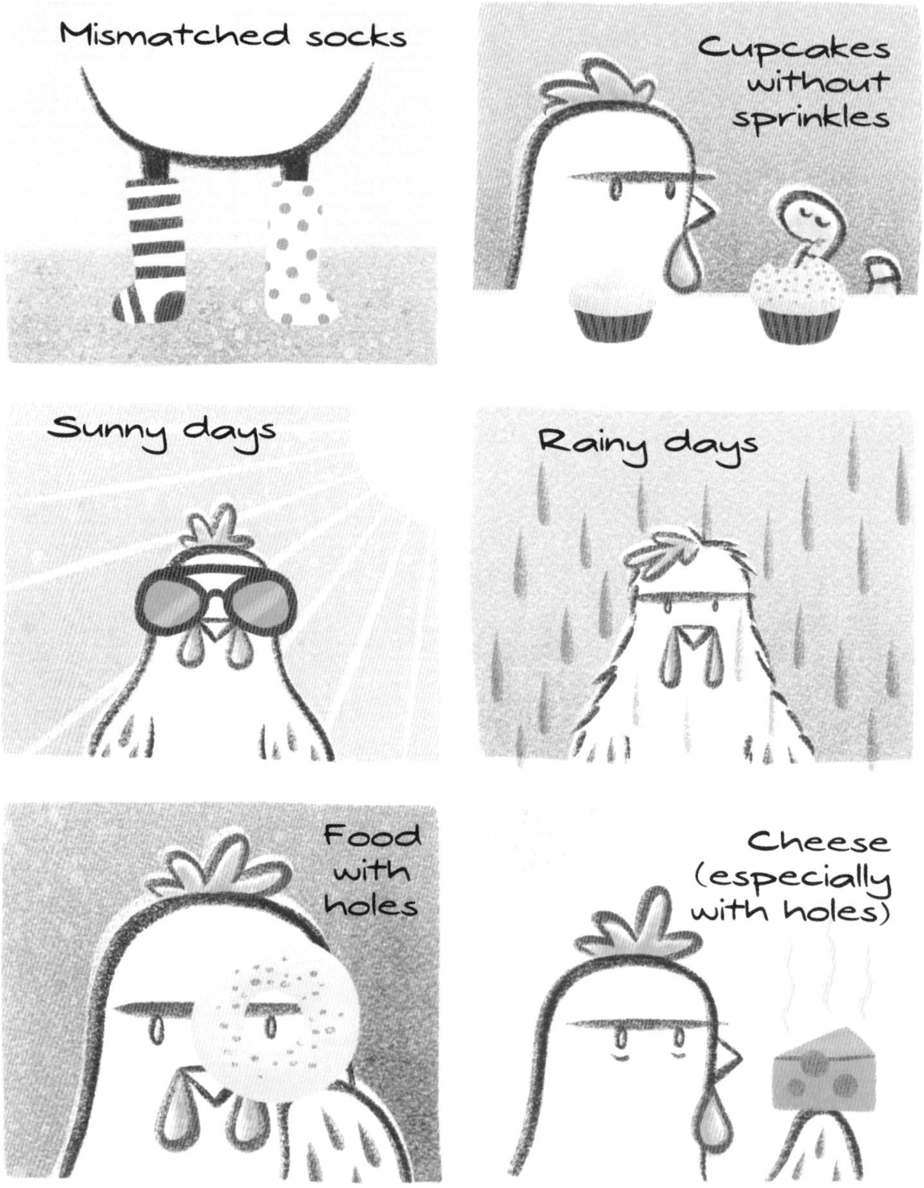
Mismatched socks
Cupcakes without sprinkles
Sunny days
Rainy days
Food with holes
Cheese (especially with holes)

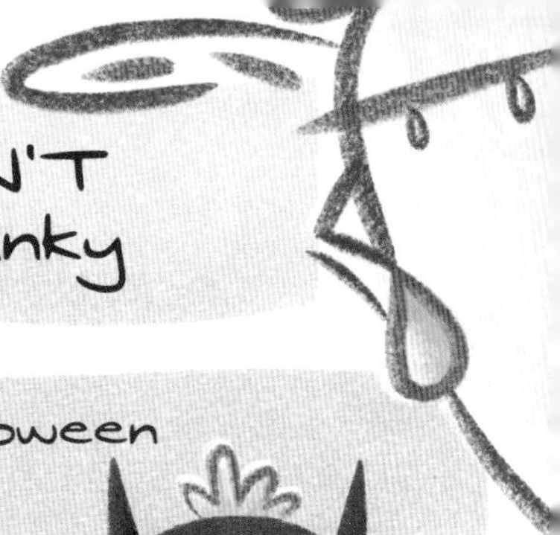

Things That DON'T Make Chicken Cranky

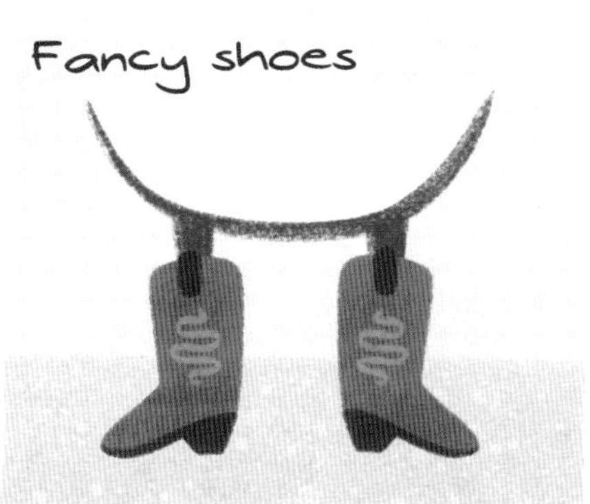
Fancy shoes

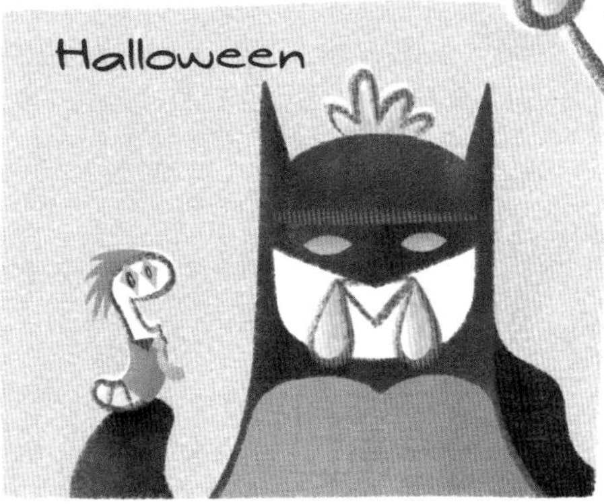
Halloween

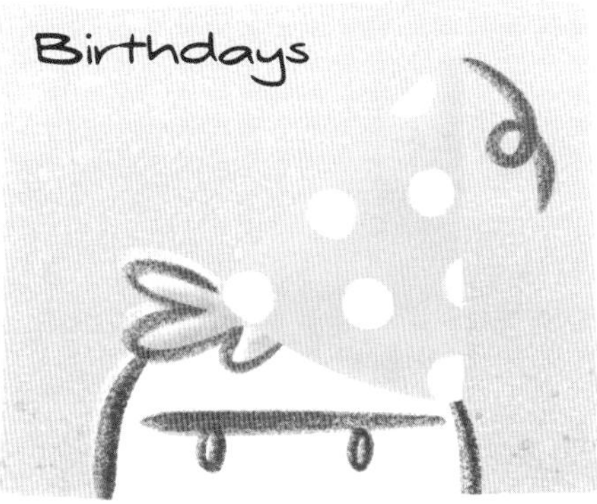
Birthdays

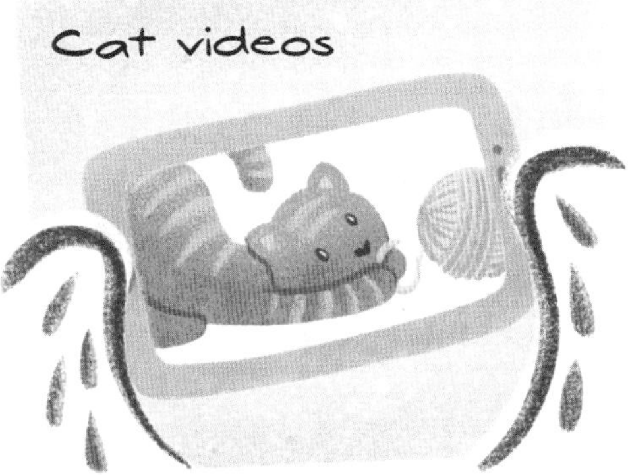
Cat videos

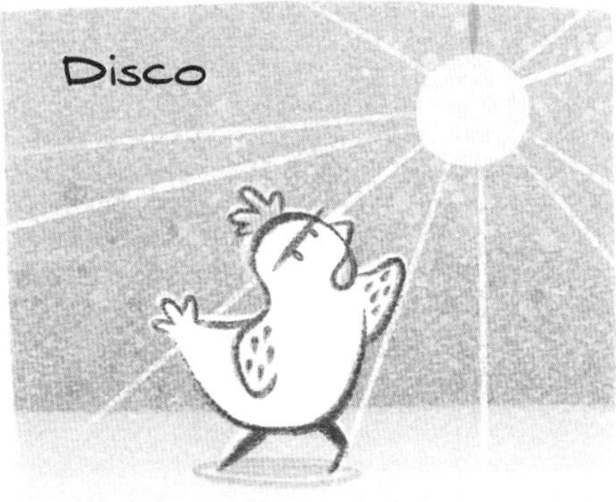
Disco

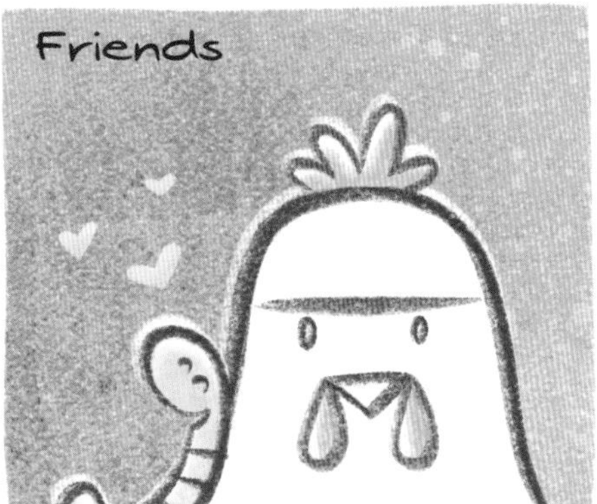
Friends

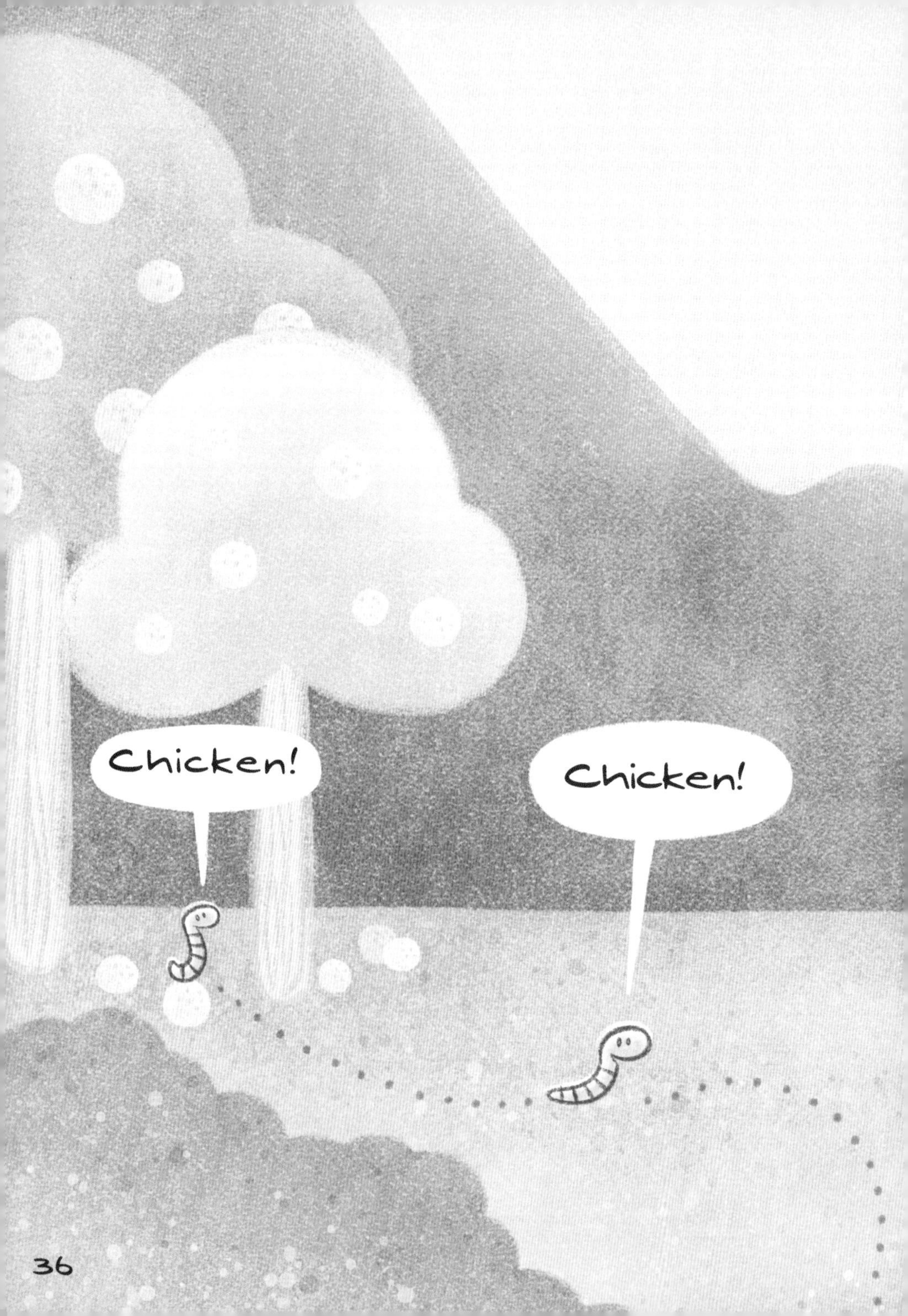
Chicken!
Chicken!

2

BEST FEATHERED FRIENDS

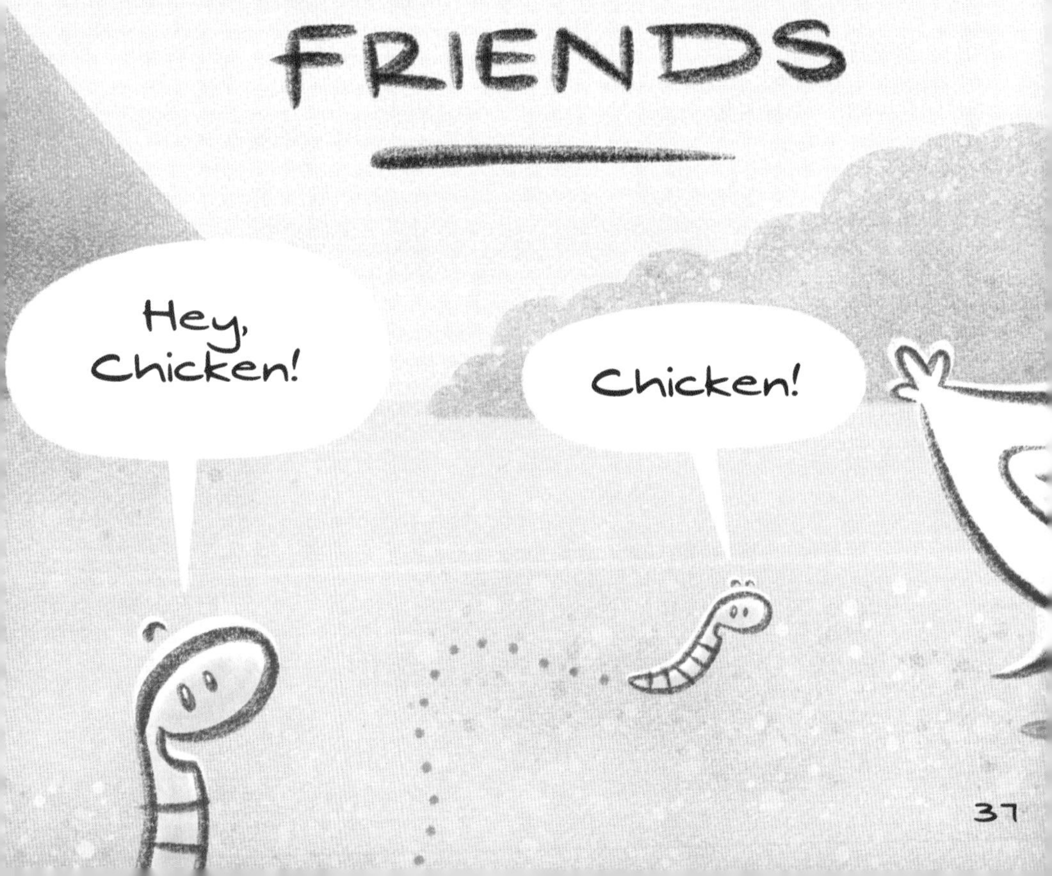
Hey, Chicken!
Chicken!

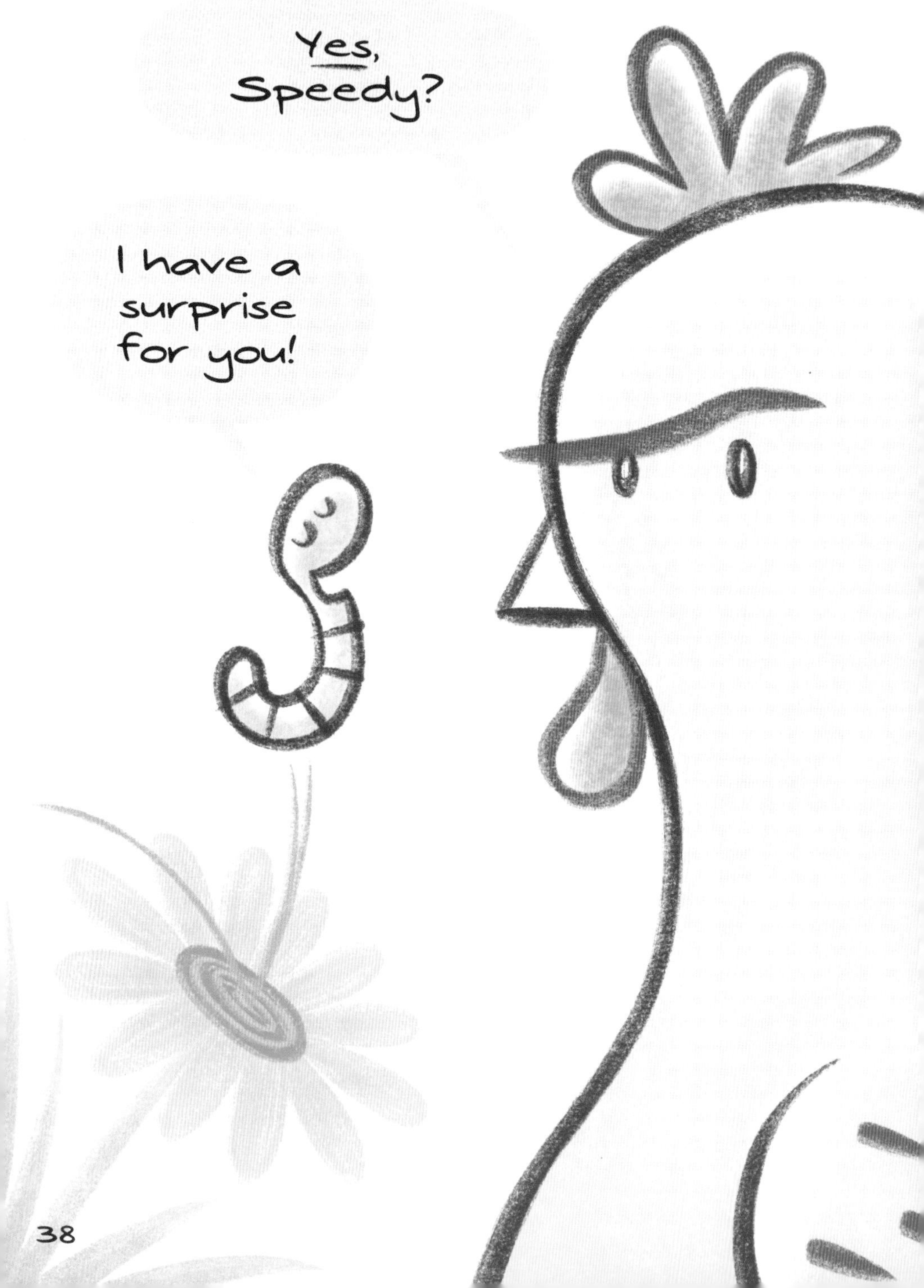
Yes, Speedy?
I have a surprise for you!

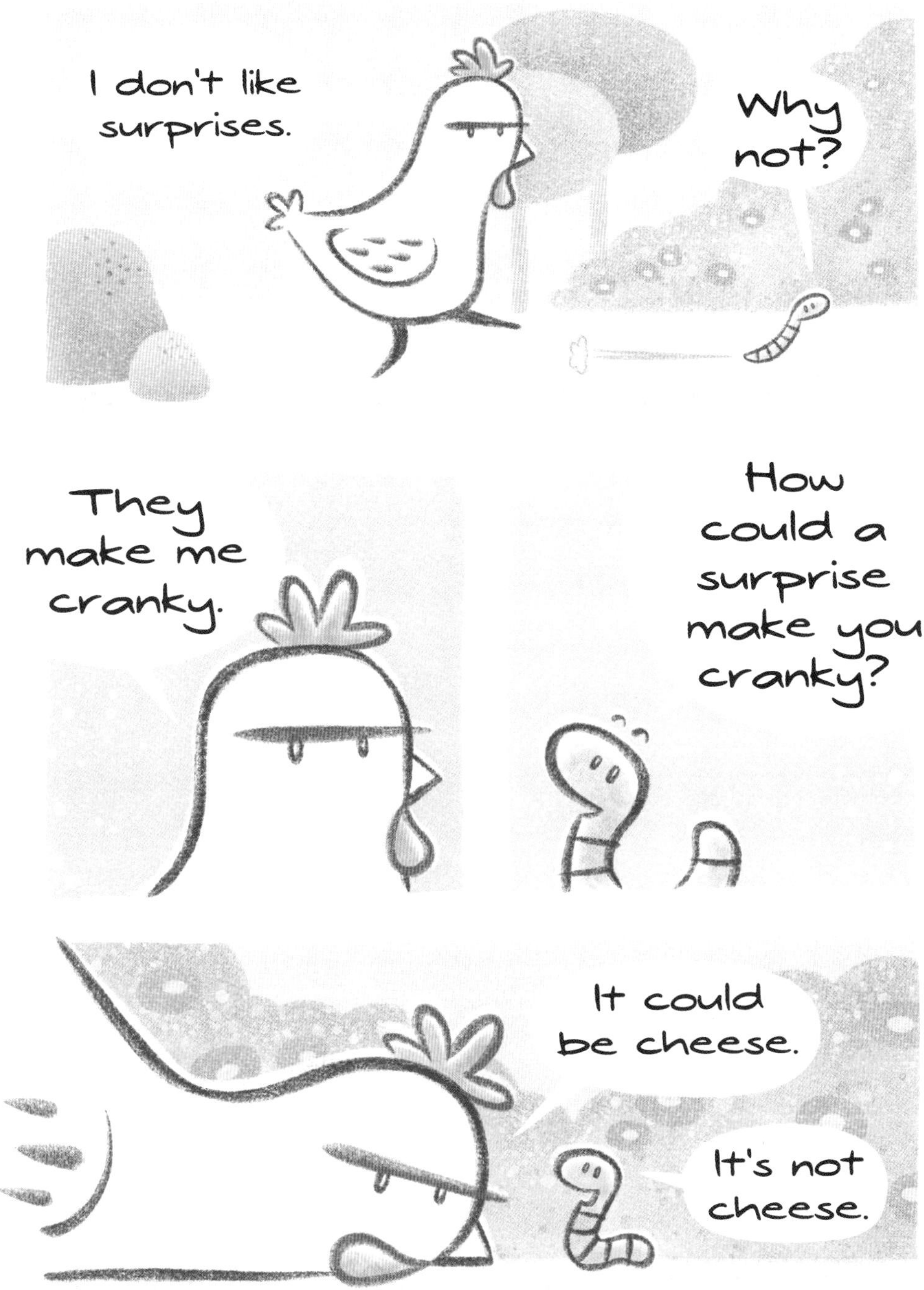
I don't like surprises.
Why not?
They make me cranky.
How could a surprise make you cranky?
It could be cheese.
It's not cheese.

What
if it's a
spider?

Hi!

Aaaaaaagh!

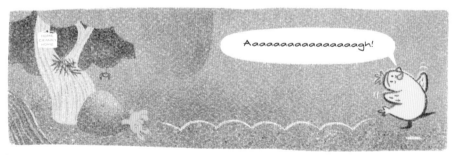

Aaaaaaaaaaaaaaaaagh!

It's a GOOD surprise, I promise.

Ready . . .

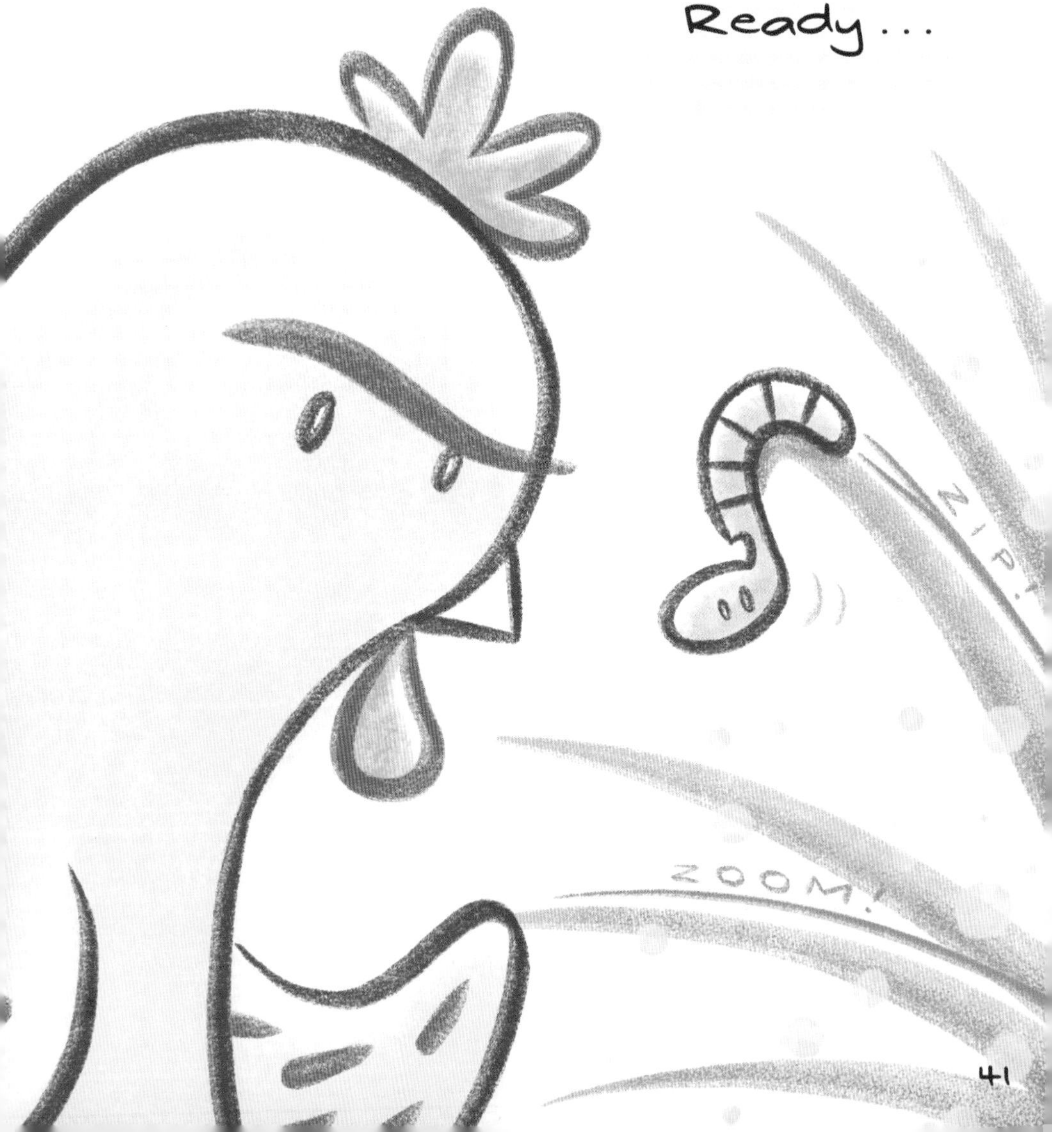
ZIP!
ZOOM!

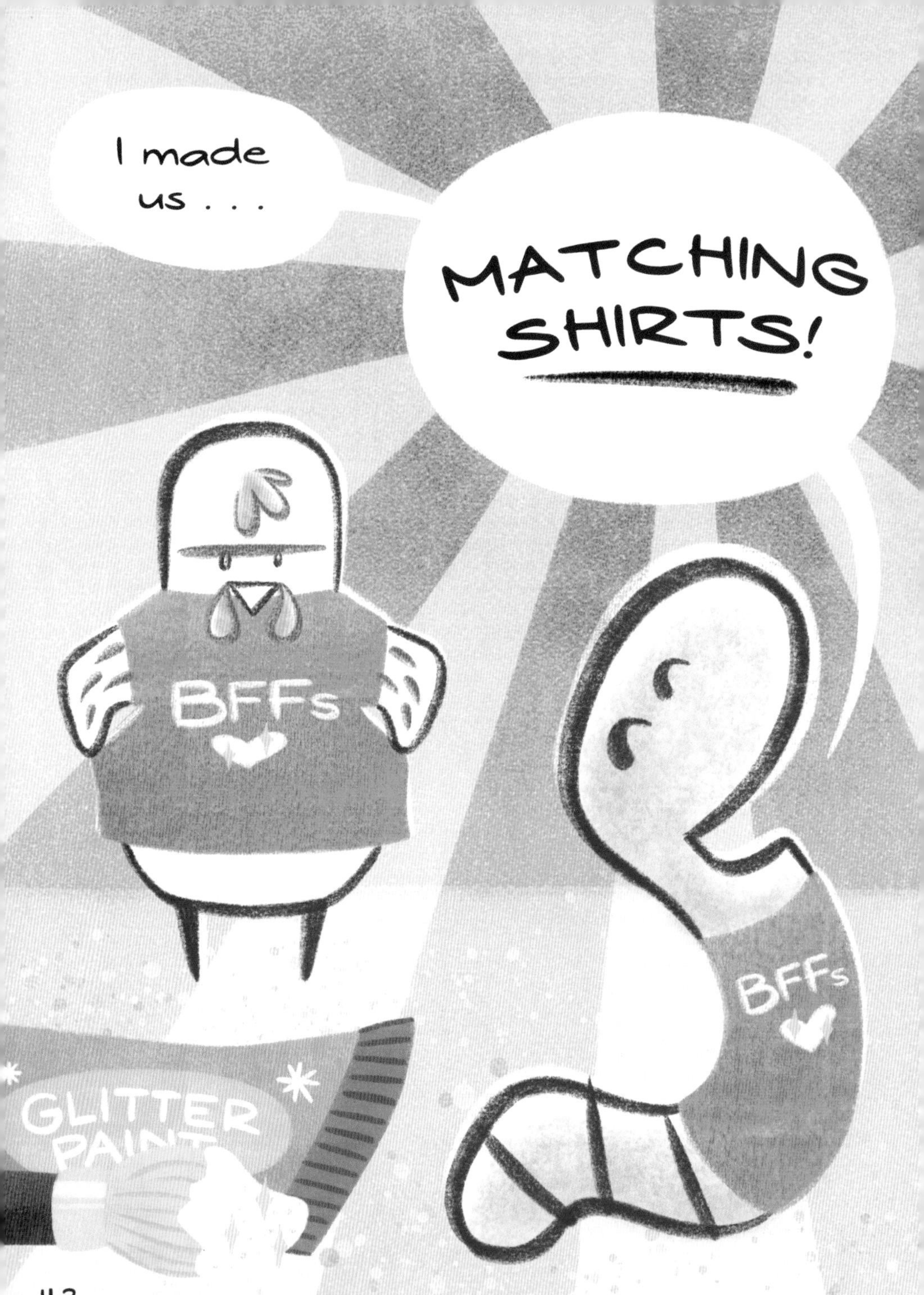
I made us . . .
MATCHING SHIRTS!
BFFs
BFFs
GLITTER PAINT

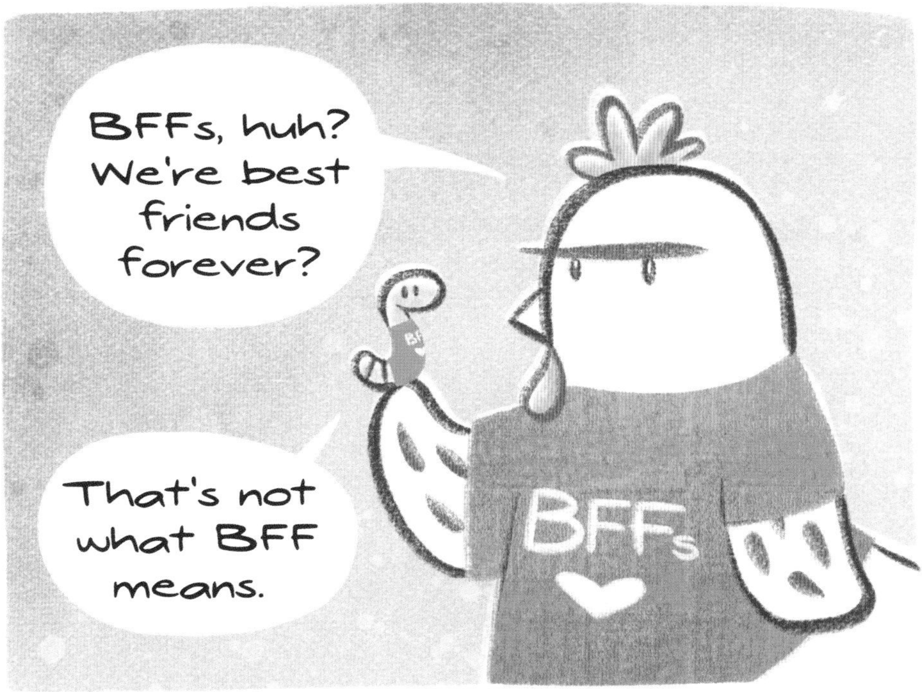
BFFs, huh? We're best friends forever?
That's not what BFF means.
BFFs

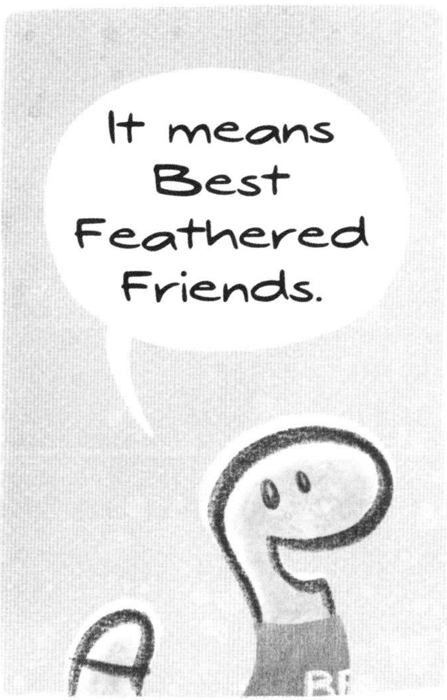
It means Best Feathered Friends.

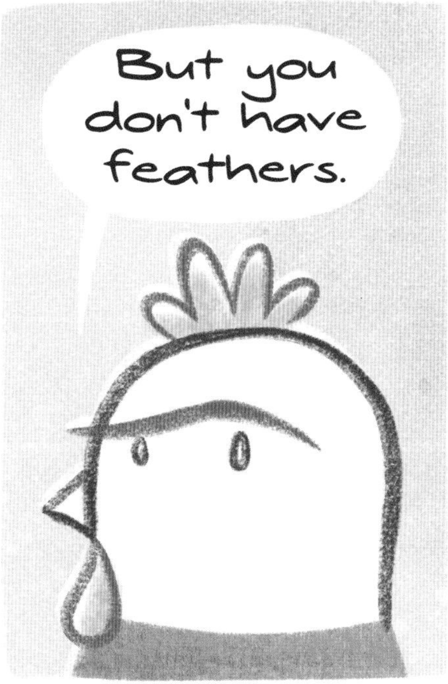
But you don't have feathers.

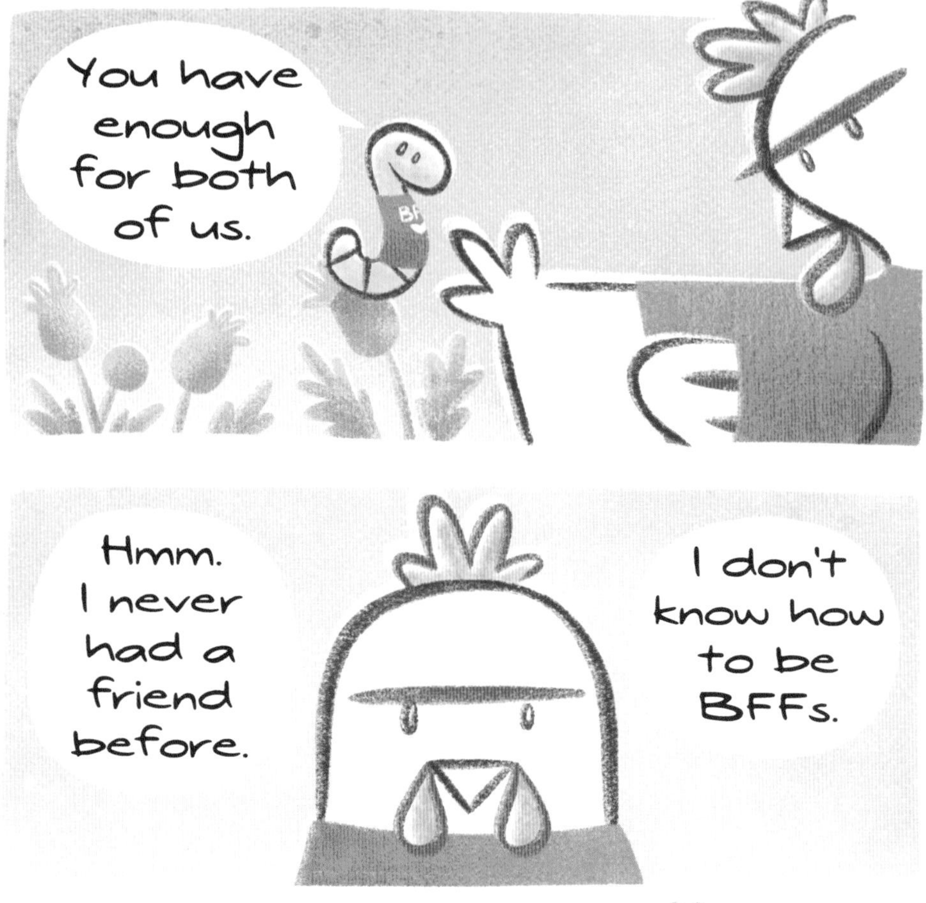
You have enough for both of us.
Hmm. I never had a friend before.
I don't know how to be BFFs.
Don't worry, Chicken. I'll teach you.

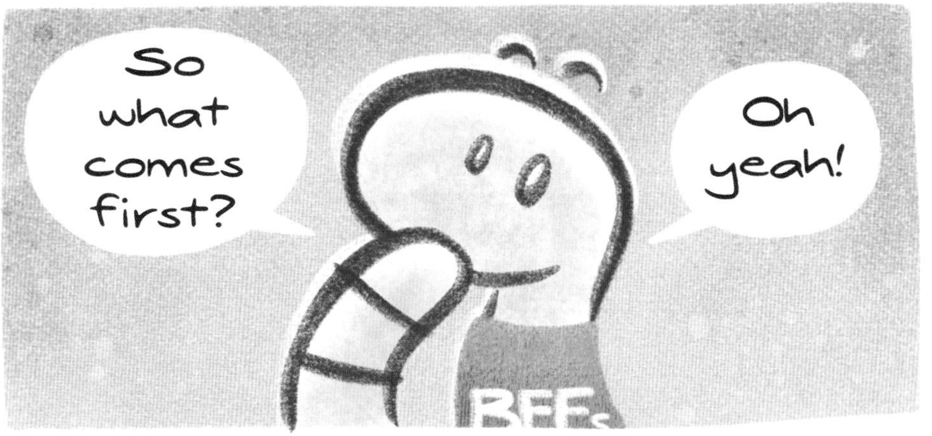
So what comes first?
Oh yeah!
BFFs

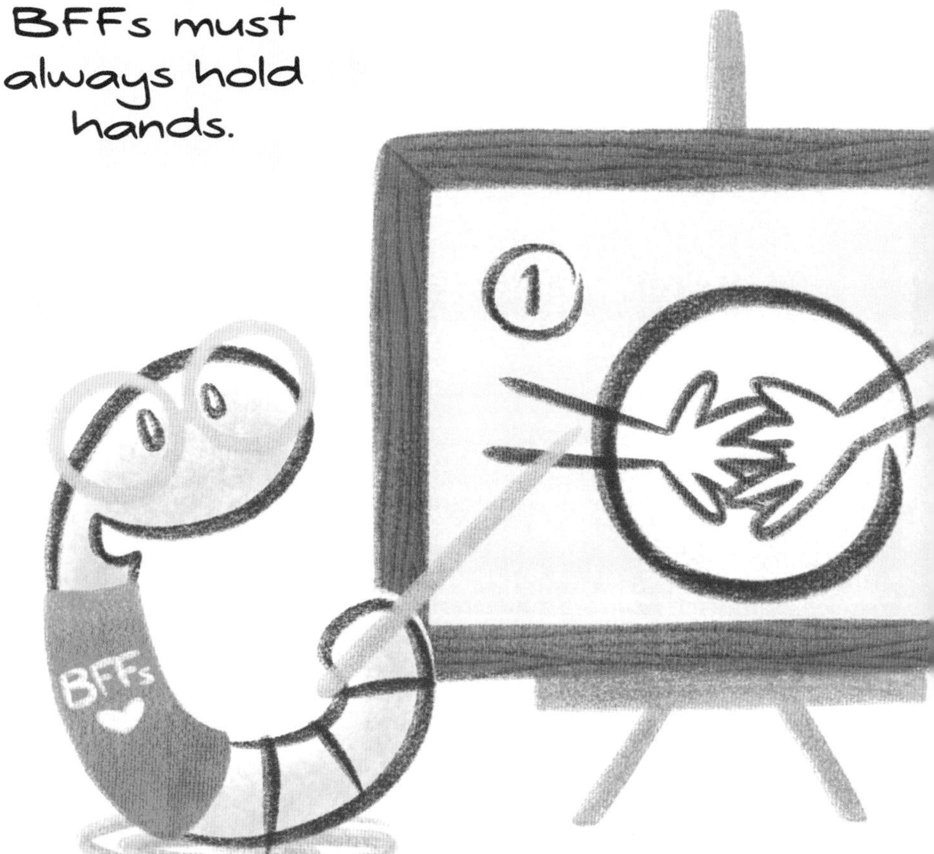
BFFs must always hold hands.
1
BFFs

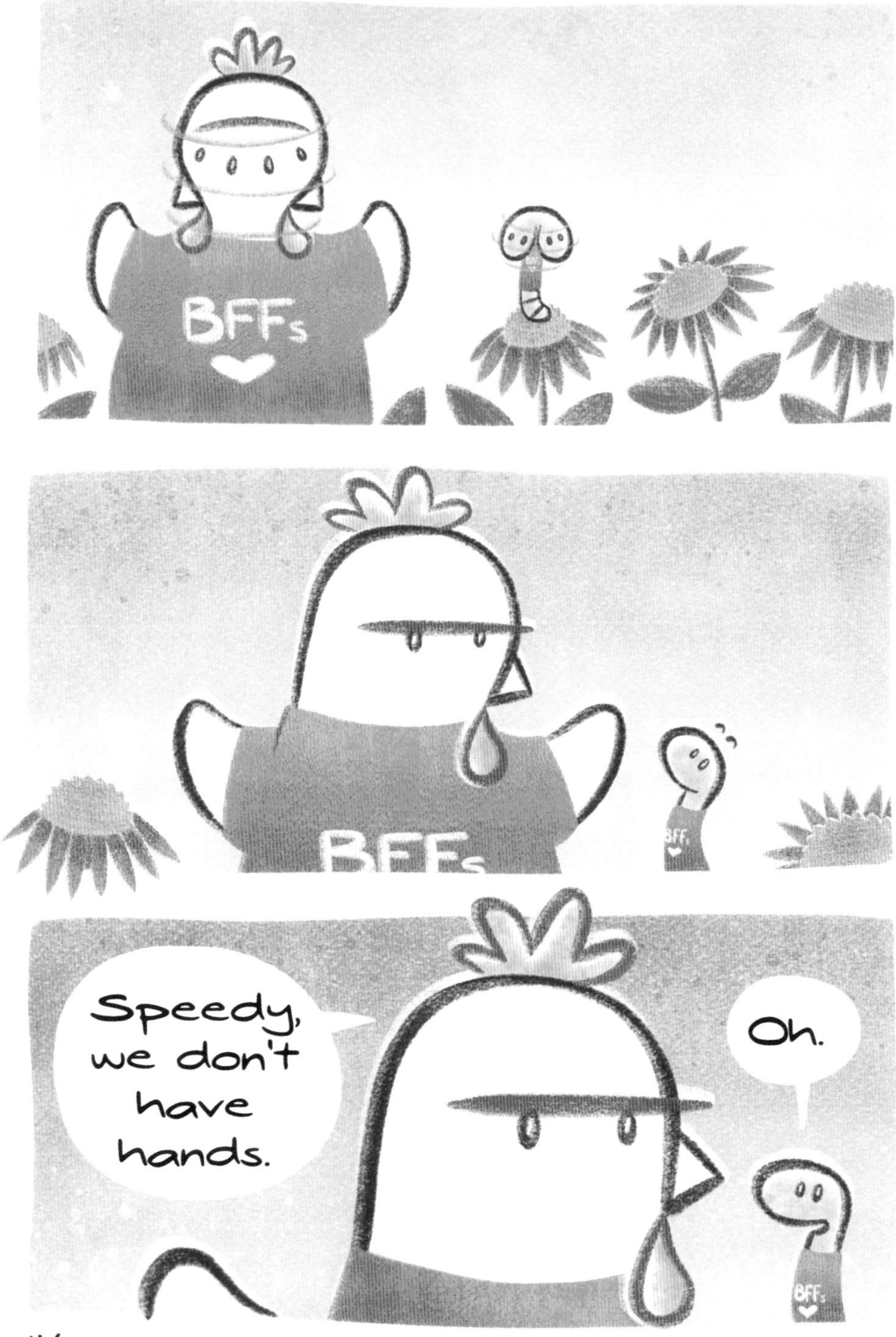
BFFs
Speedy, we don't have hands.
Oh.

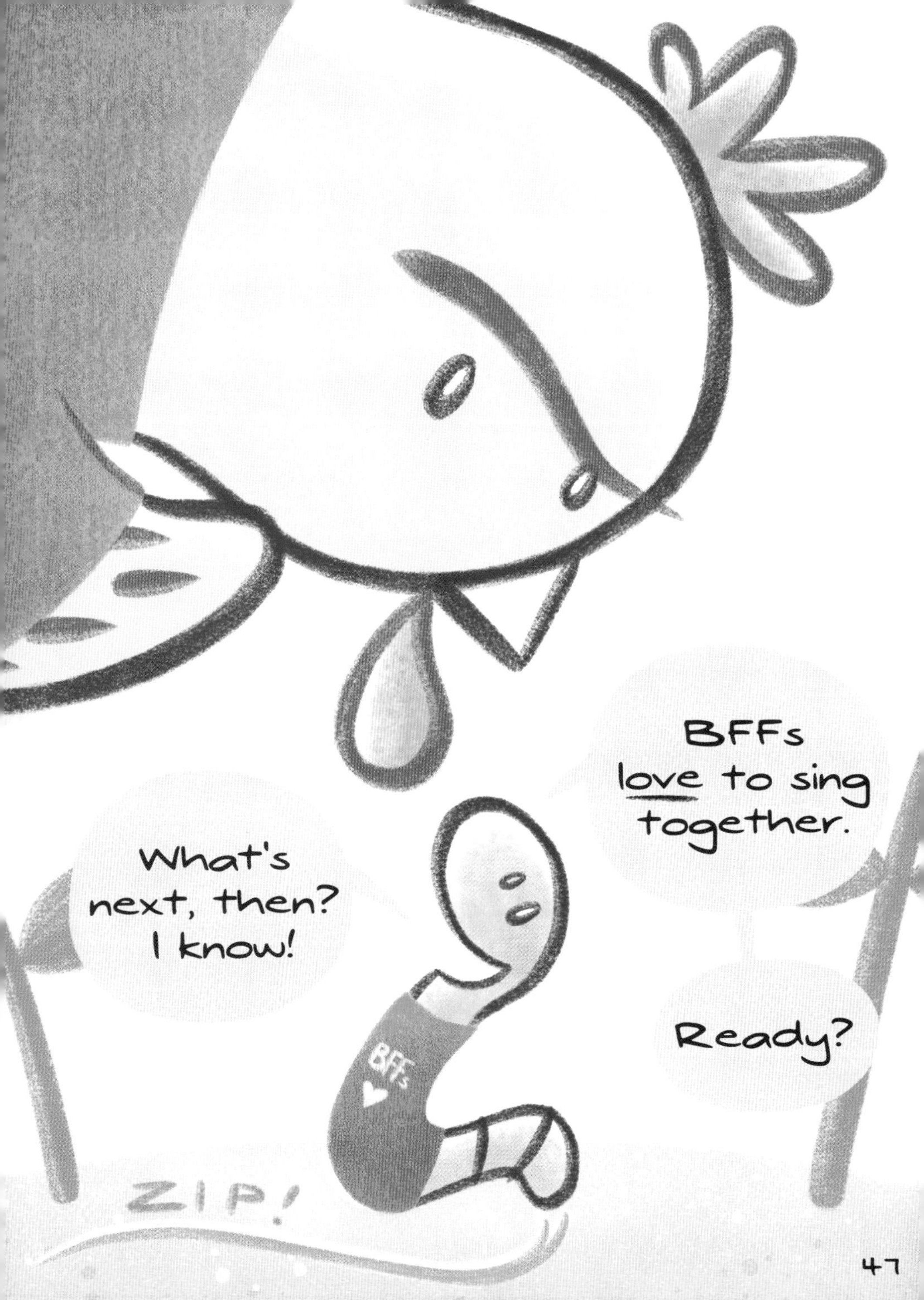
BFFs love to sing together.
What's next, then? I know!
Ready?
BFFs
ZIP!

We are
FRIENDS!
We are really friendly
FRIENDS!

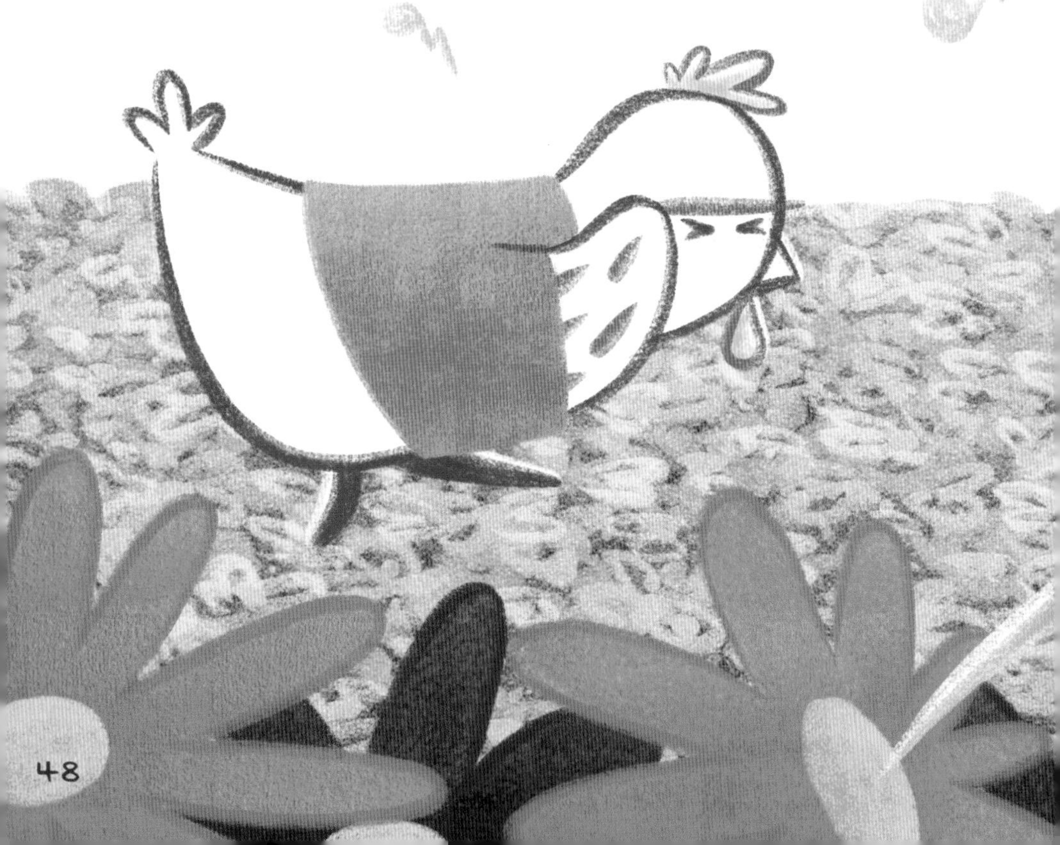

We are the
FRIENDLIEST OF
FRIENDS!

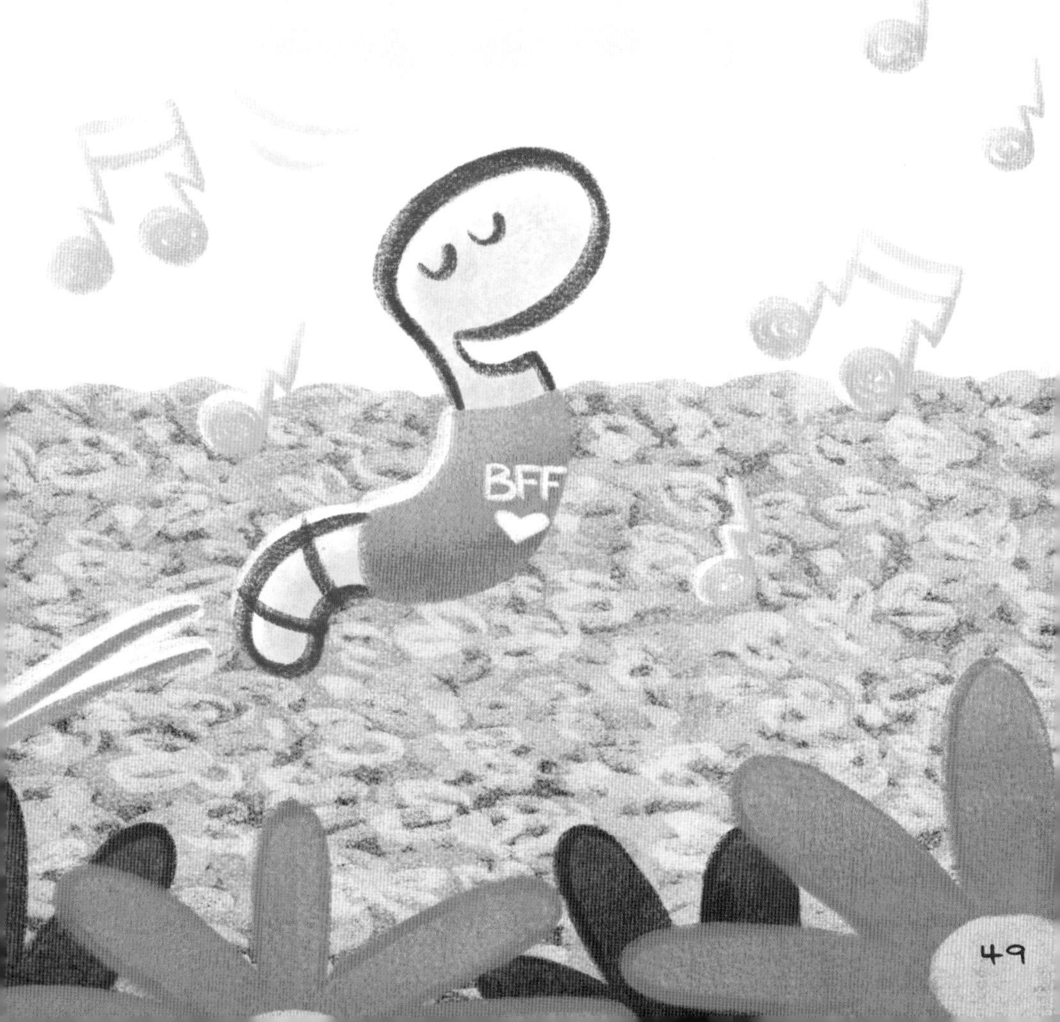
BFF

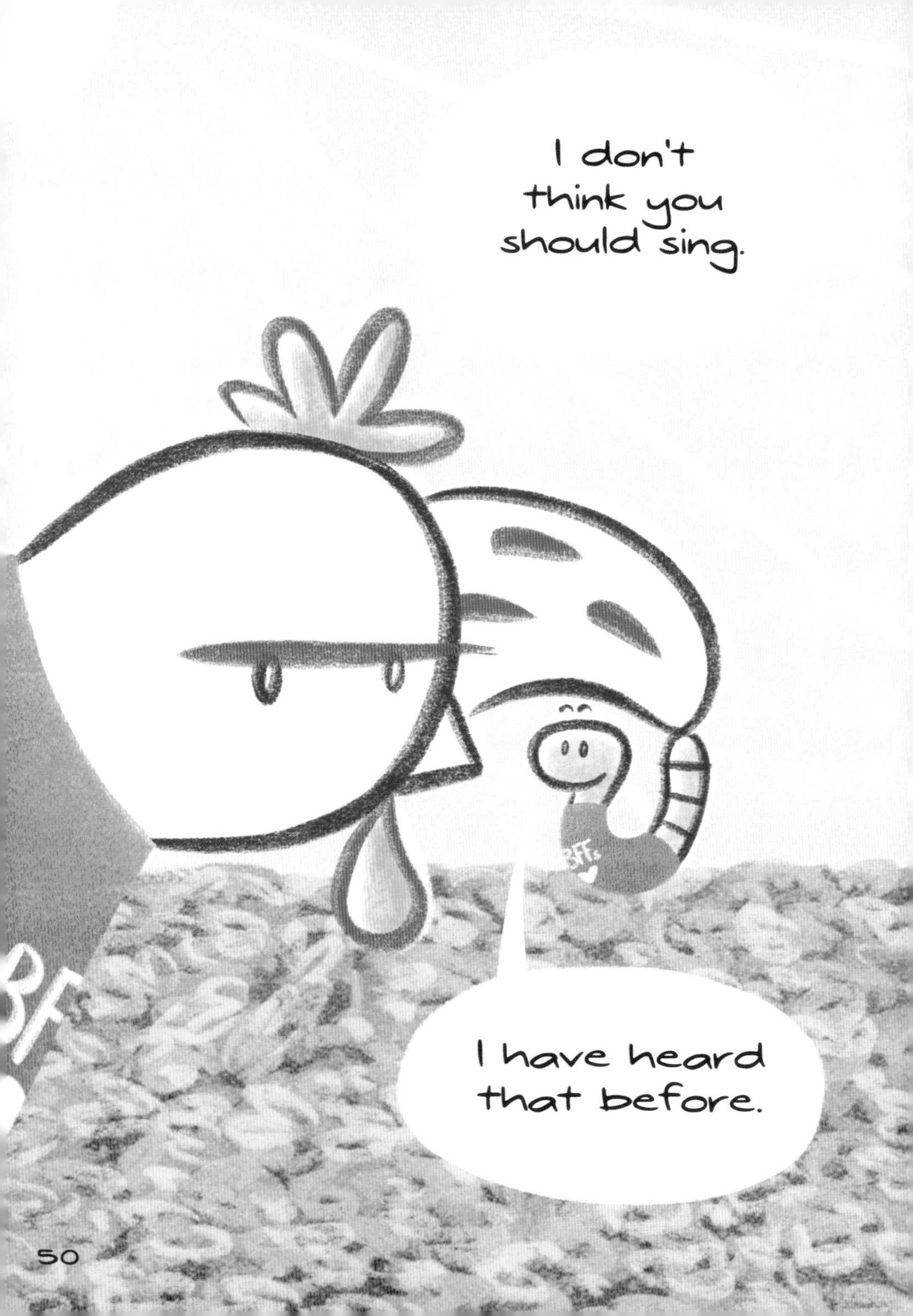
I don't think you should sing.
I have heard that before.
BFFs

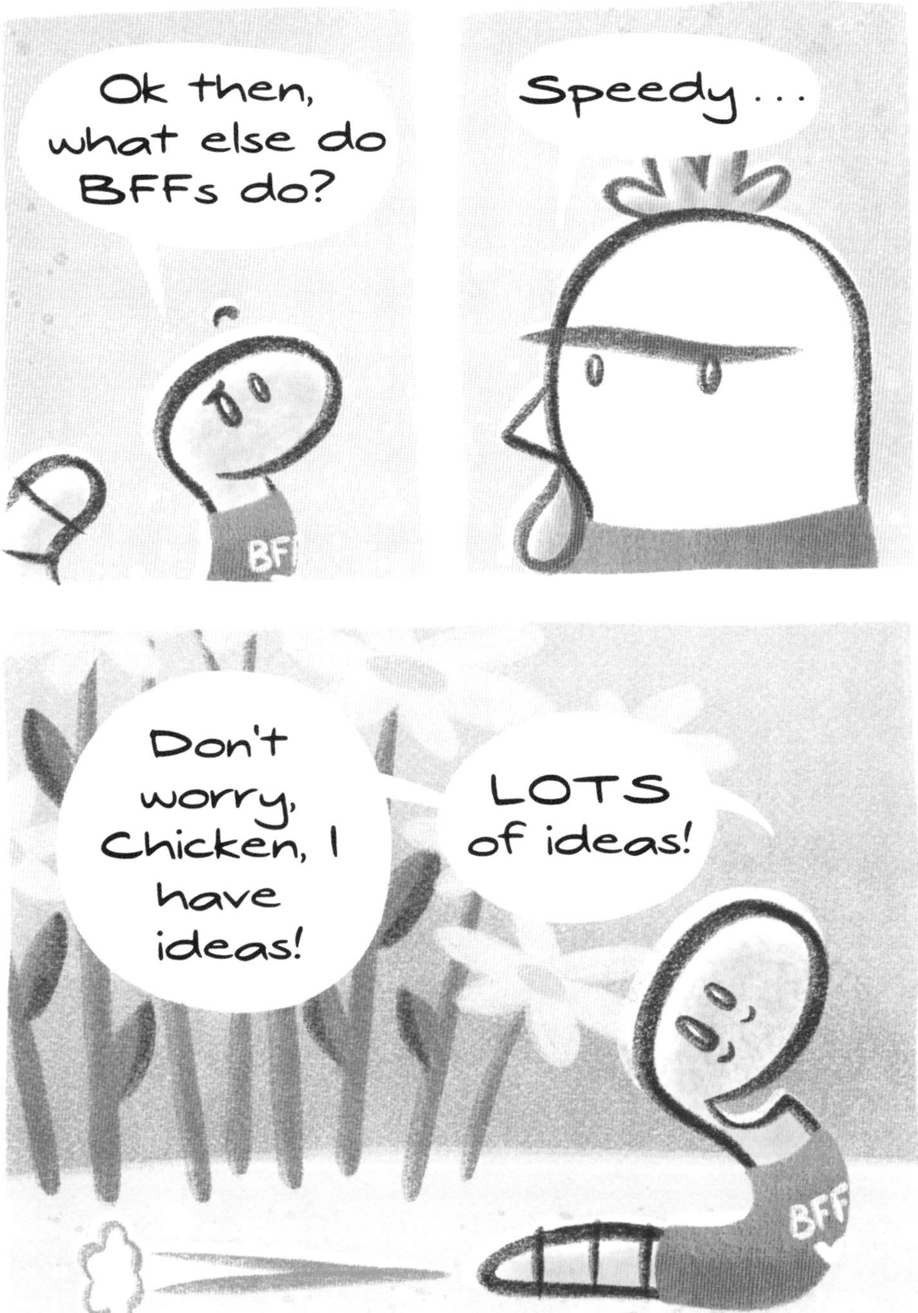

Ok then, what else do BFFs do?
Speedy . . .
Don't worry, Chicken, I have ideas!
LOTS of ideas!

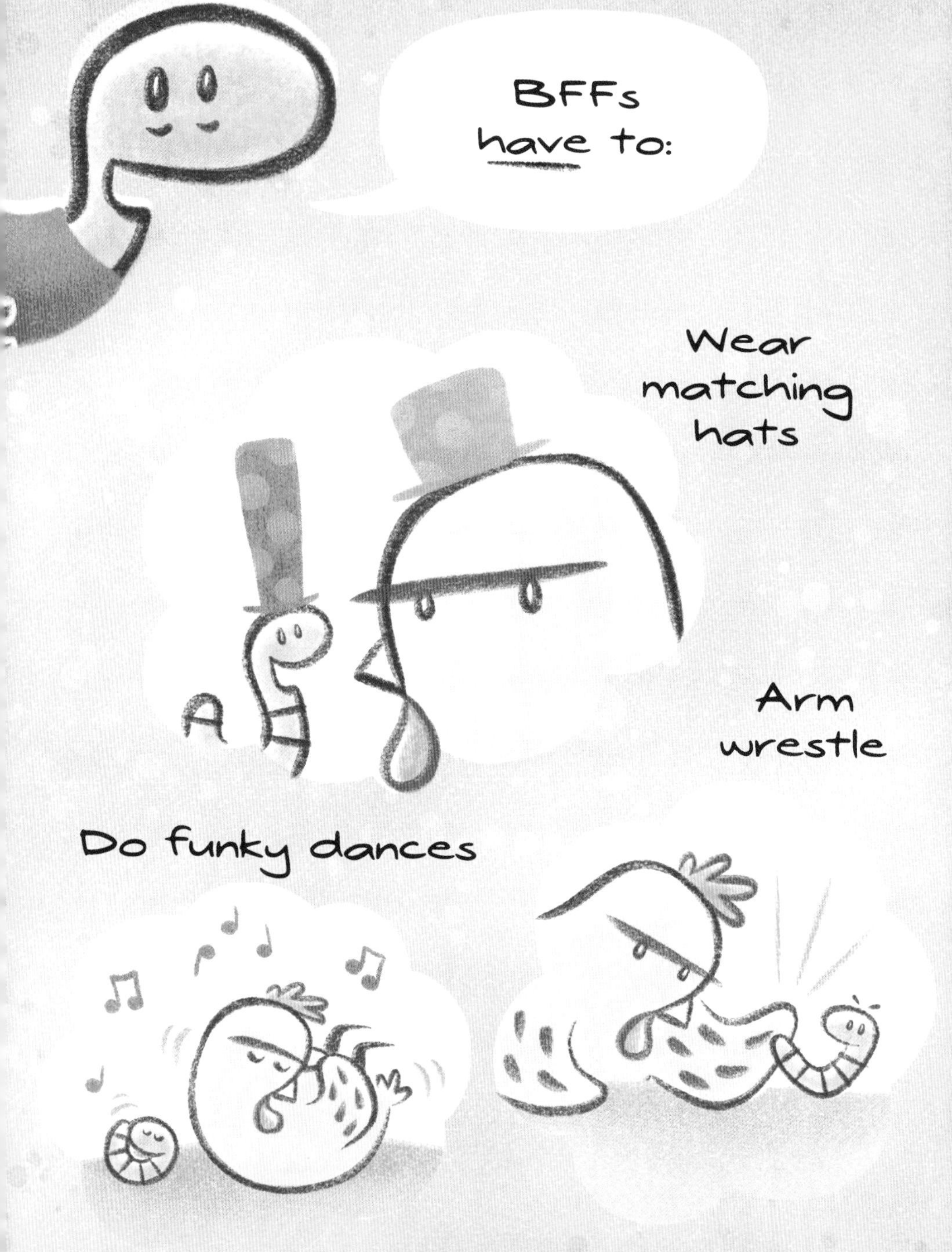

BFFs have to:
Wear matching hats
Arm wrestle
Do funky dances

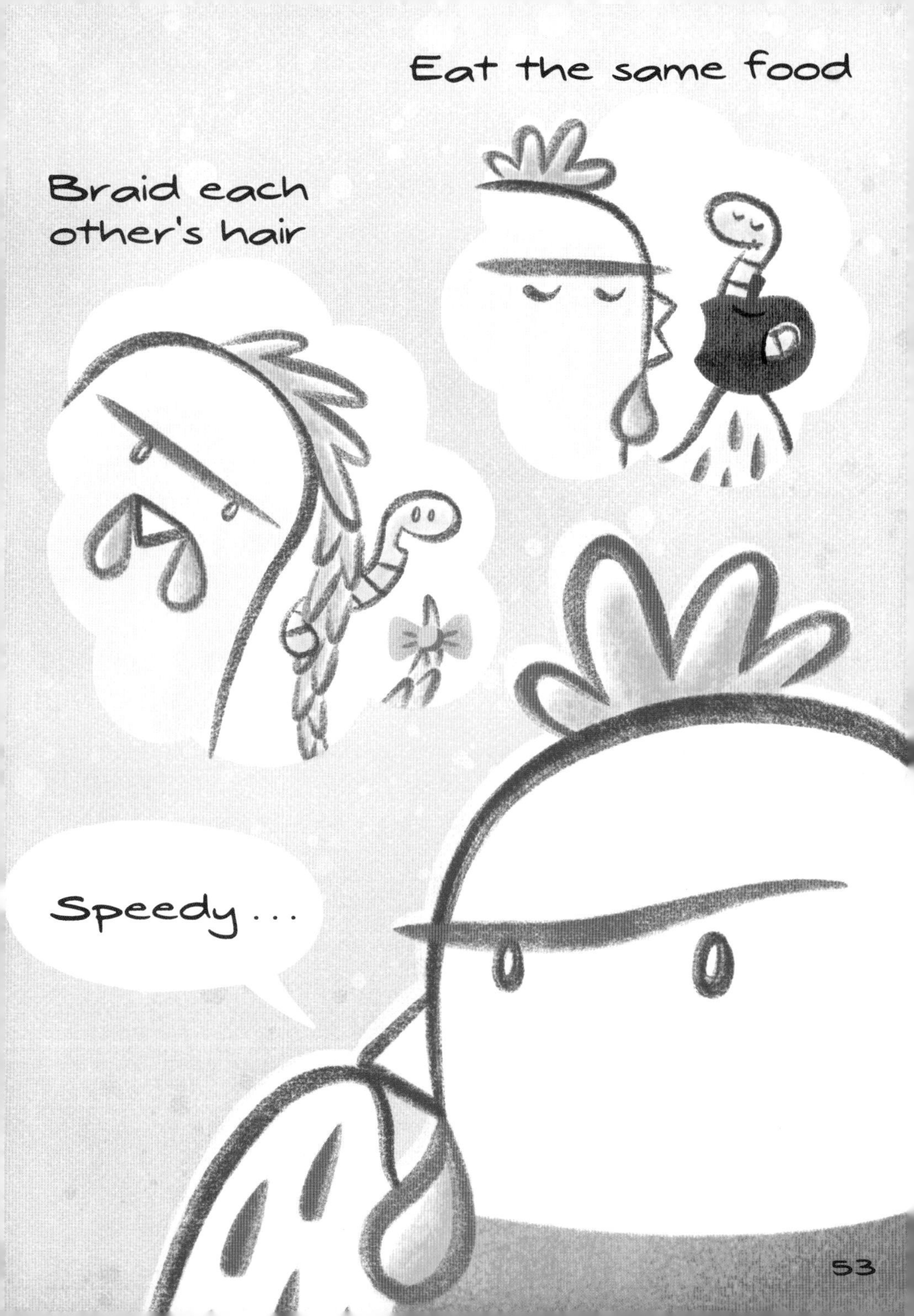
Eat the same food
Braid each other's hair
Speedy . . .

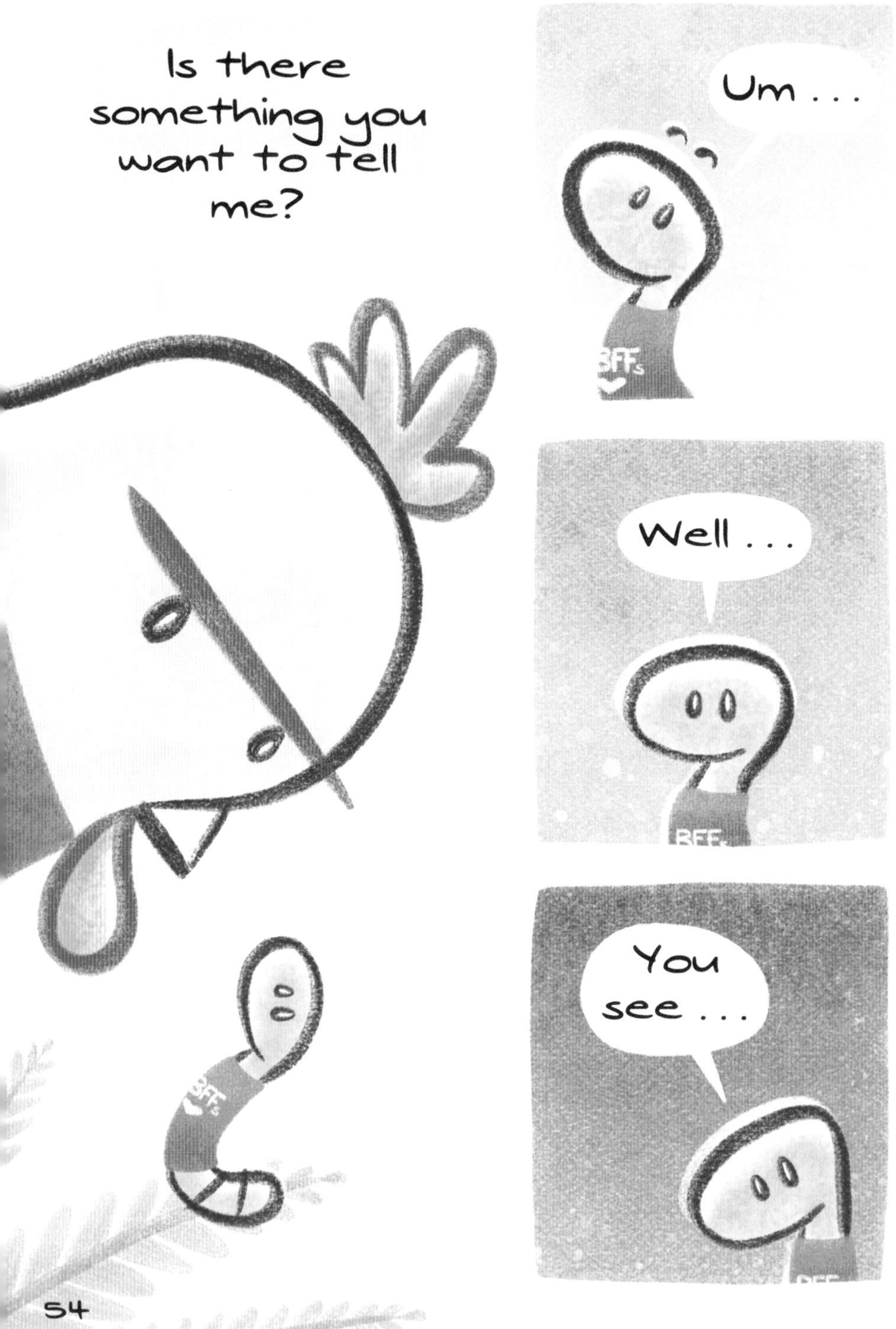
Is there something you want to tell me?
Um . . .
Well . . .
You see . . .

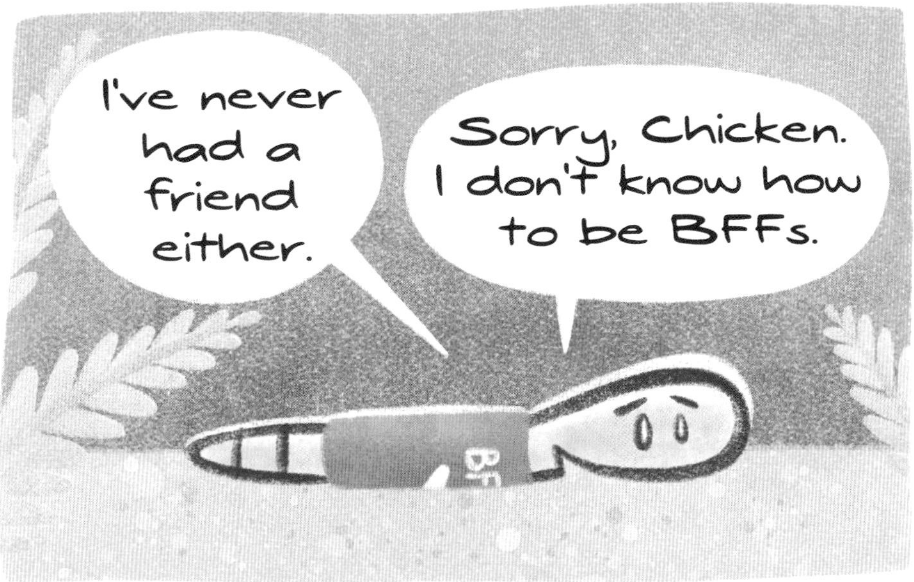
I've never had a friend either.
Sorry, Chicken. I don't know how to be BFFs.
BF

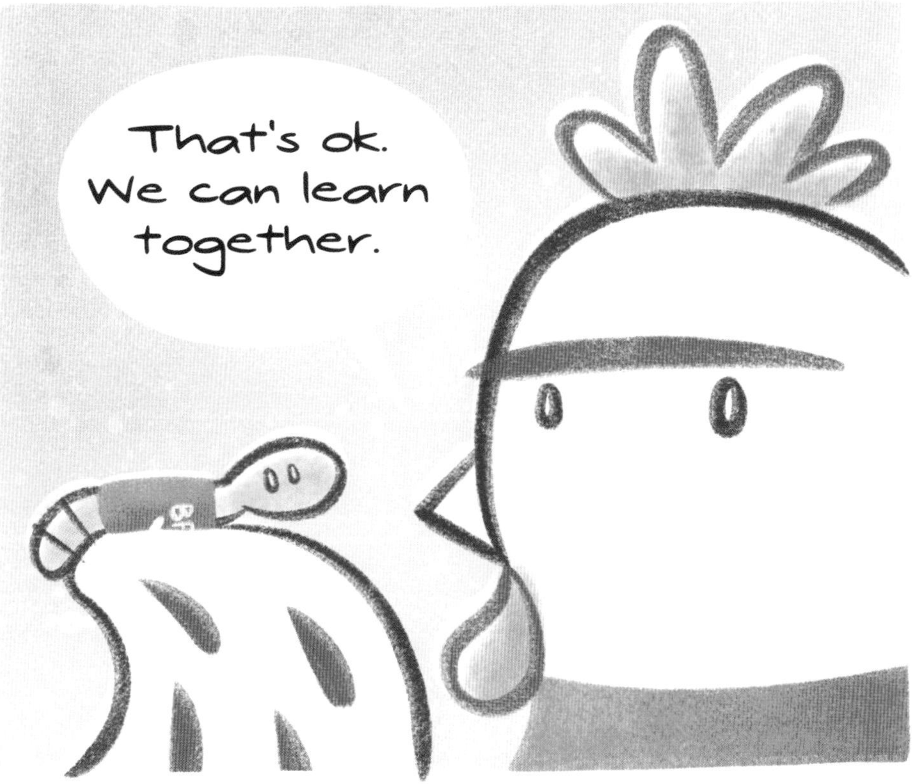
That's ok. We can learn together.

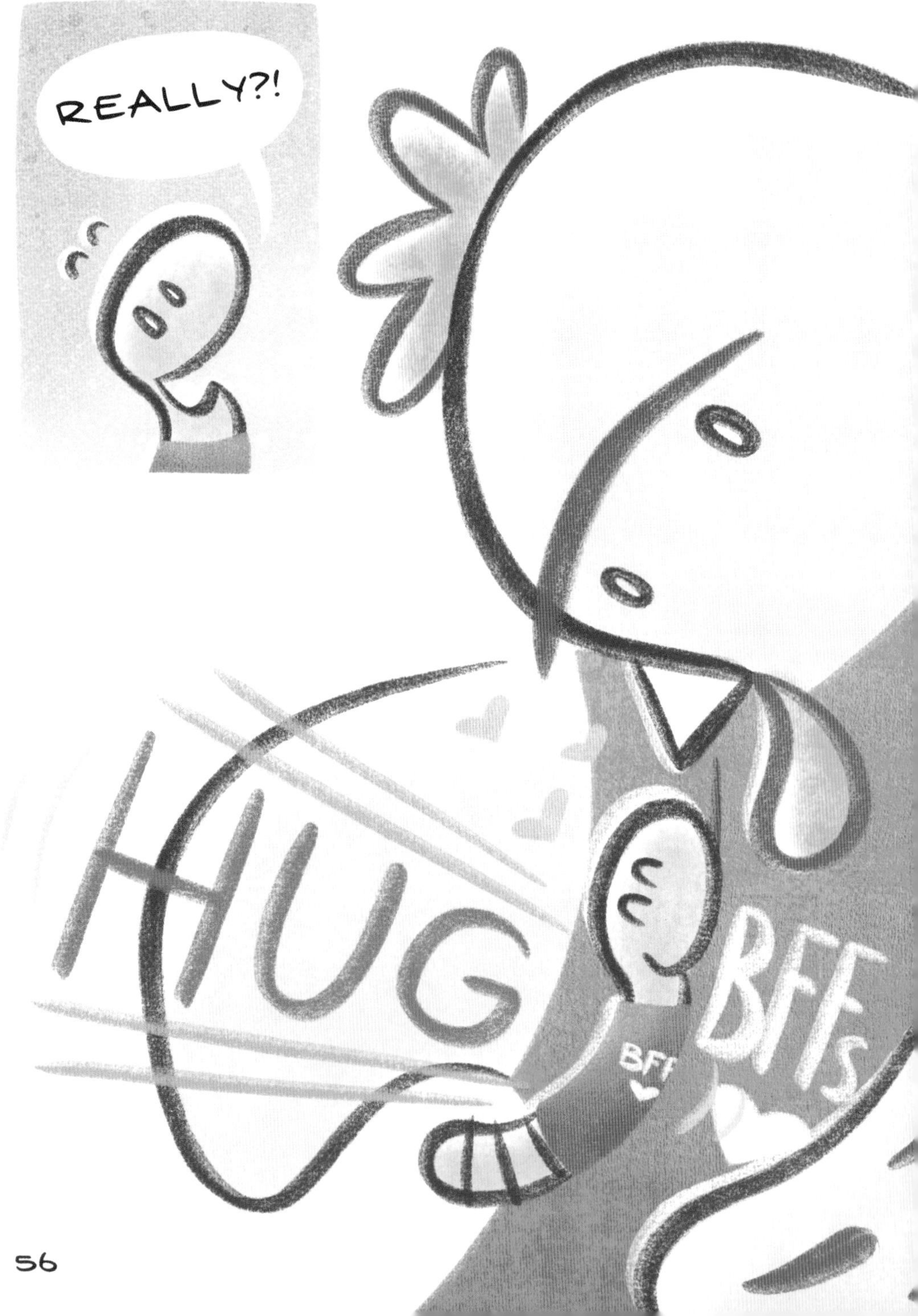
REALLY?!
HUG
BFFS
BFF

So what are our BFF rules?

Maybe there are no rules. Maybe it's just whatever makes us . . . not cranky.

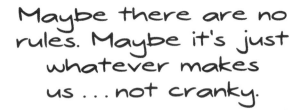

What would make you happy?

Well . . . I think friends don't keep secrets.

Ooh, that's a good one! I'll start . . .

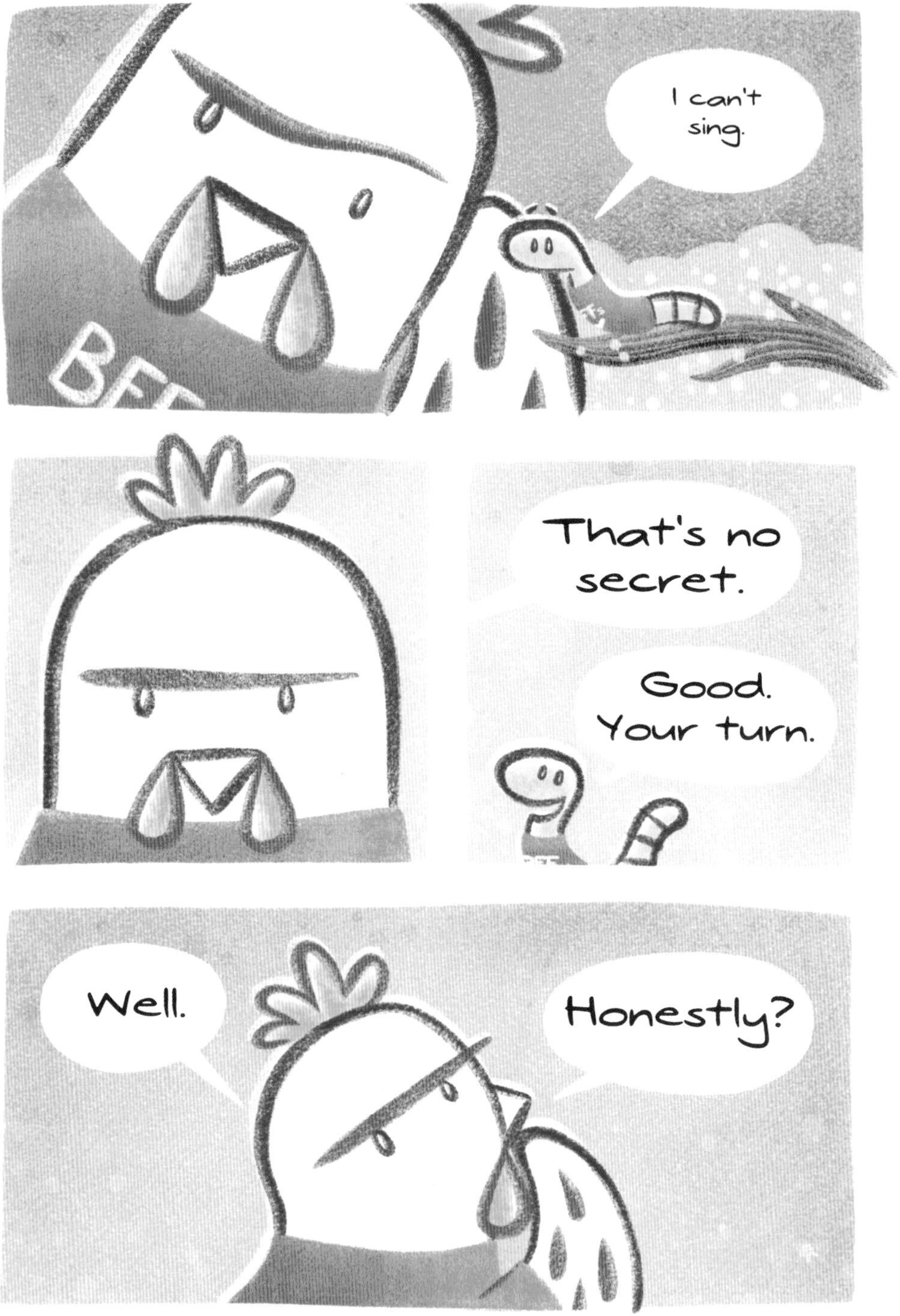
I can't sing.
That's no secret.
Good. Your turn.
Well.
Honestly?

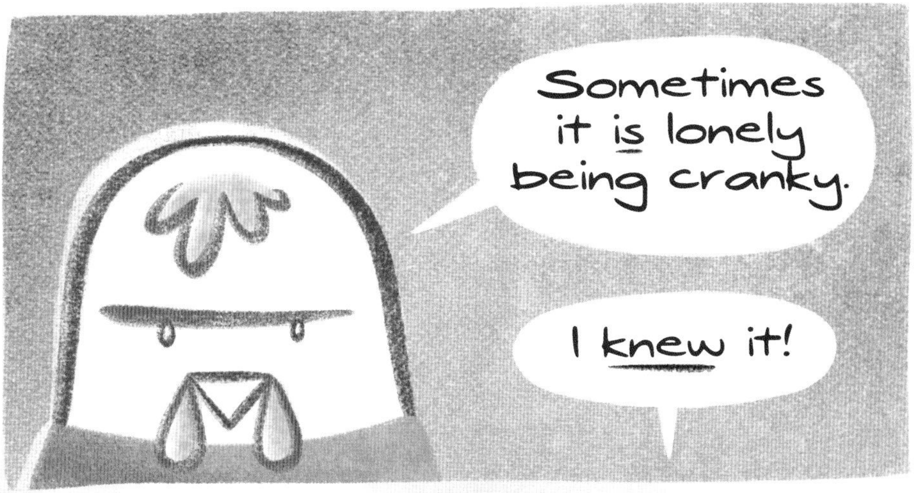
Sometimes it is lonely being cranky.
I knew it!

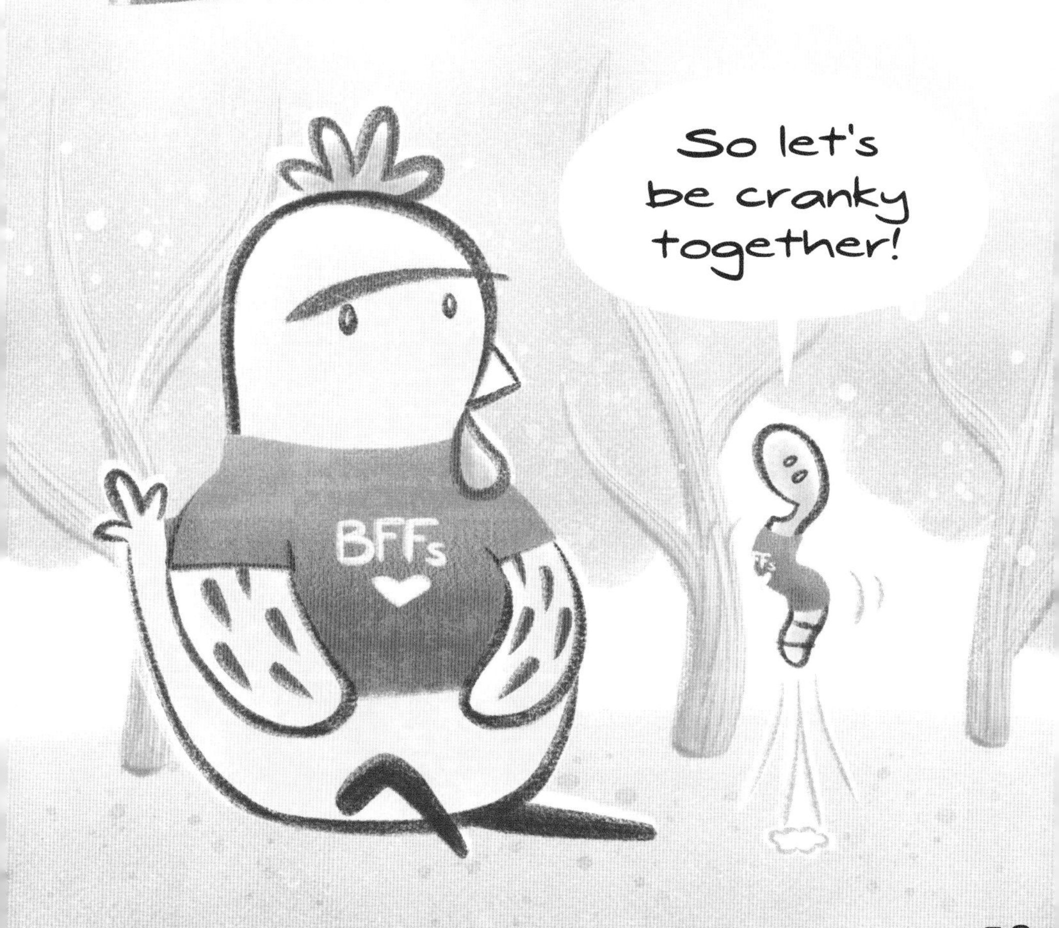
So let's be cranky together!
BFFs
BFFs

HOW TO BE CRANKY

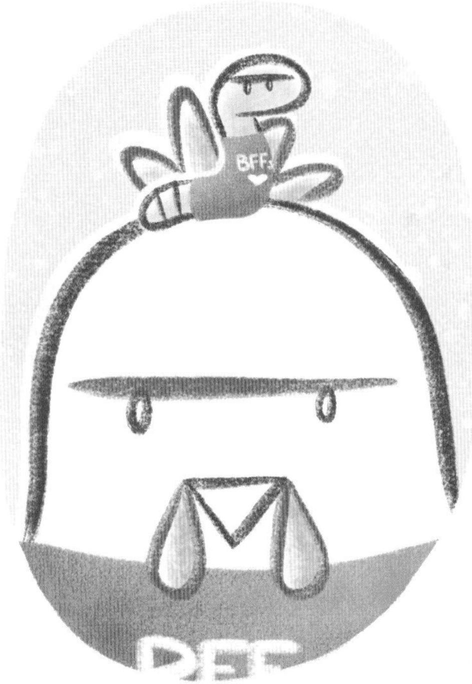

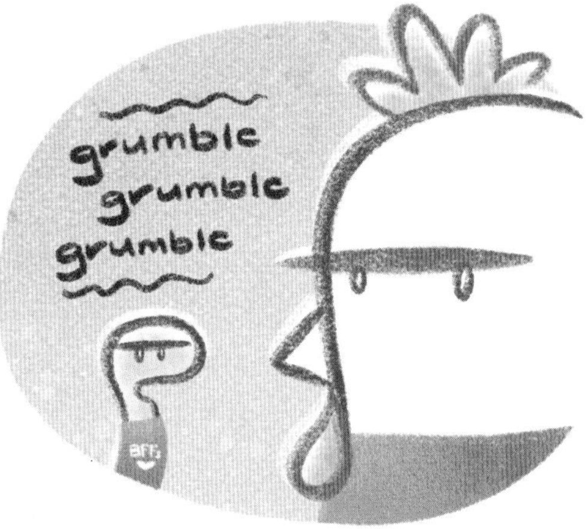
grumble
grumble
grumble

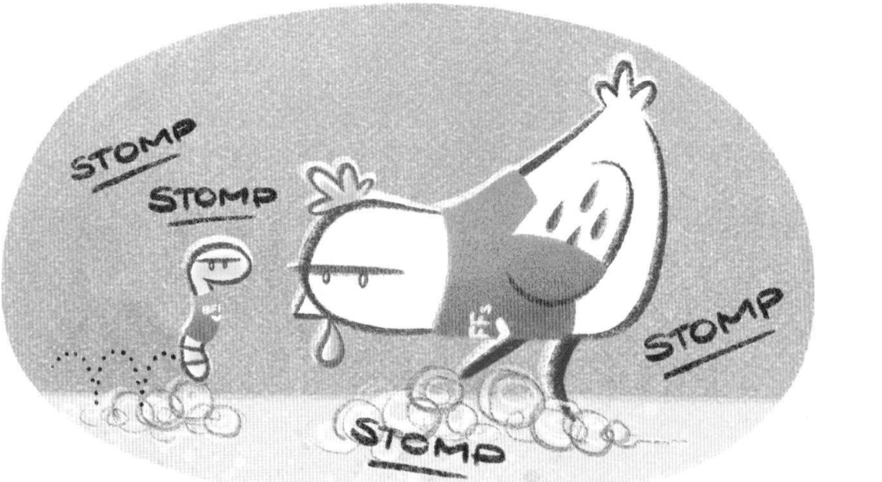
STOMP
STOMP
STOMP
STOMP

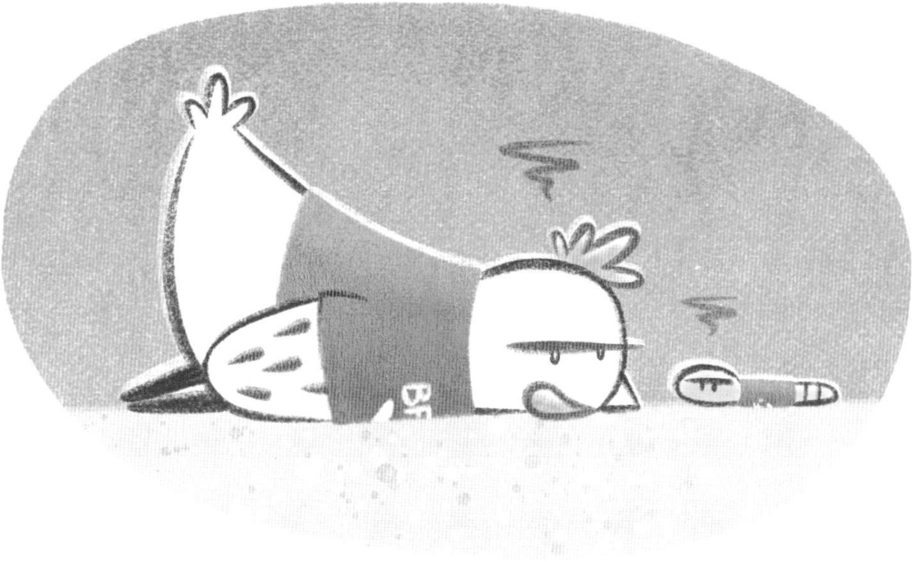
BFFs

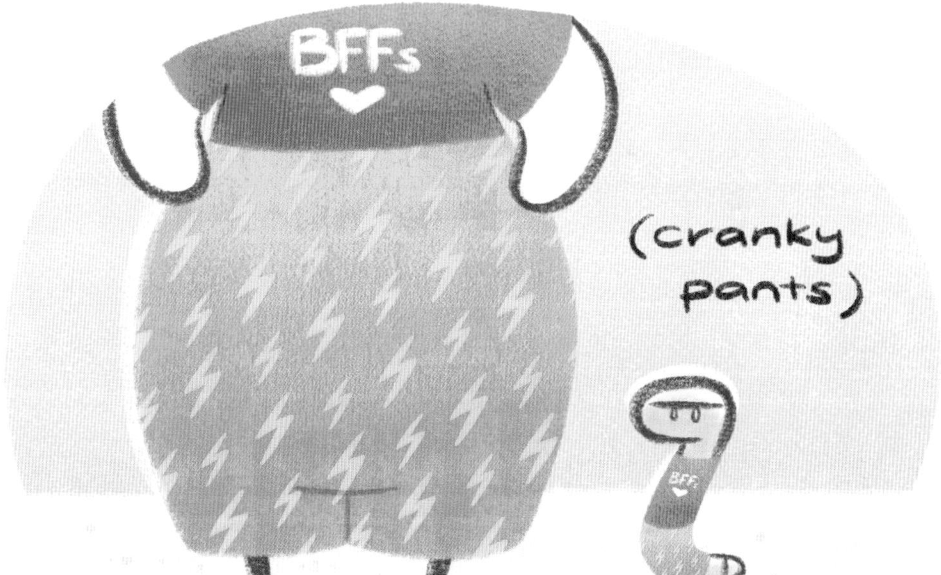
BFFs
(cranky
pants)
BFFs

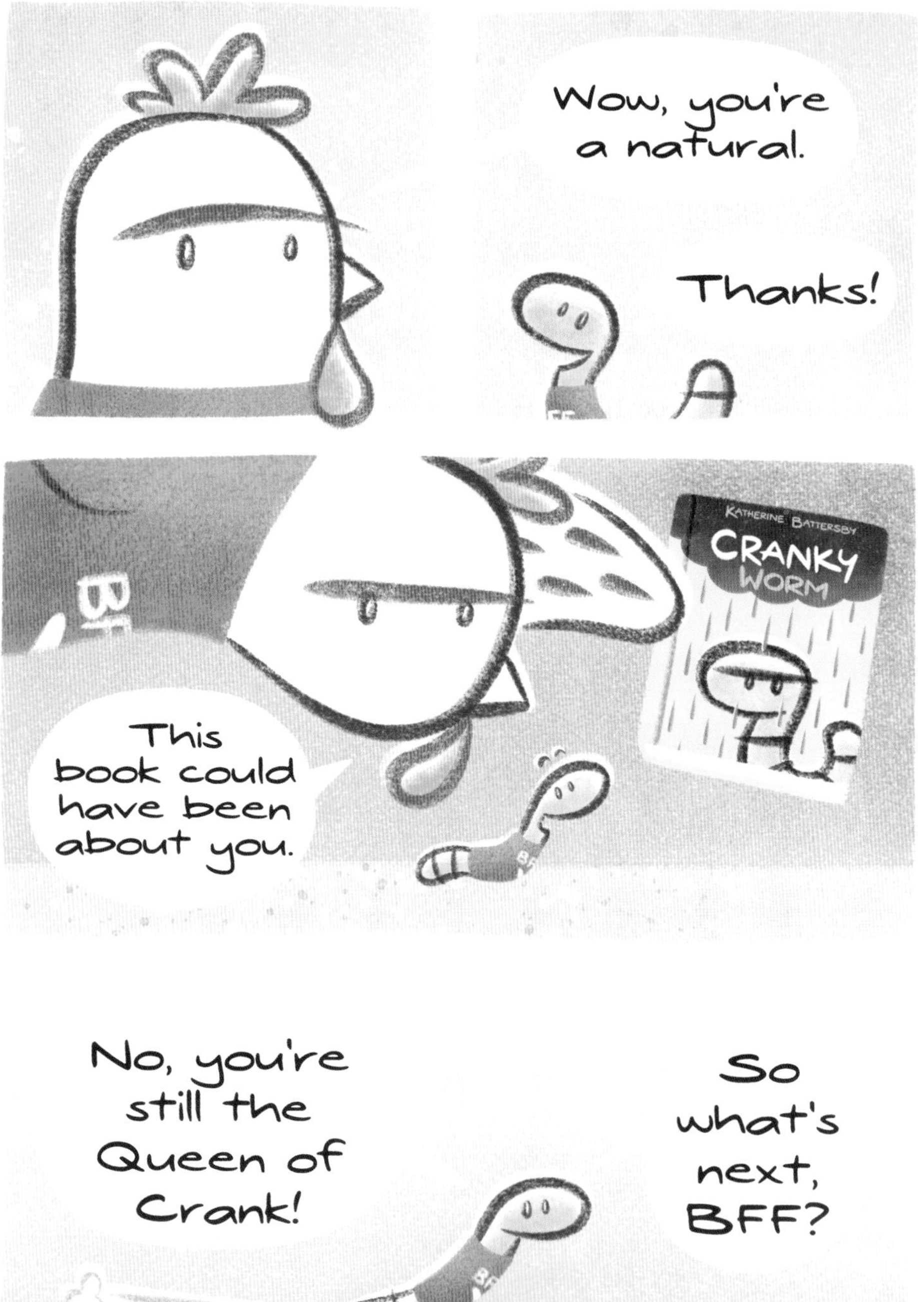
Wow, you're a natural.
Thanks!
KATHERINE BATTERSBY
CRANKY WORM
This book could have been about you.
No, you're still the Queen of Crank!
So what's next, BFF?

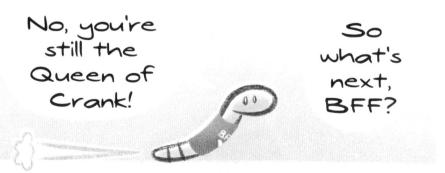

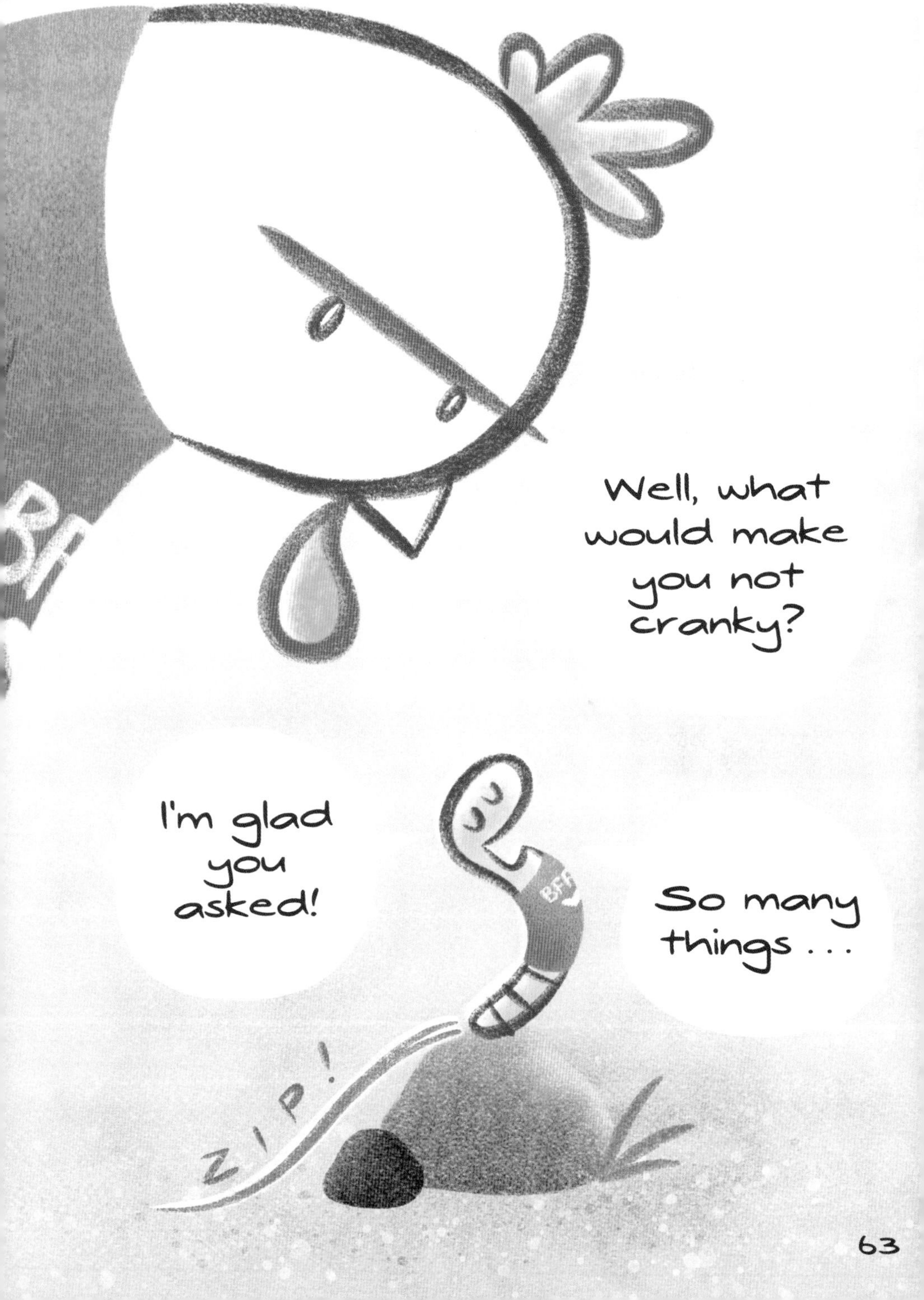

Well, what would make you not cranky?
I'm glad you asked!
So many things . . .
ZIP!

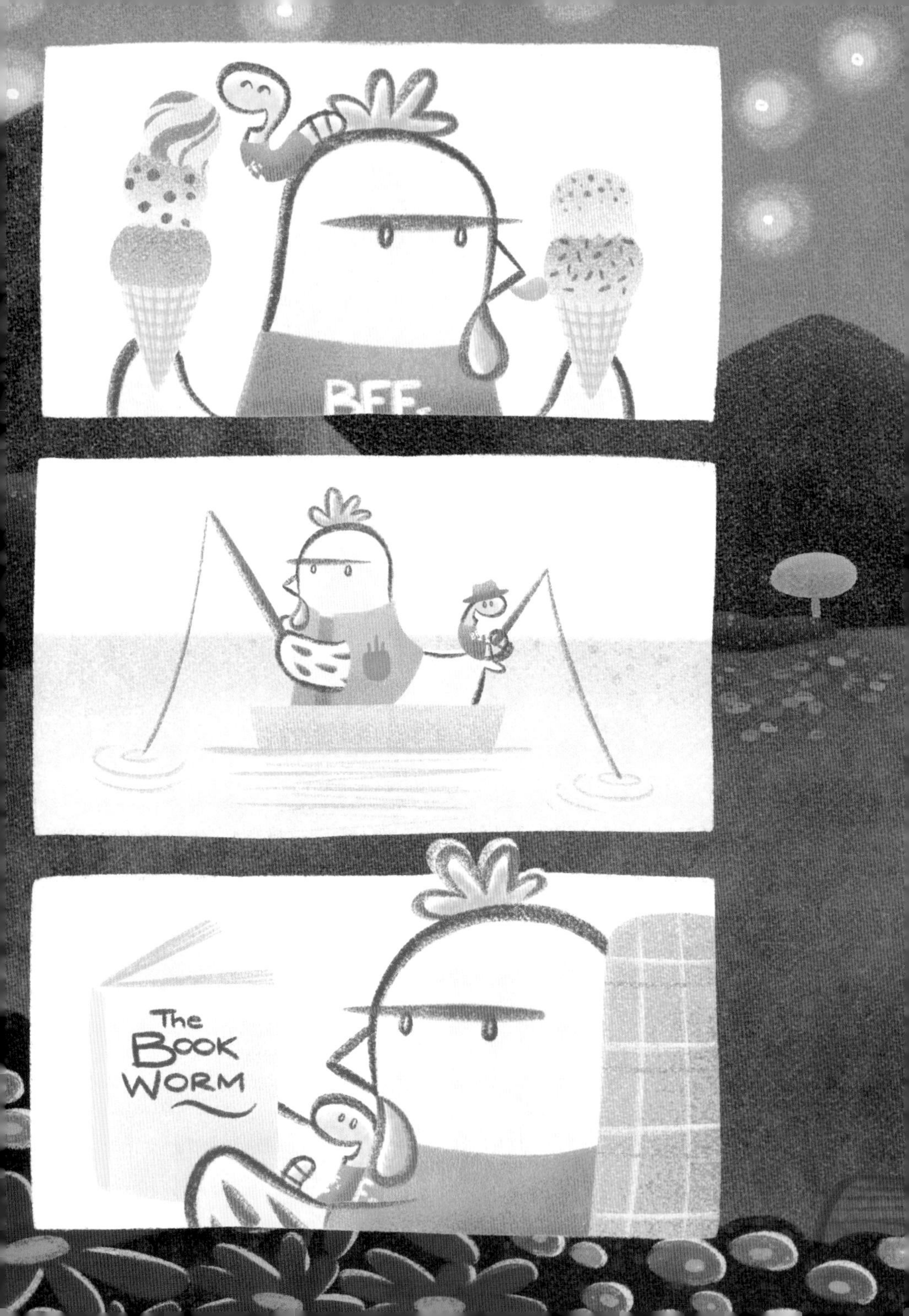
BFF
The Book Worm

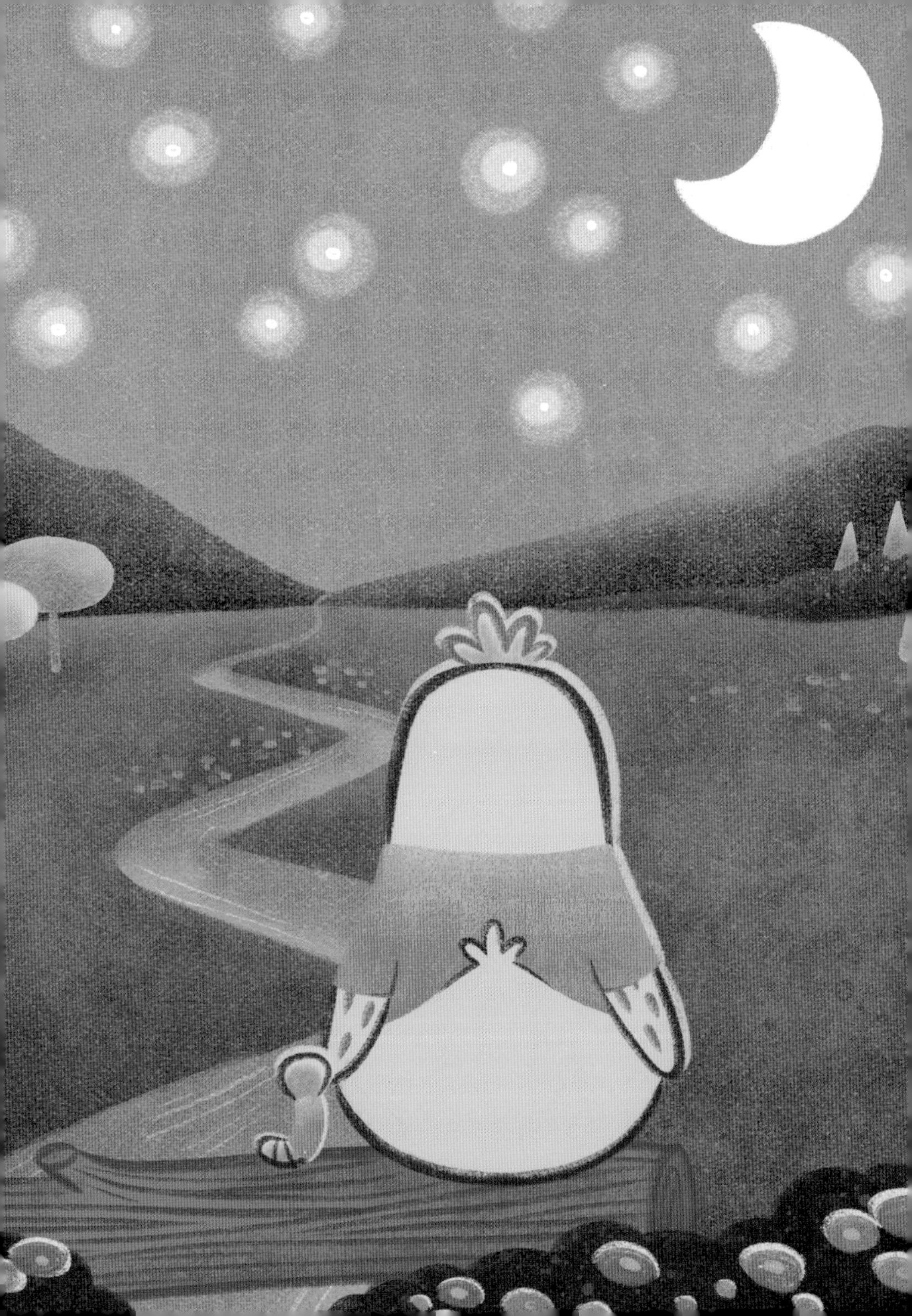

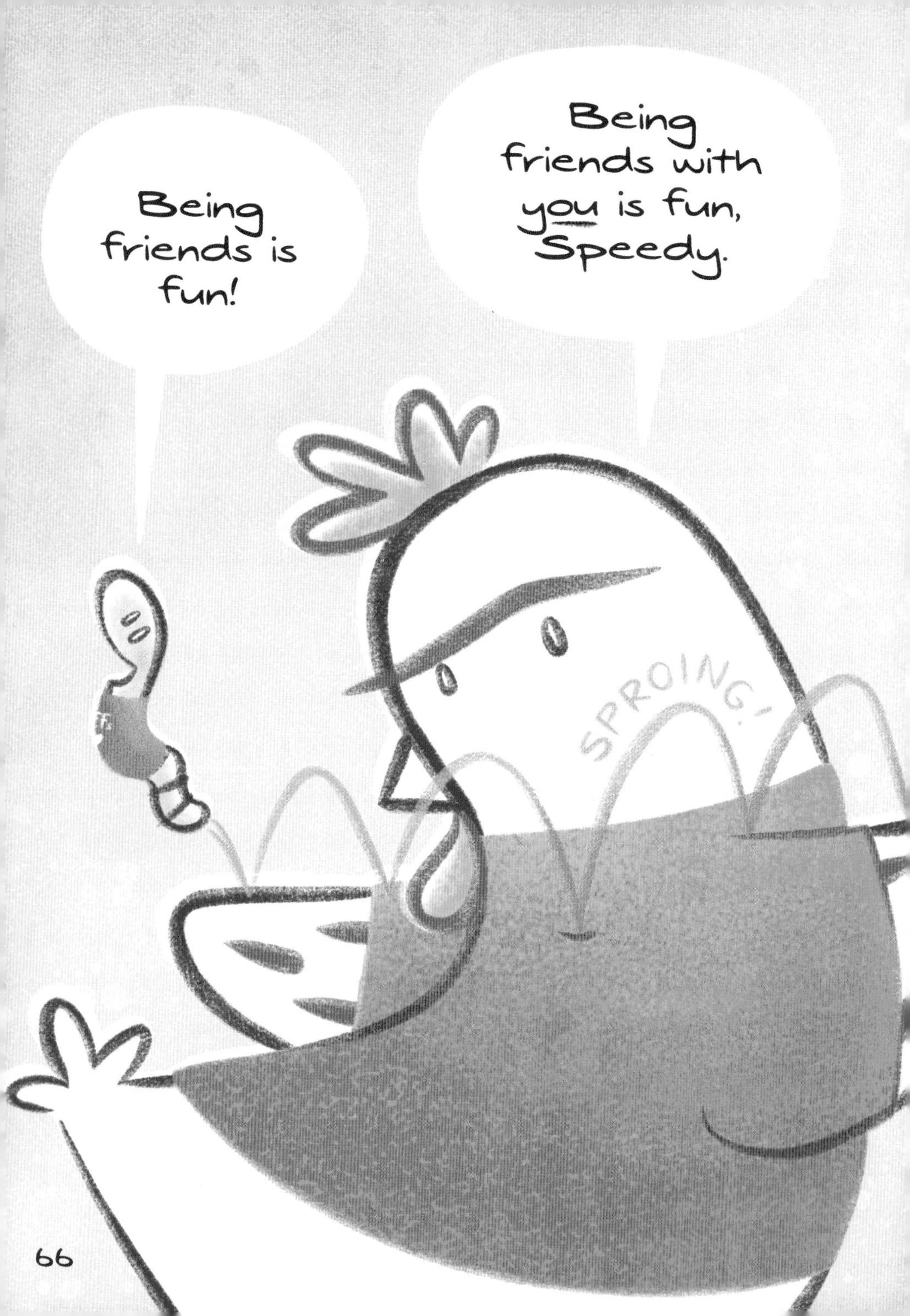
Being friends is fun!
Being friends with you is fun, Speedy.
SPROING!

Best
feathered
friends
forever!

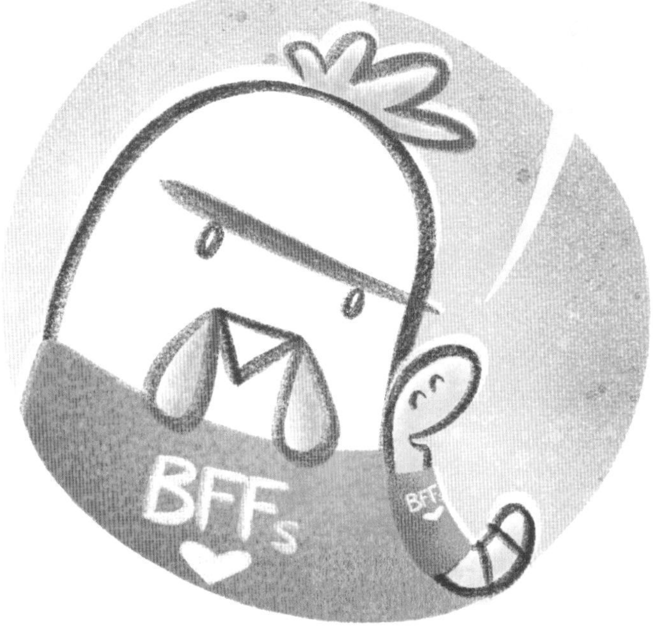
BFFs
BFF

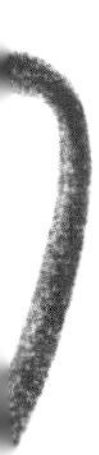

More CHICKEN FACTS

Why Did the Chicken REALLY Cross the Road?

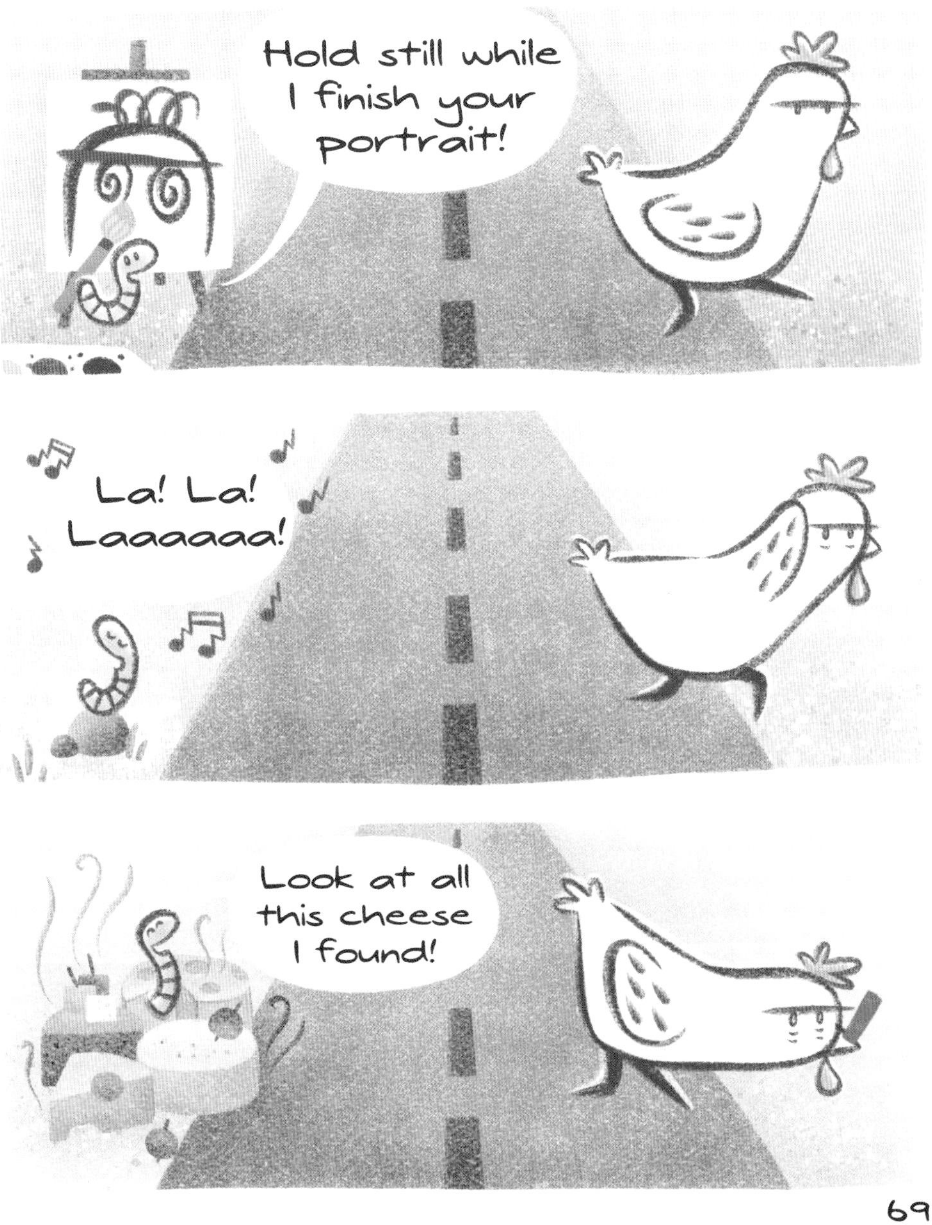
Hold still while I finish your portrait!
La! La! Laaaaaa!
Look at all this cheese I found!

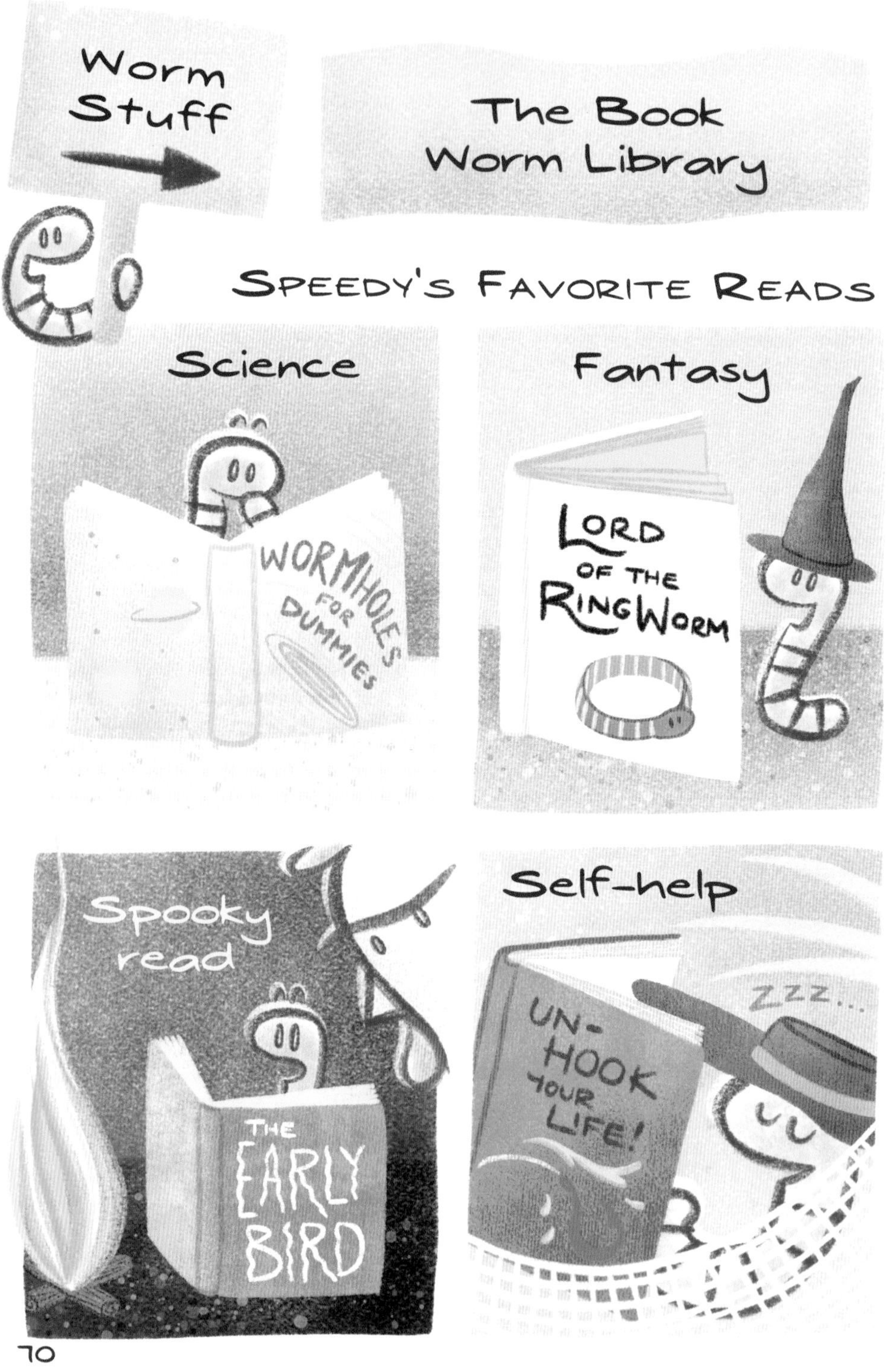
Worm Stuff
The Book Worm Library
SPEEDY'S FAVORITE READS
Science
WORMHOLES FOR DUMMIES
Fantasy
LORD OF THE RINGWORM
Spooky read
THE EARLY BIRD
Self-help
UN-HOOK YOUR LIFE!
ZZZ...

Speedy: The Fastest Draw in the West

Famous Dirt Drawings

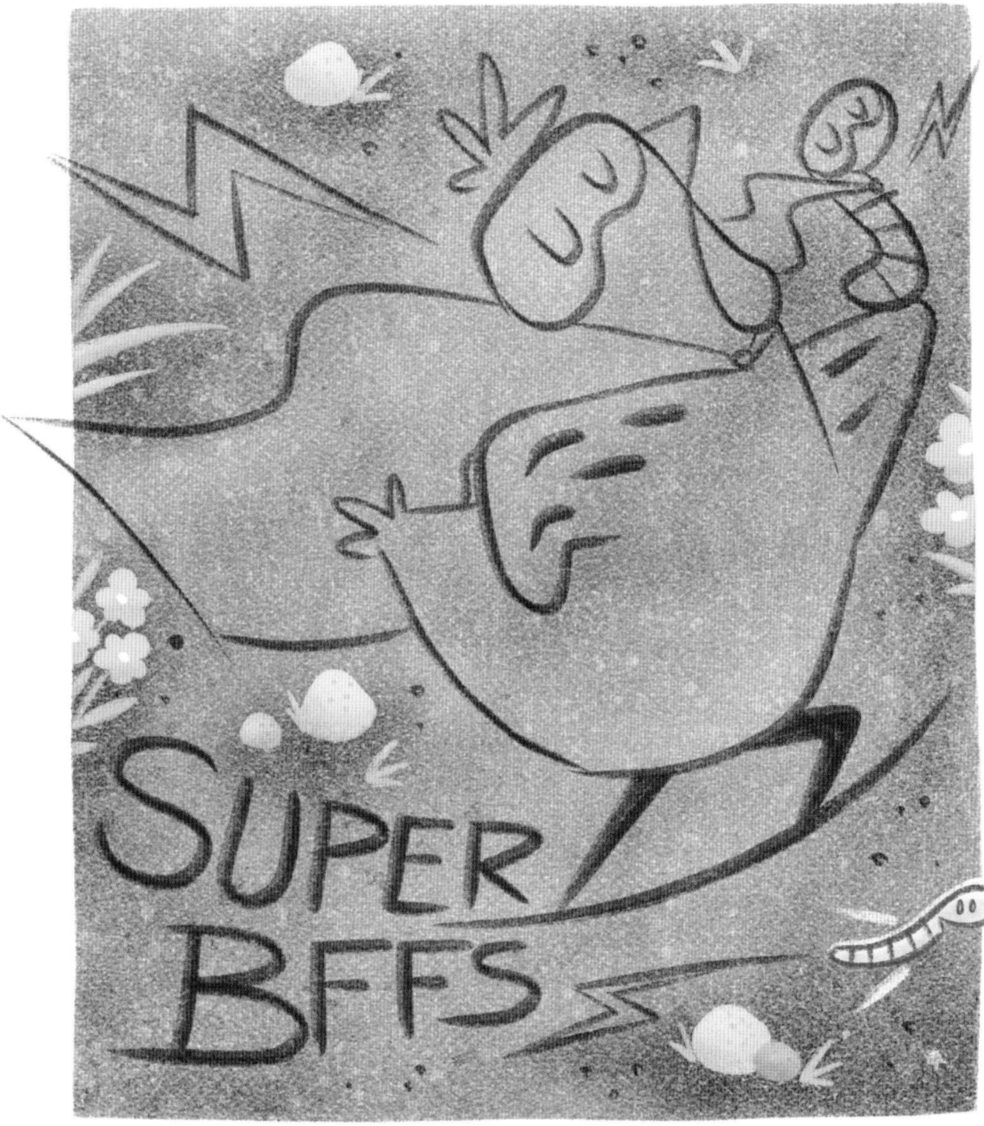
SUPER
BFFS

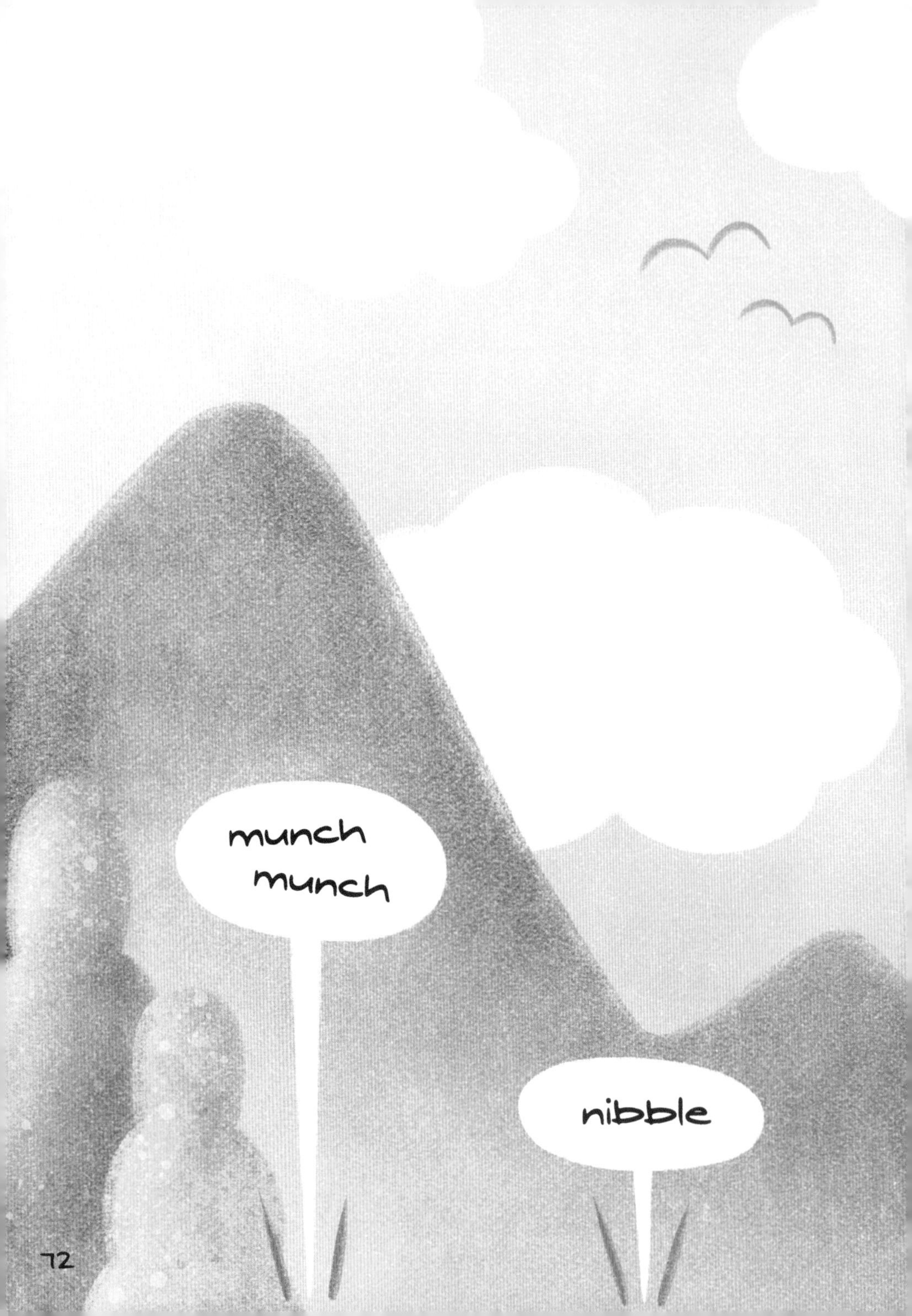
munch munch
nibble

3

THE AMAZING FLYING WING WORM

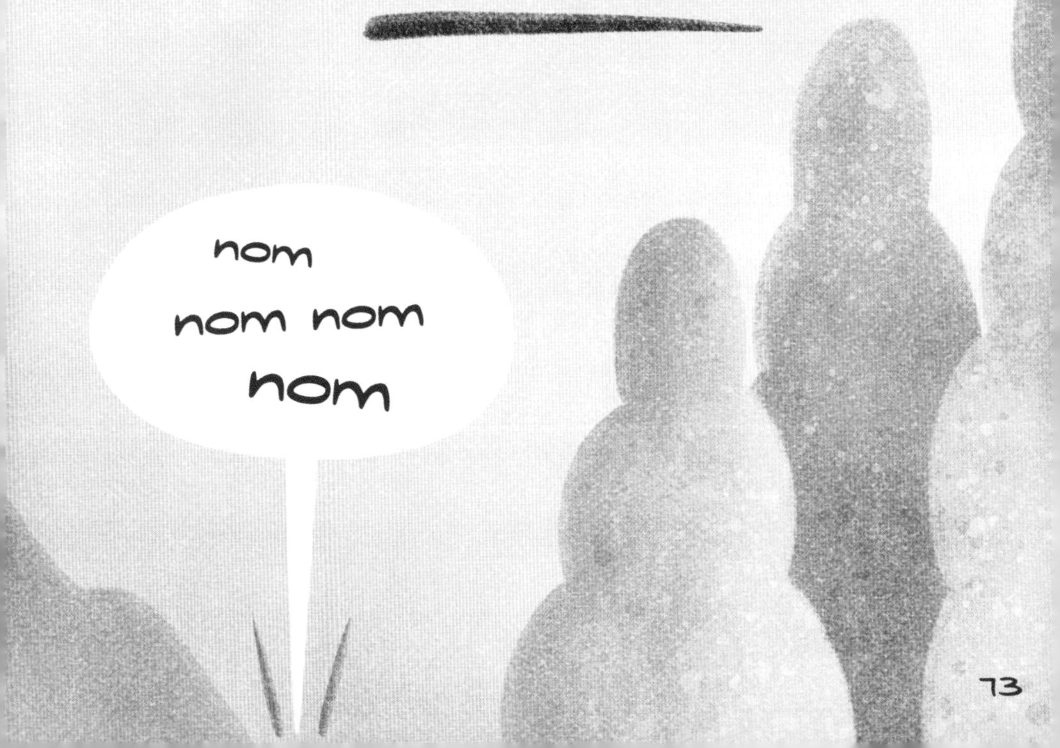
nom
nom nom nom
nom

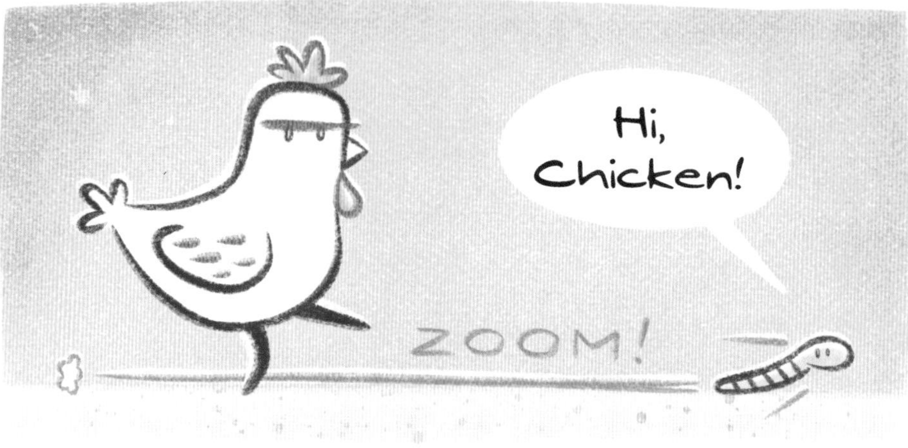
Hi, Chicken!
ZOOM!

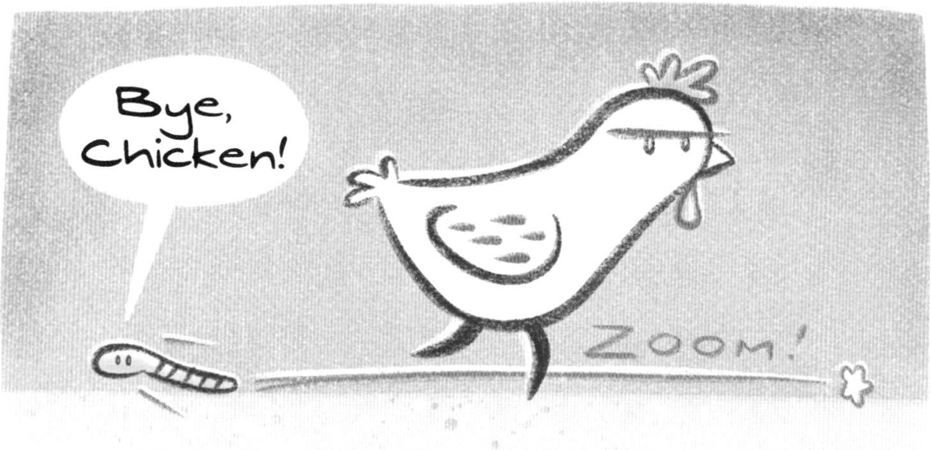
Bye, Chicken!
ZOOM!

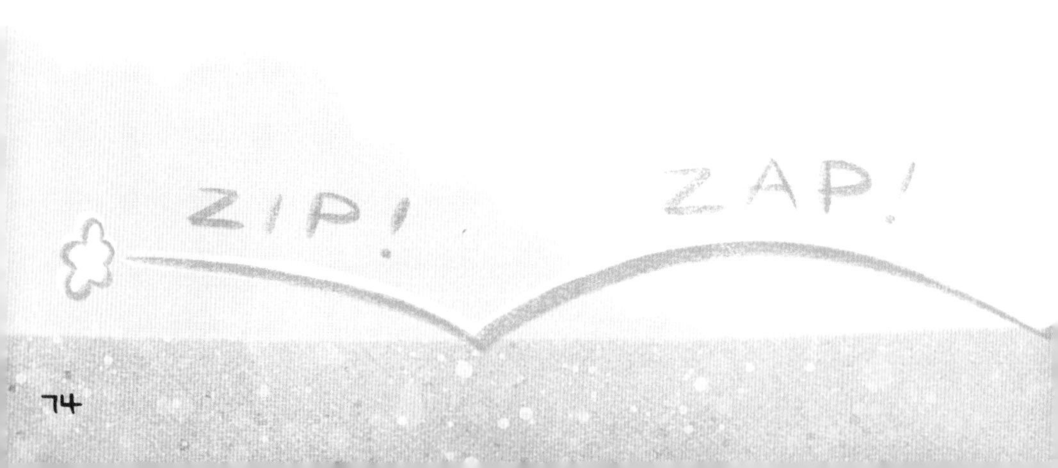
ZIP!
ZAP!

Watch
me fly,
Chicken!

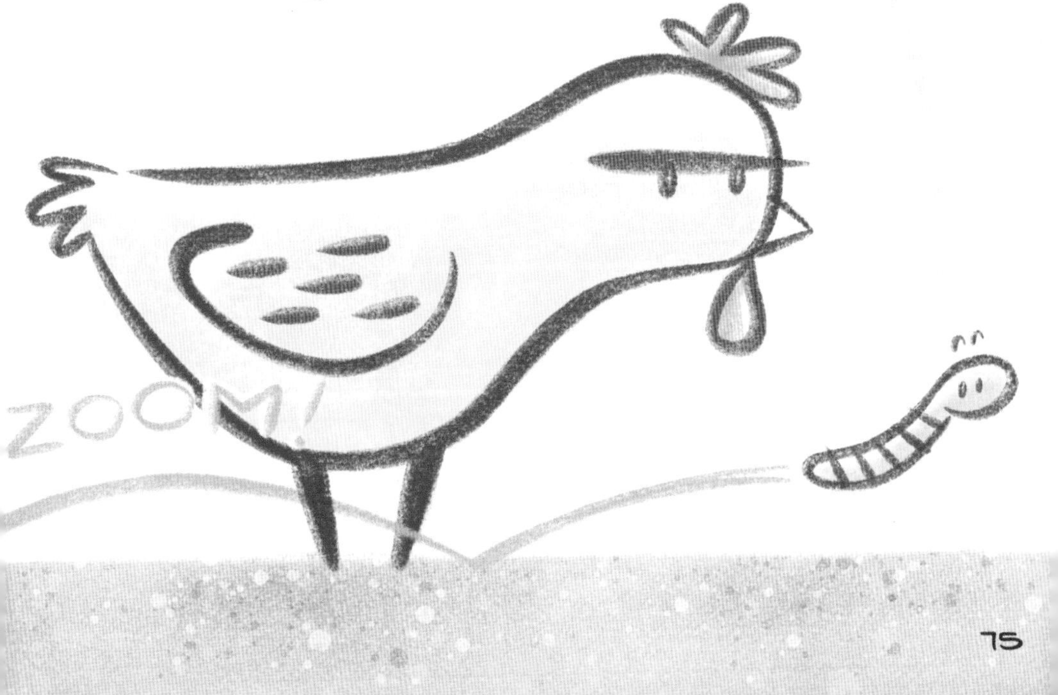
ZOOM!

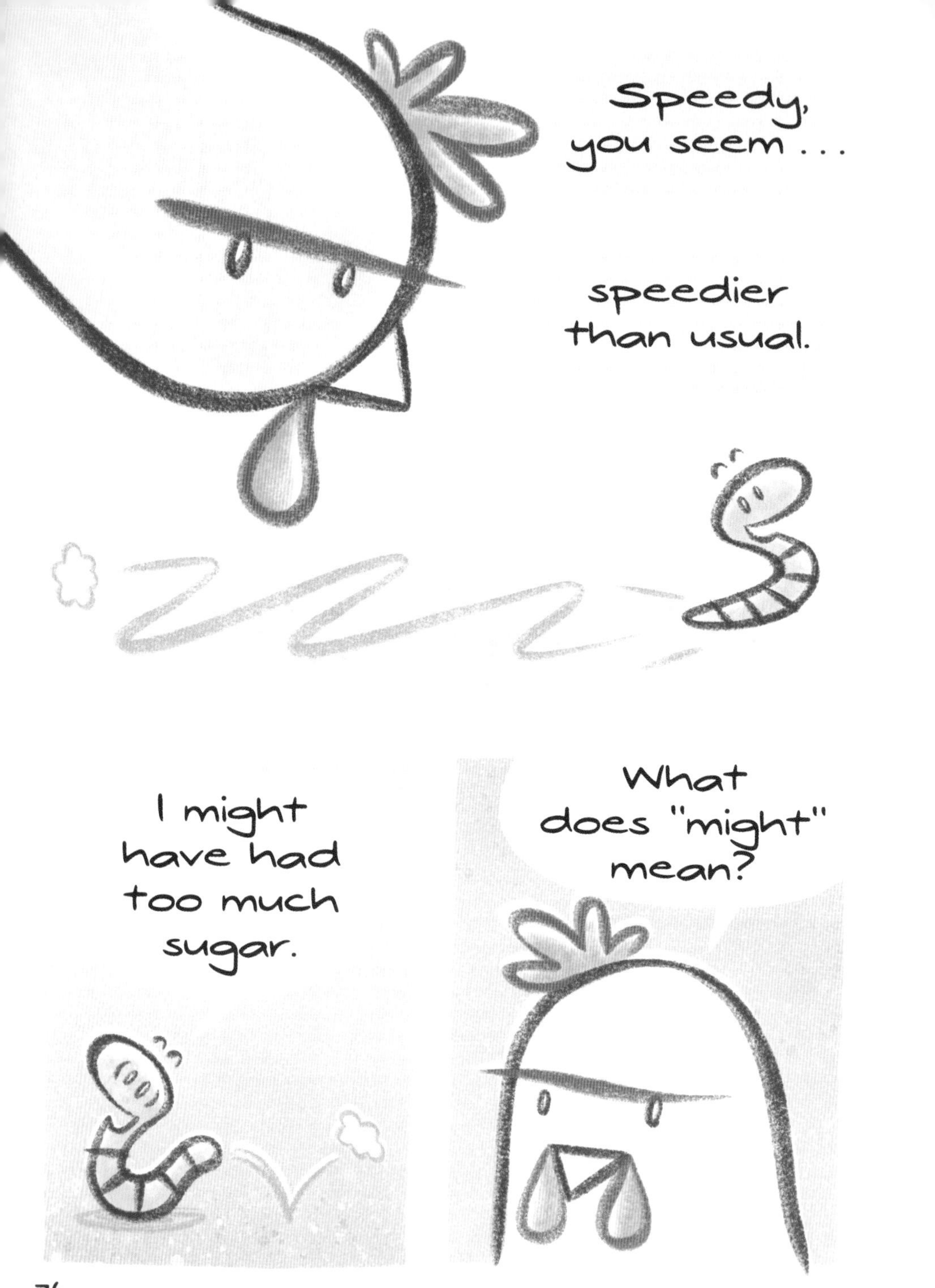
Speedy, you seem . . .
speedier than usual.
I might have had too much sugar.
What does "might" mean?

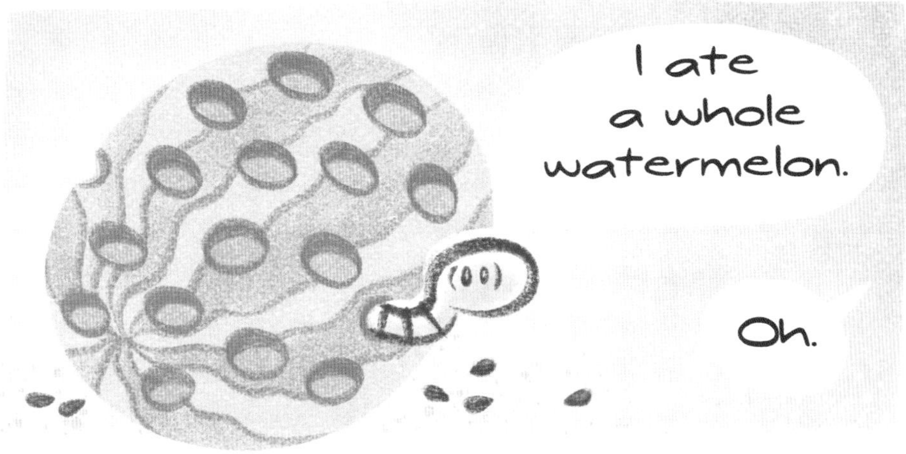

I ate
a whole
watermelon.
Oh.

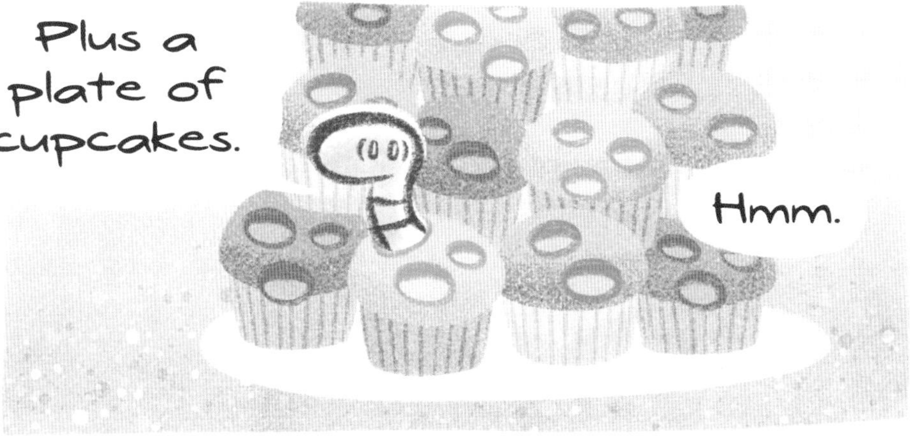

Plus a
plate of
cupcakes.
Hmm.

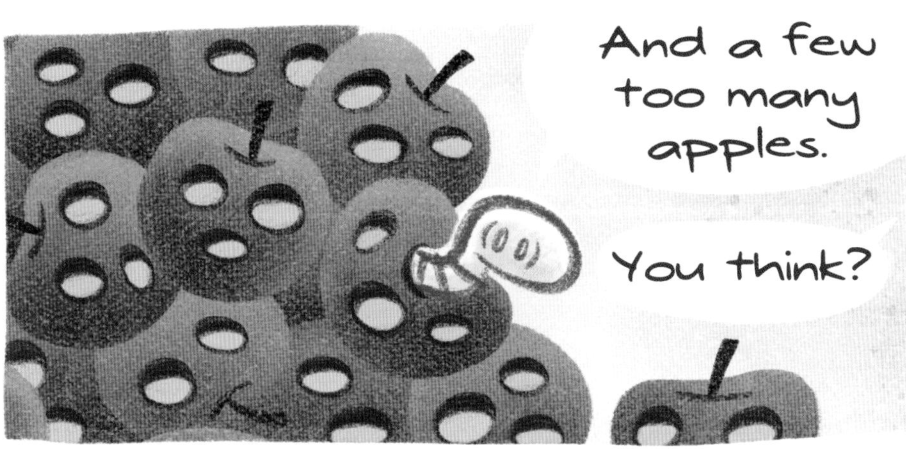

And a few
too many
apples.
You think?

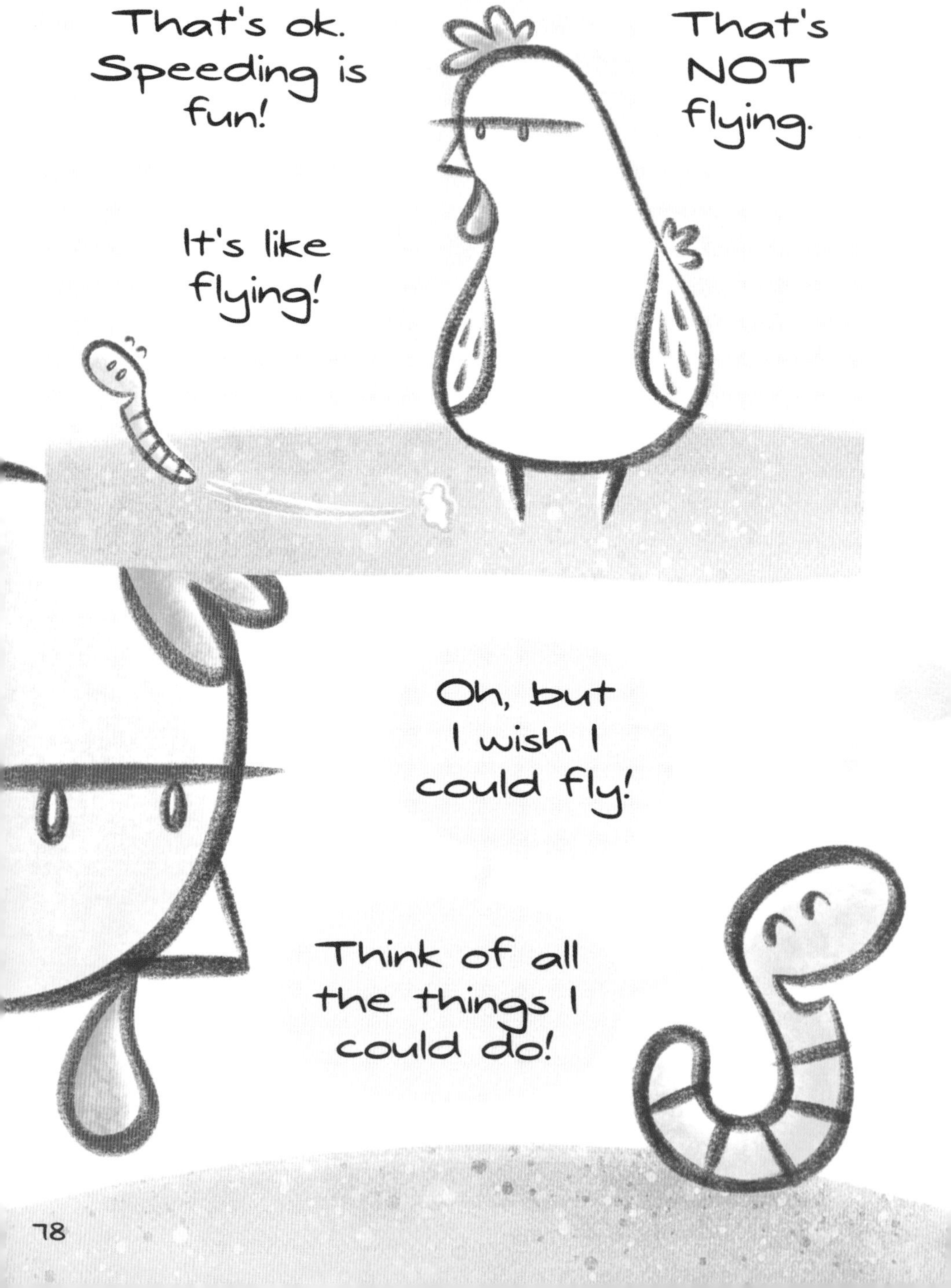
That's ok. Speeding is fun!
That's NOT flying.
It's like flying!
Oh, but I wish I could fly!
Think of all the things I could do!

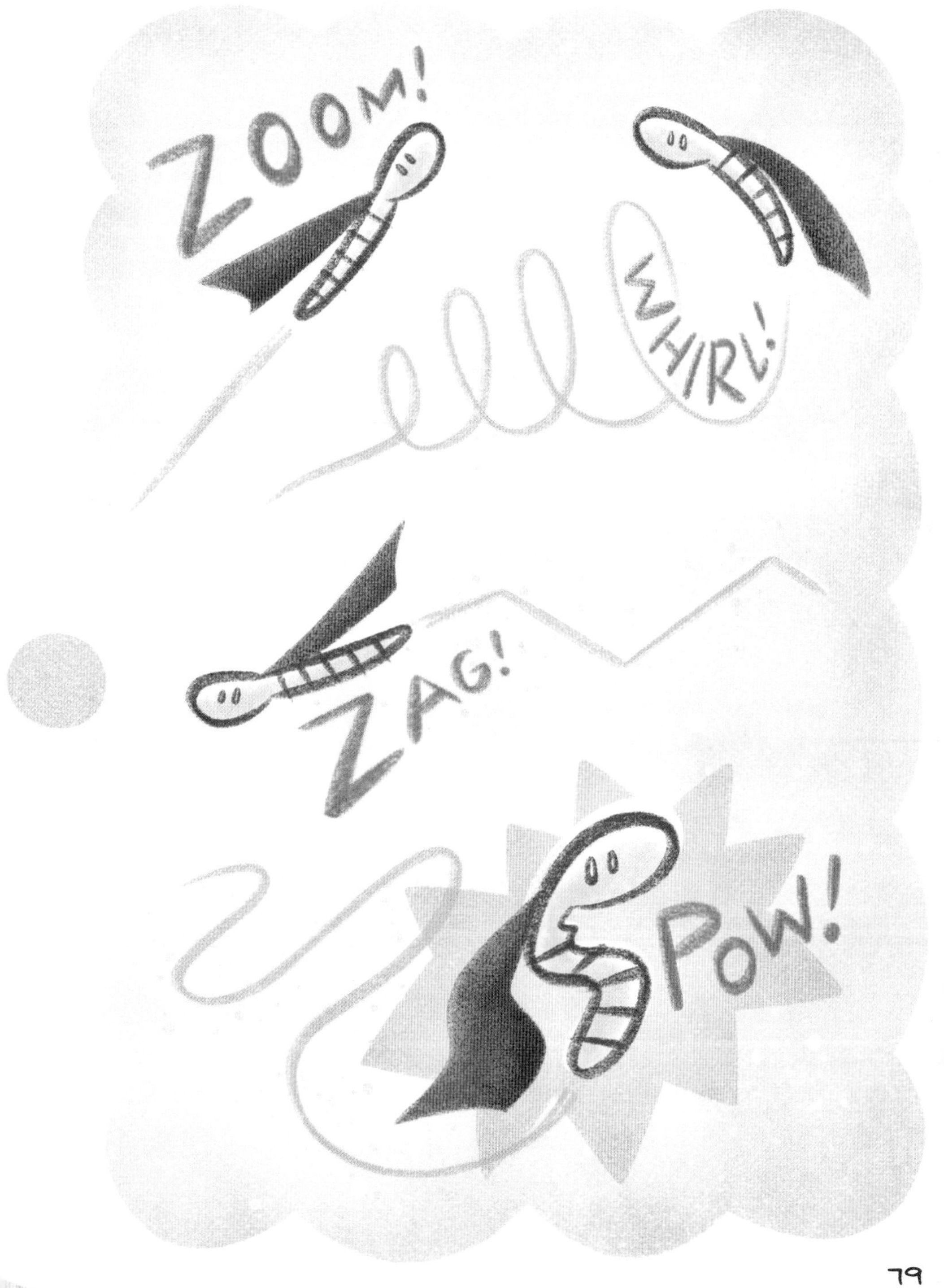
ZOOM!
WHIRL!
ZAG!
POW!

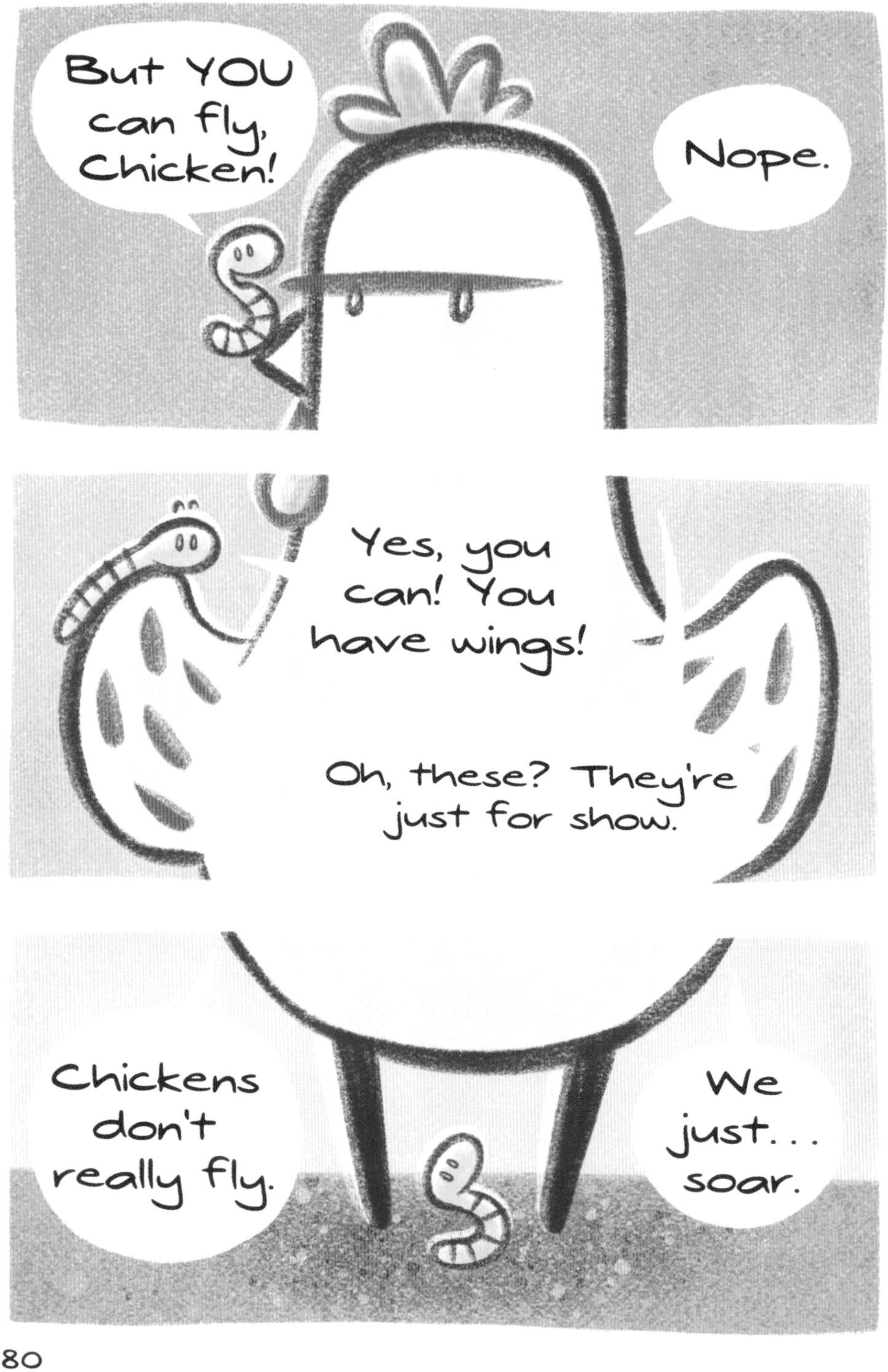
But YOU can fly, Chicken!
Nope.
Yes, you can! You have wings!
Oh, these? They're just for show.
Chickens don't really fly.
We just... soar.

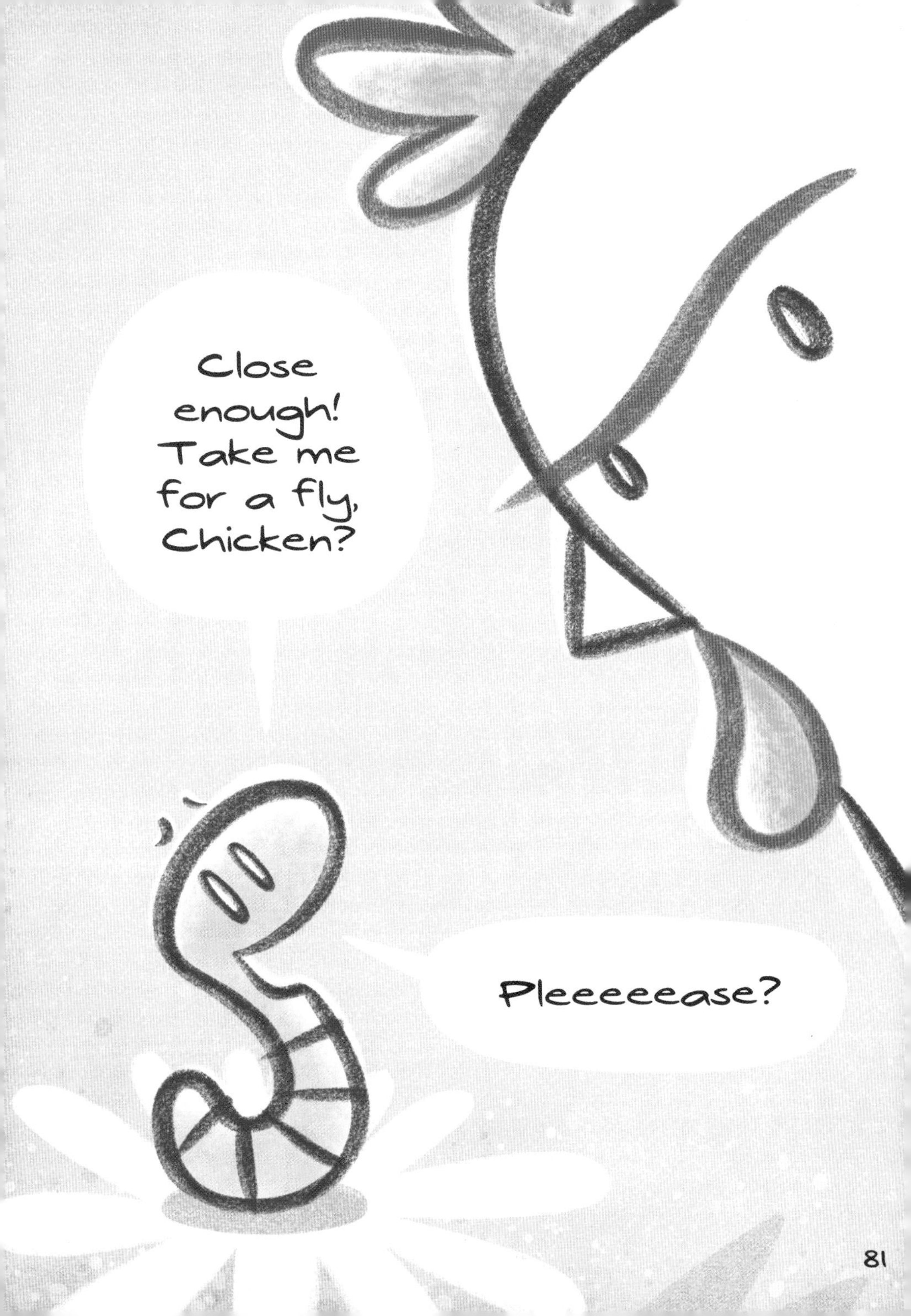
Close enough! Take me for a fly, Chicken?
Pleeeeease?

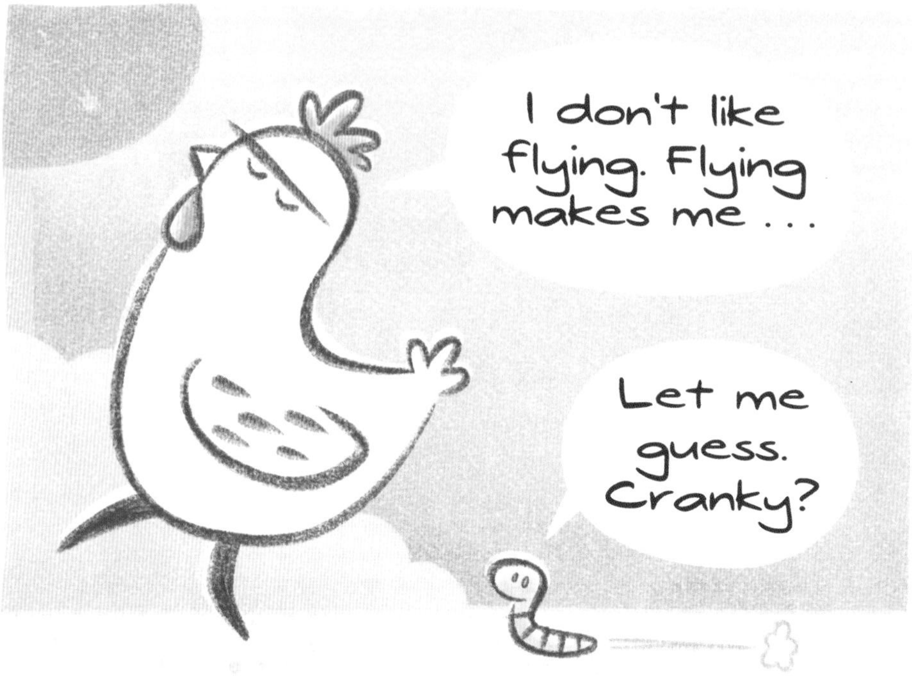
I don't like flying. Flying makes me . . .
Let me guess. Cranky?

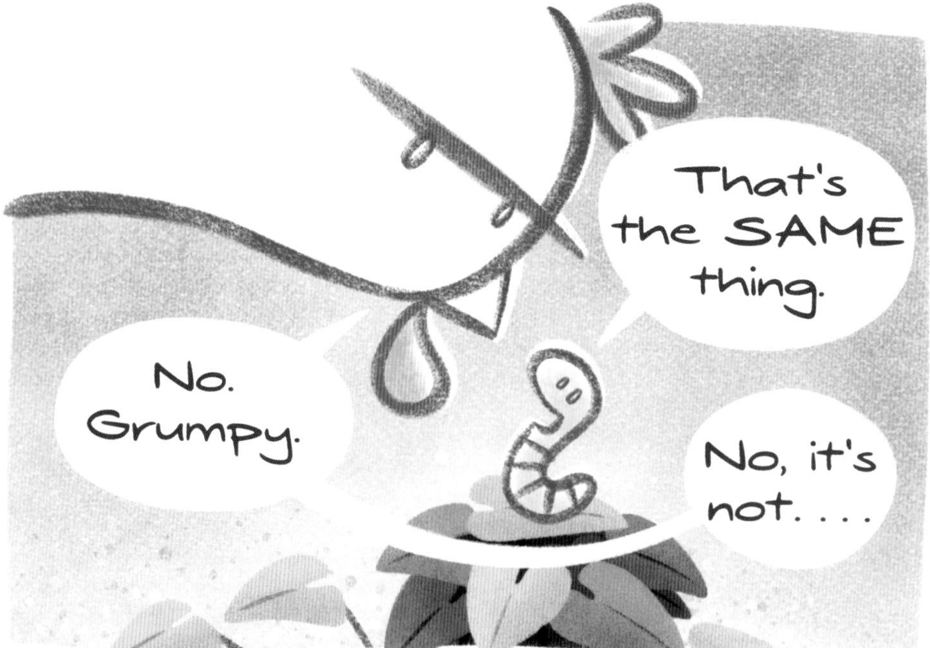
That's the SAME thing.
No. Grumpy.
No, it's not. . . .

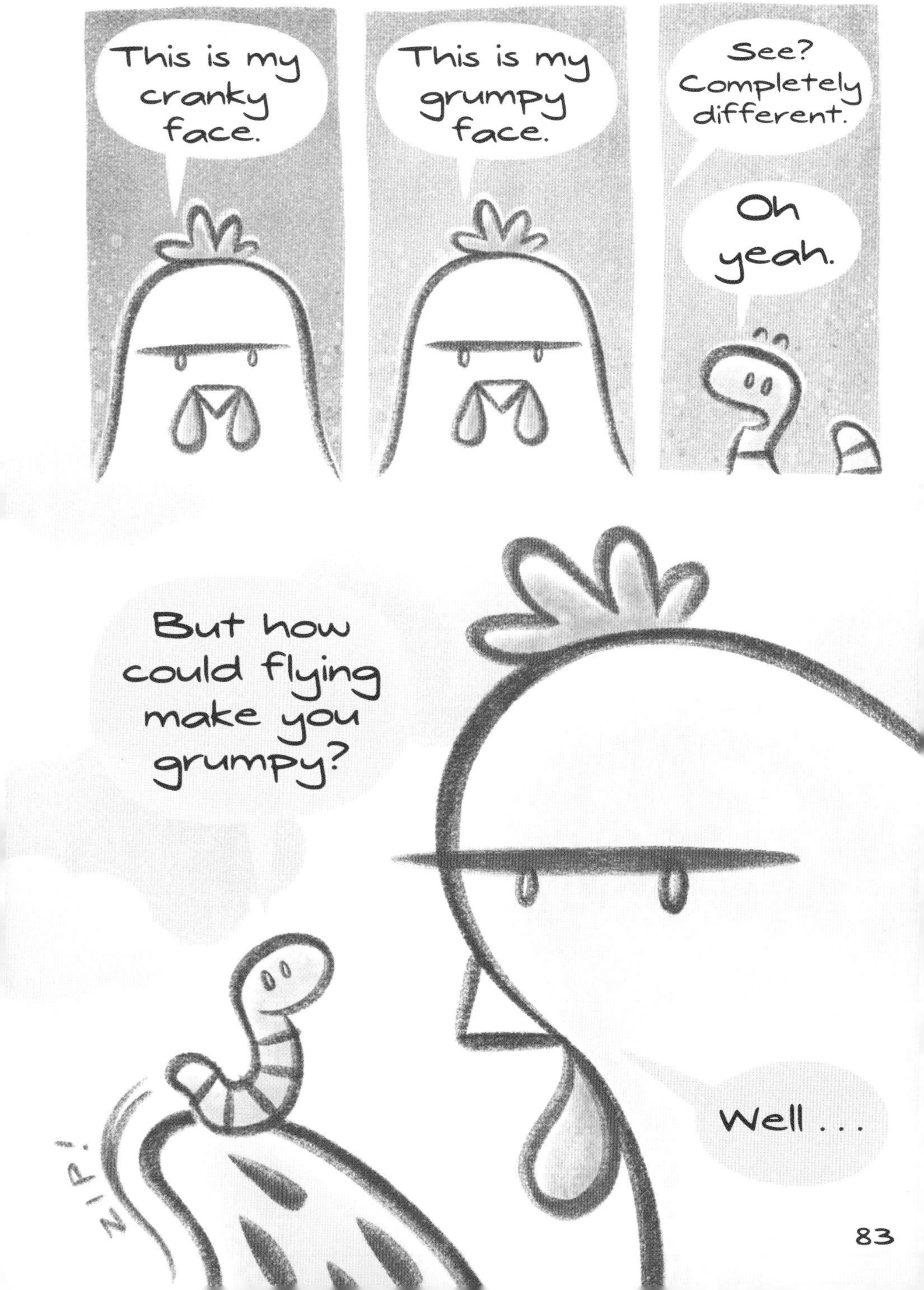
This is my cranky face.
This is my grumpy face.
See? Completely different.
Oh yeah.
But how could flying make you grumpy?
Well . . .
ZIP!

Why Flying Makes Cranky Chicken Grumpy

Bugs splat in face

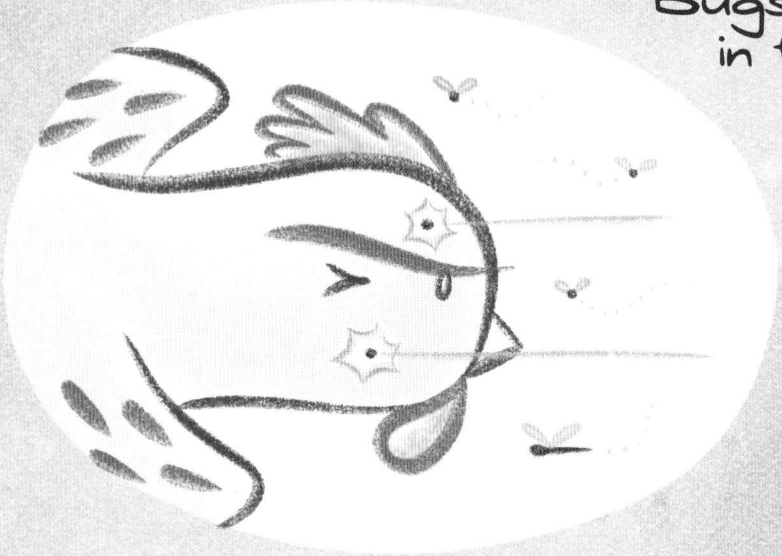

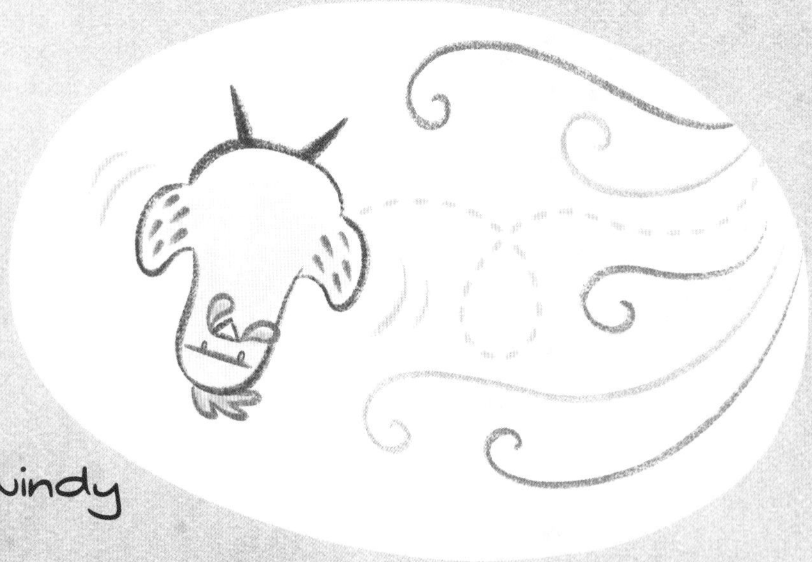

Too windy

Messes up feathers

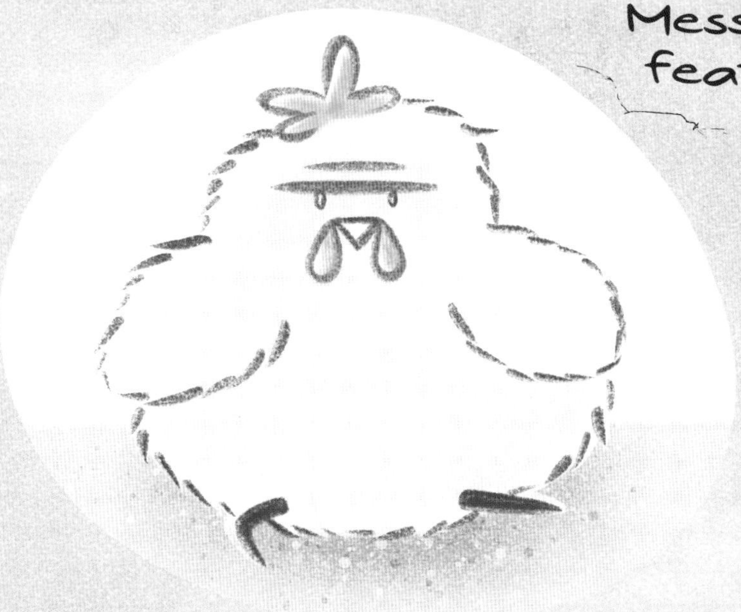

Power lines

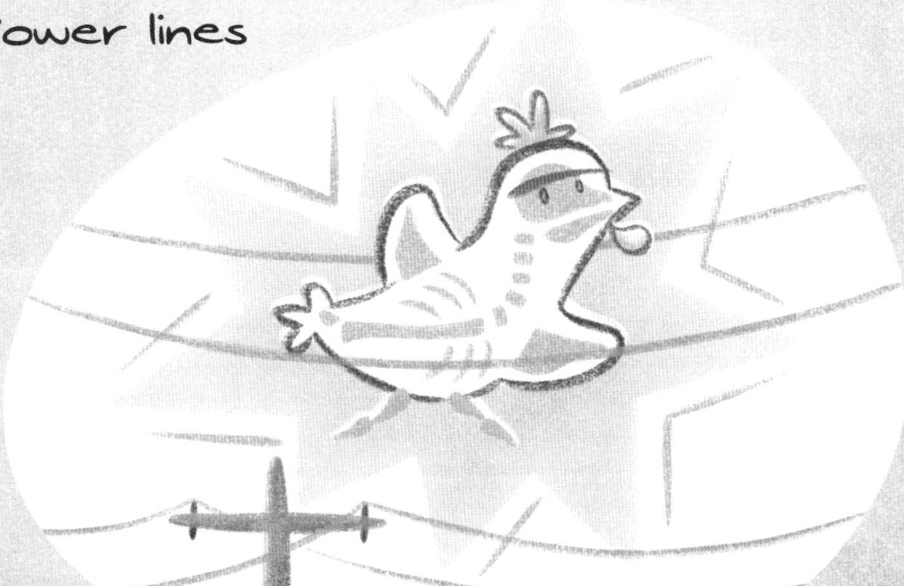

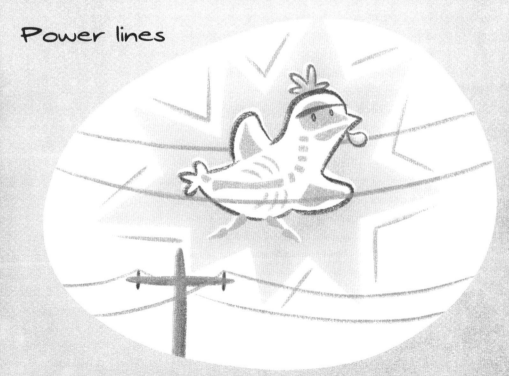

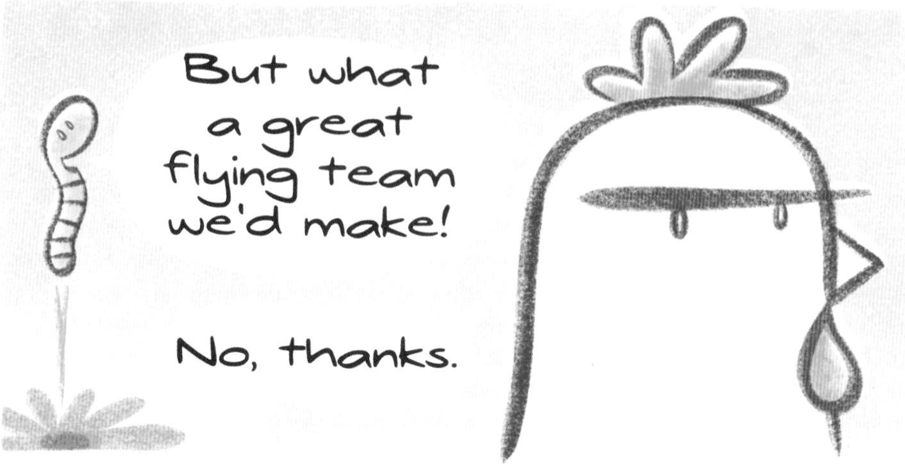
But what a great flying team we'd make!
No, thanks.

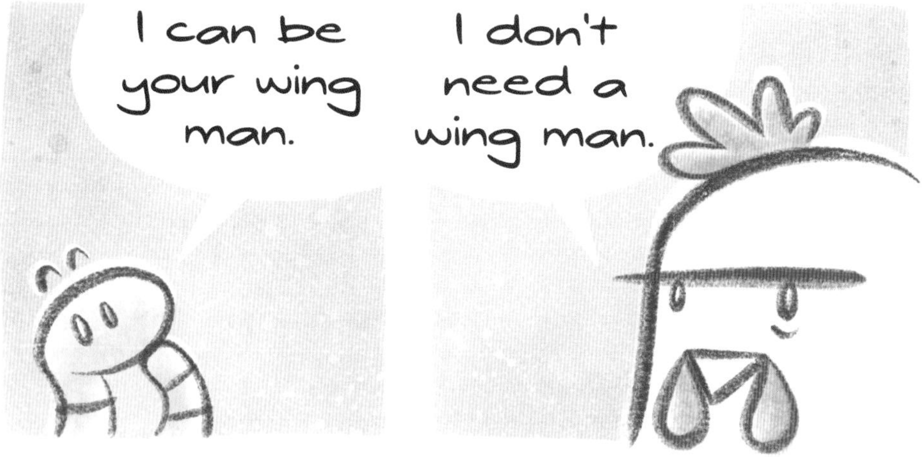
I can be your wing man.
I don't need a wing man.

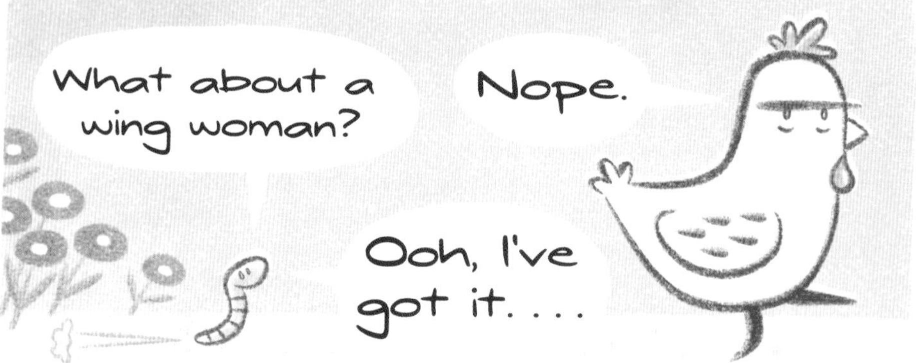
What about a wing woman?
Nope.
Ooh, I've got it. . . .

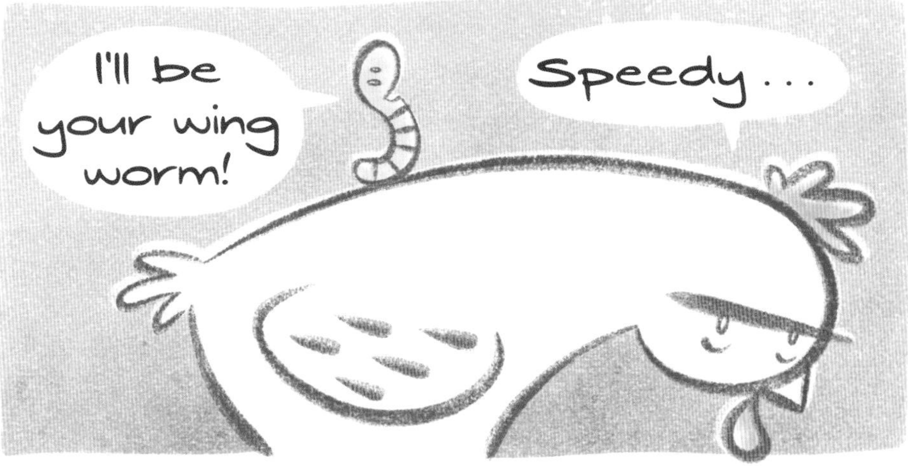
I'll be your wing worm!
Speedy . . .

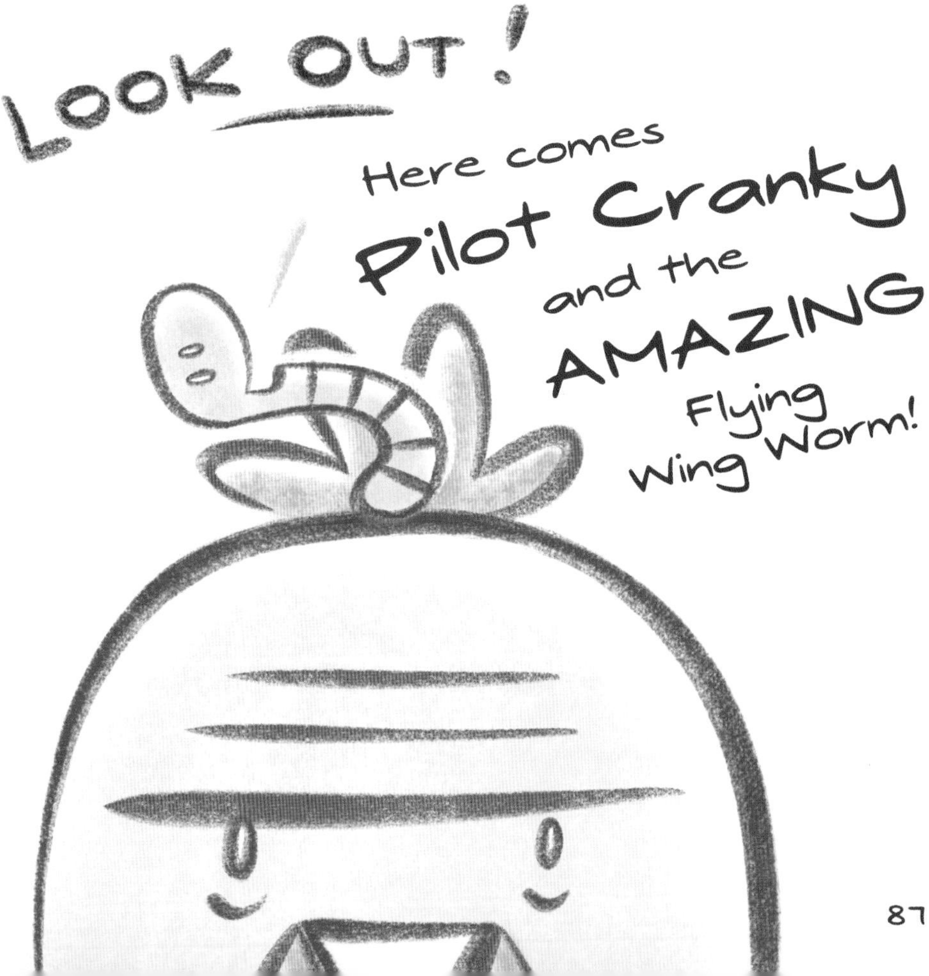
LOOK OUT!
Here comes
Pilot Cranky
and the
AMAZING
Flying
Wing Worm!

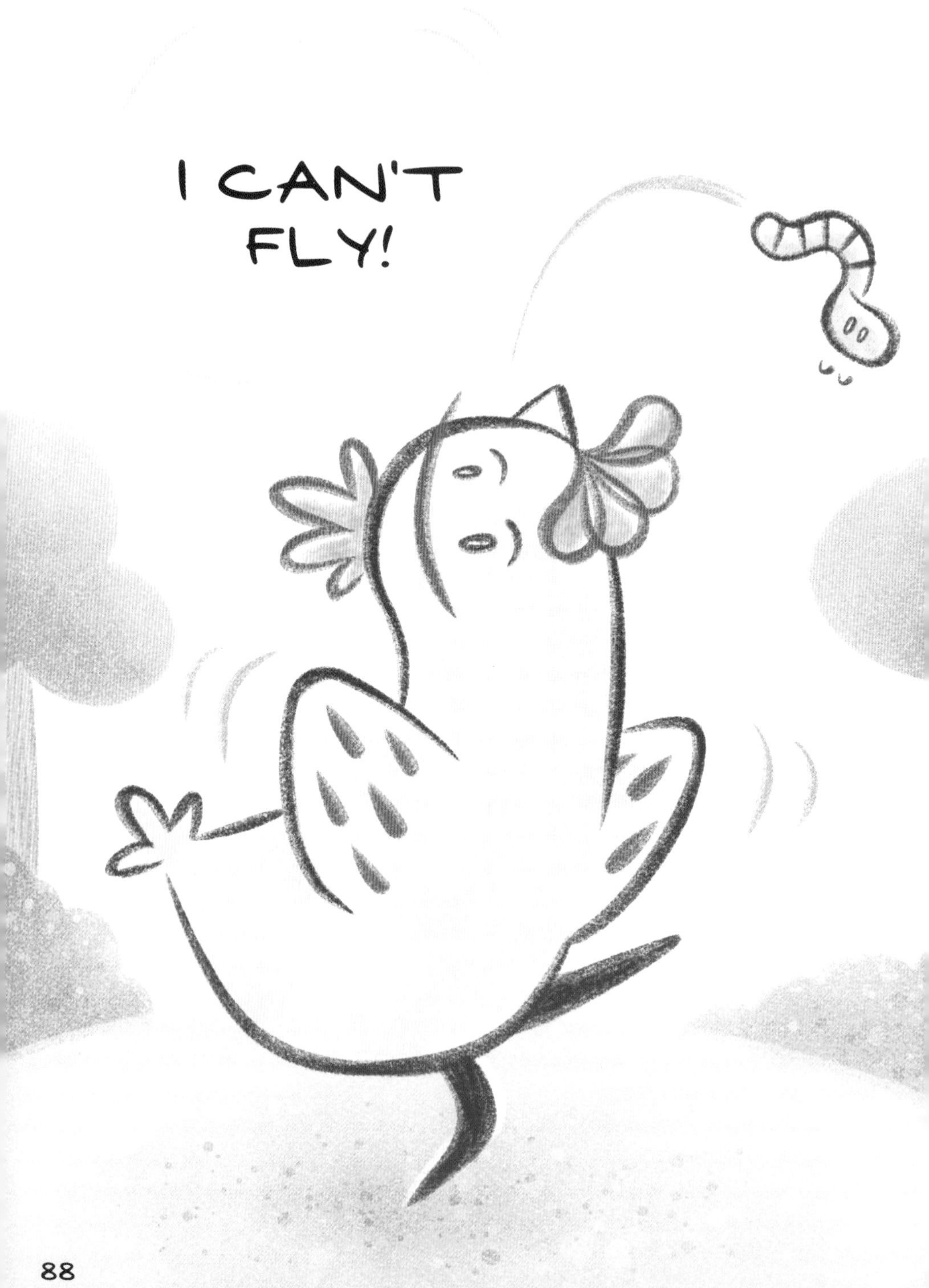
I CAN'T FLY!

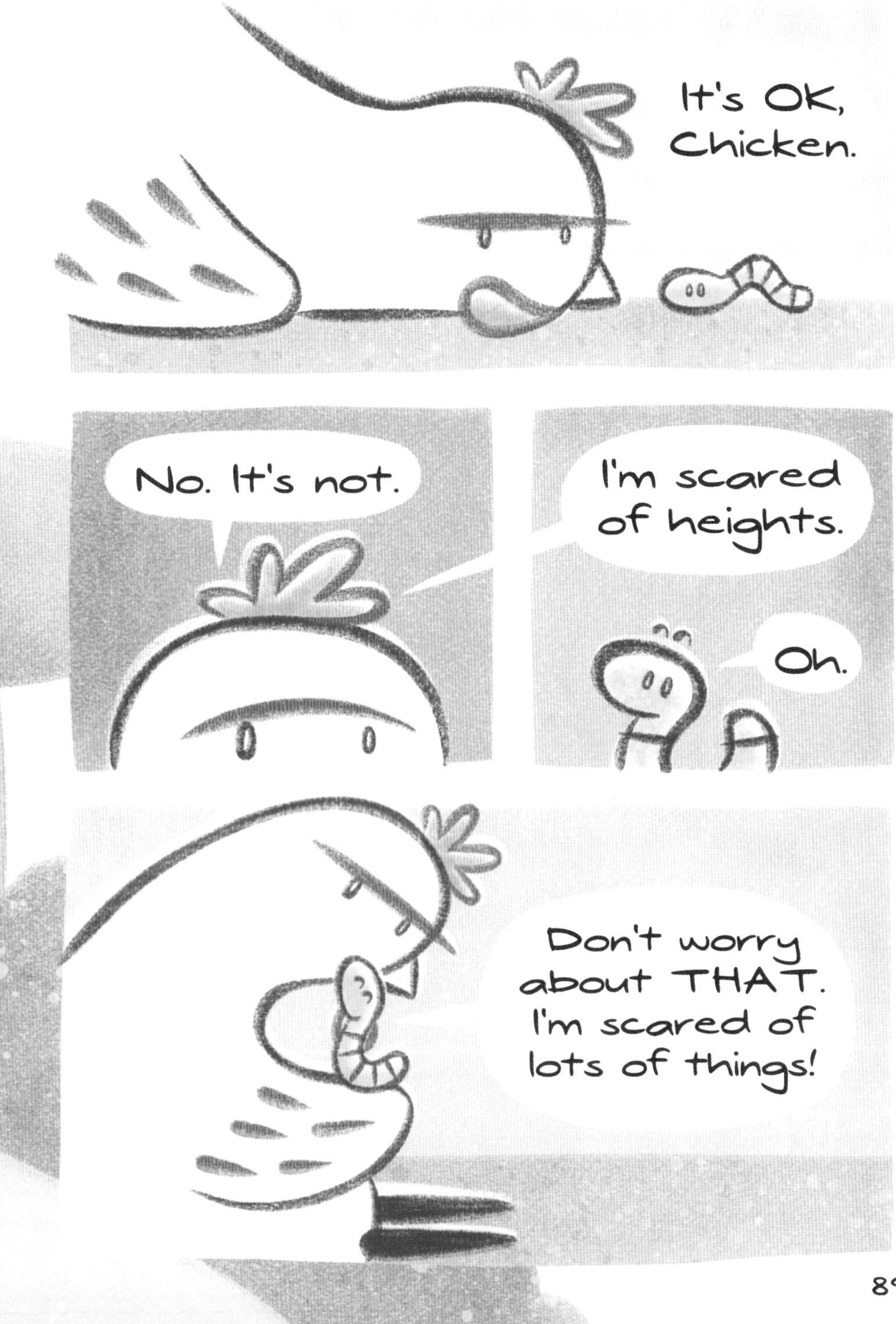
It's OK, Chicken.
No. It's not.
I'm scared of heights.
Oh.
Don't worry about THAT. I'm scared of lots of things!

Worm's Most FEARSOME Fears

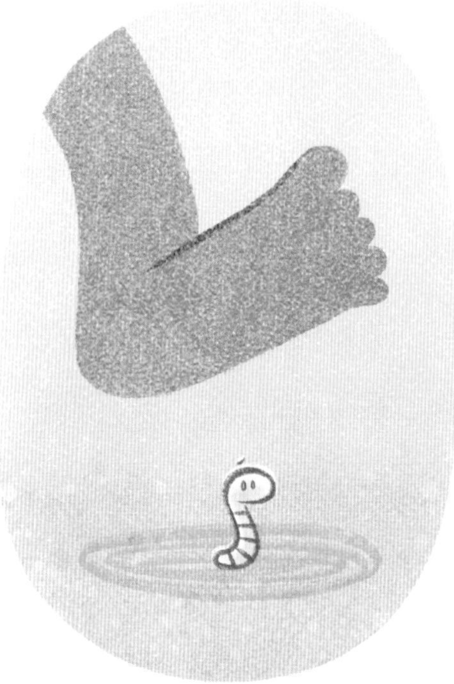

Feet

Scary movies

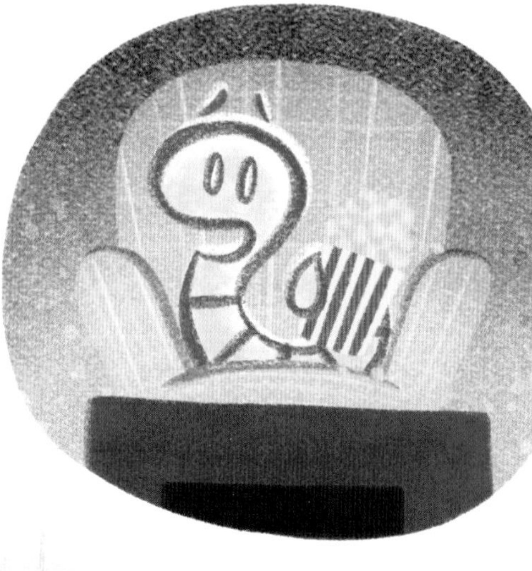

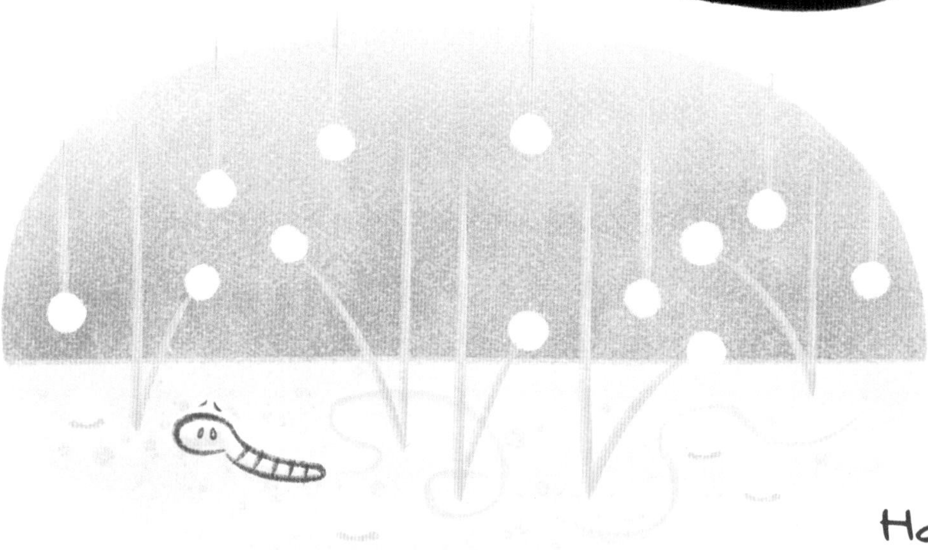

Hail

Autumn

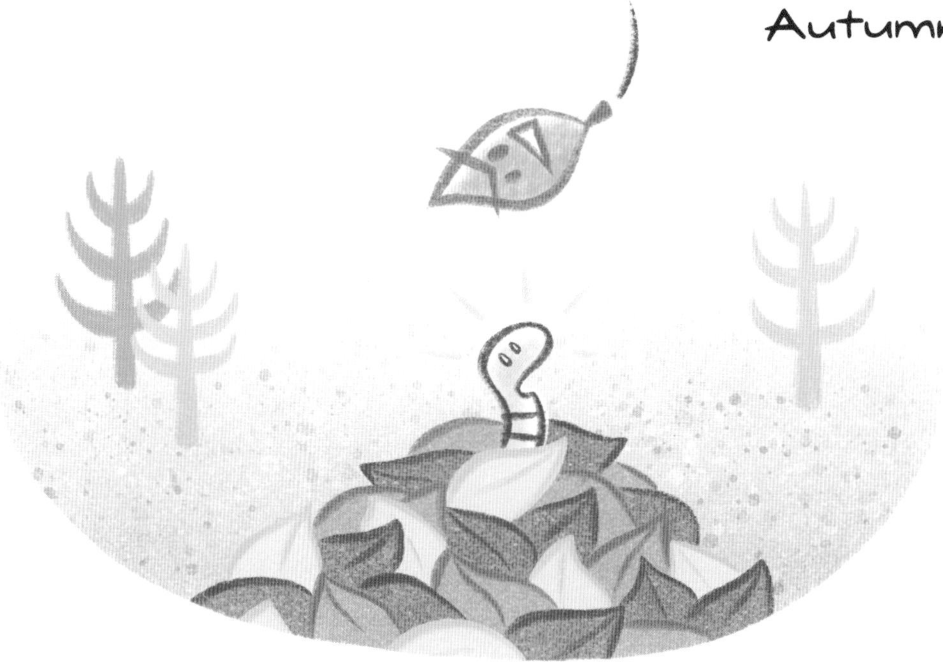

Bears

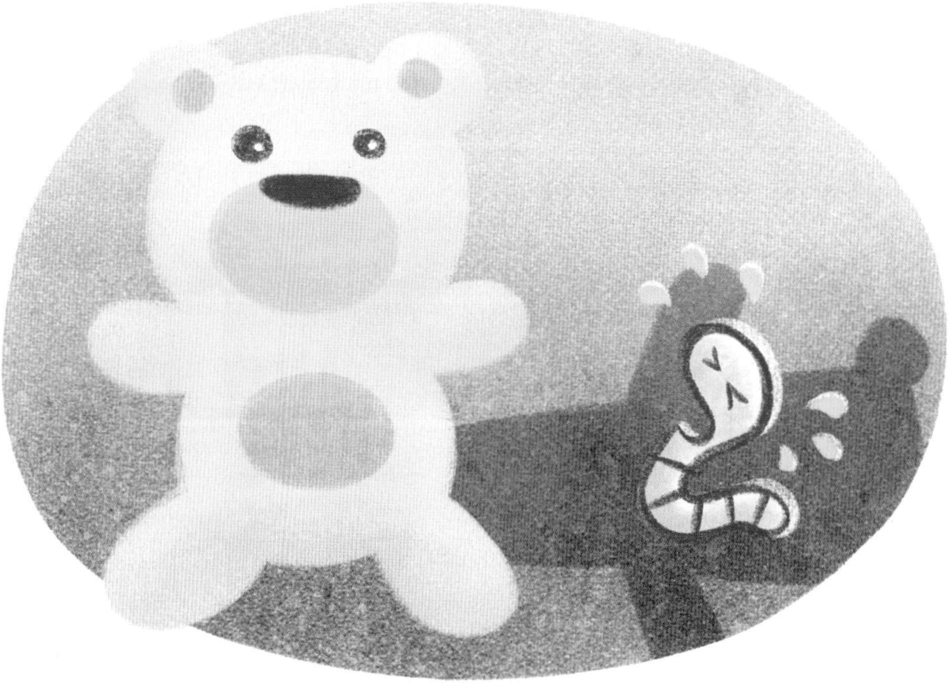

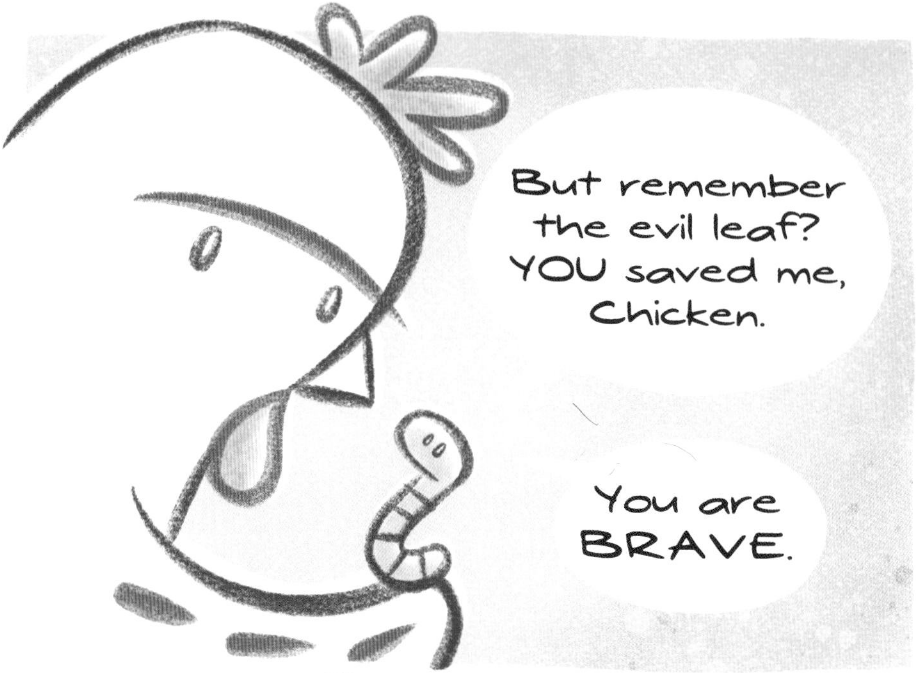
But remember the evil leaf? YOU saved me, Chicken.
You are BRAVE.

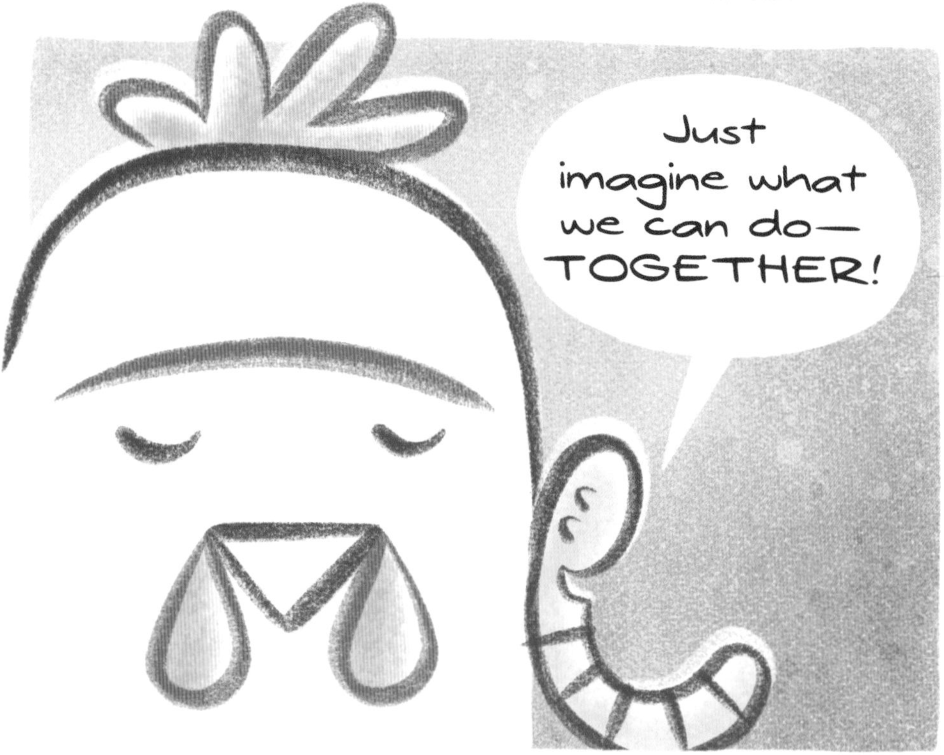
Just imagine what we can do—TOGETHER!

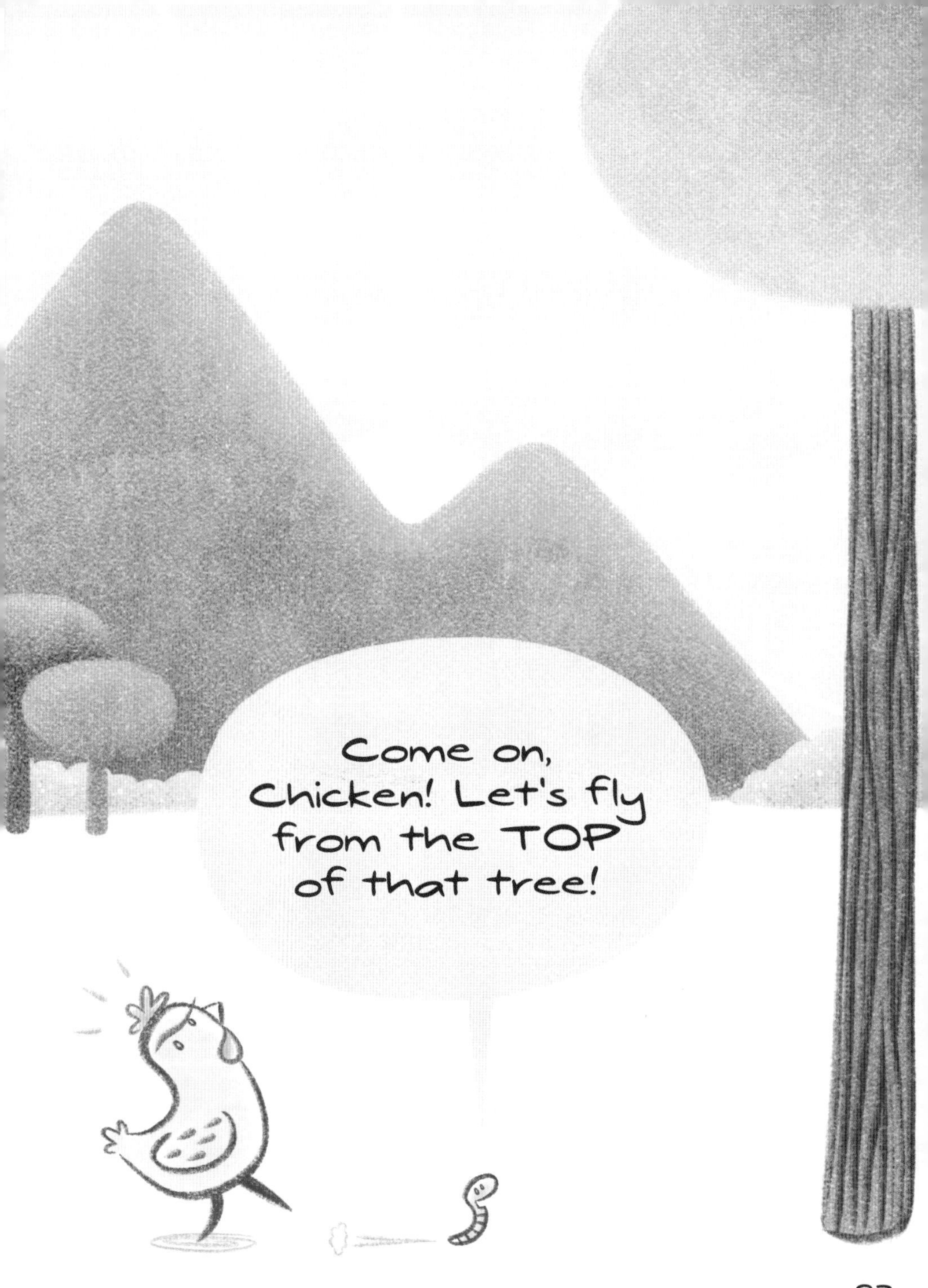
Come on, Chicken! Let's fly from the TOP of that tree!

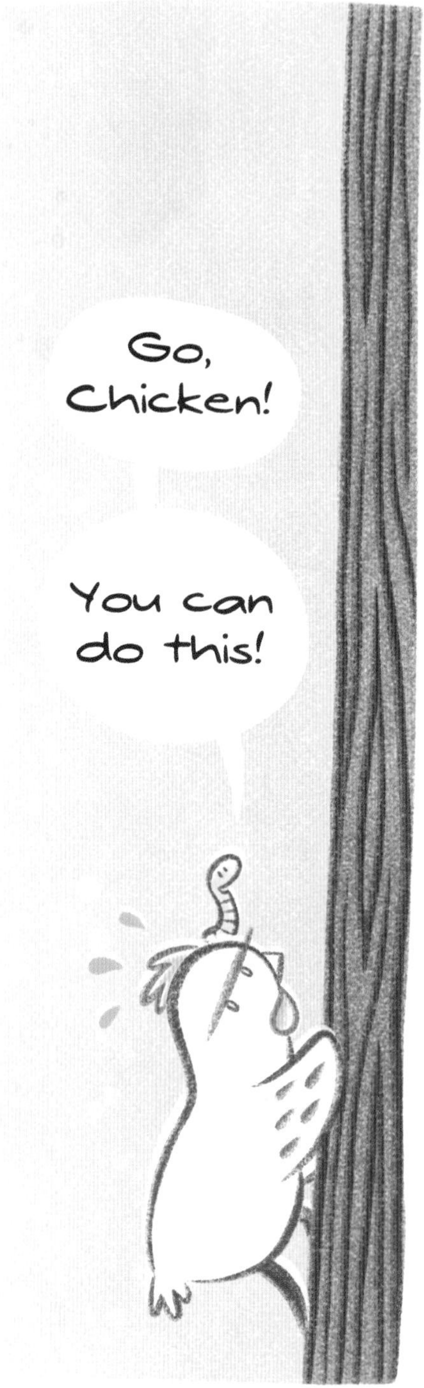
Go, Chicken!
You can do this!

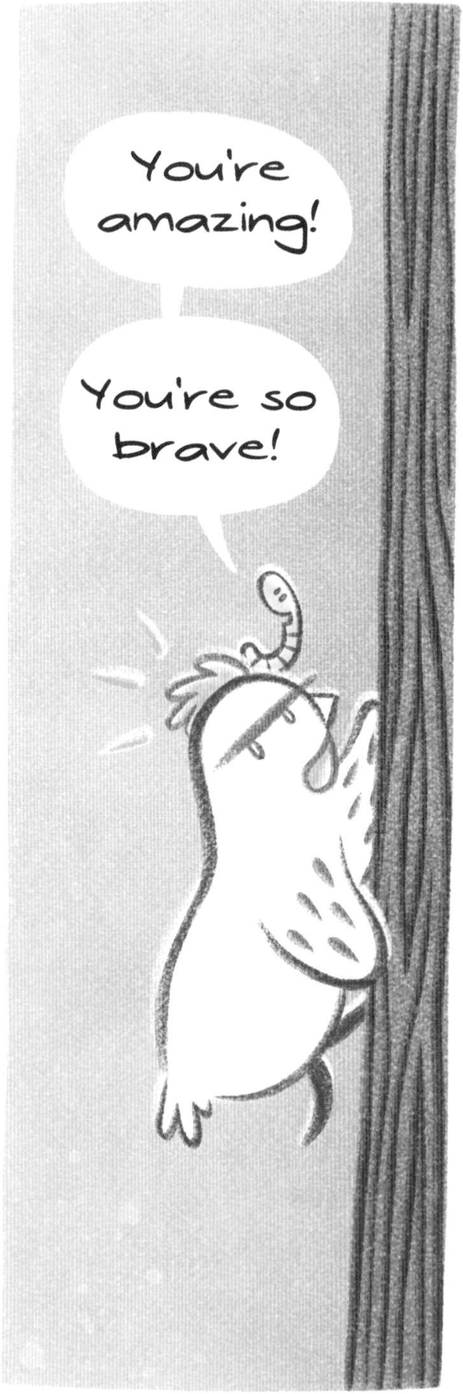
You're amazing!
You're so brave!

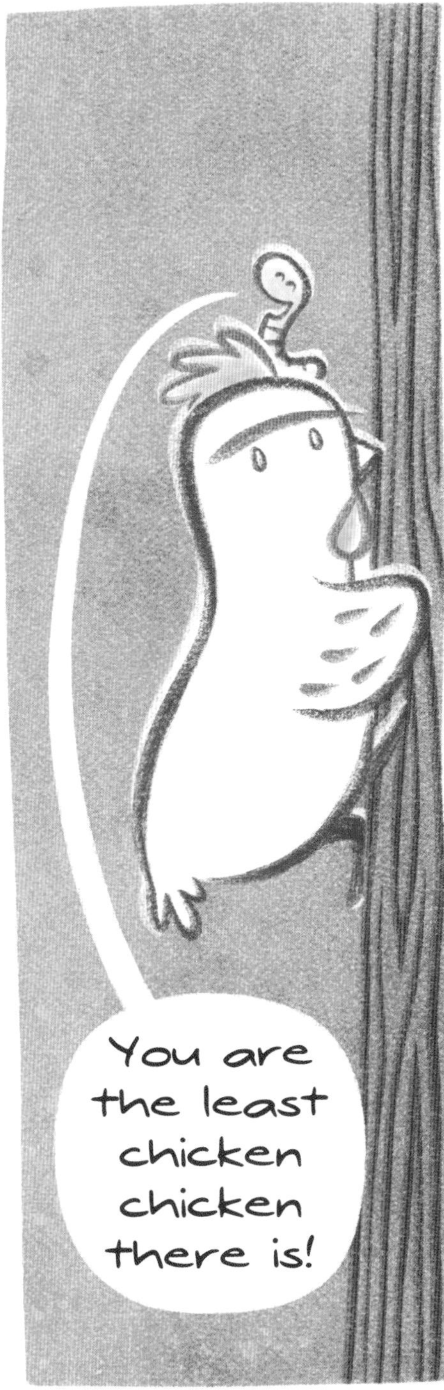
You are the least chicken chicken there is!

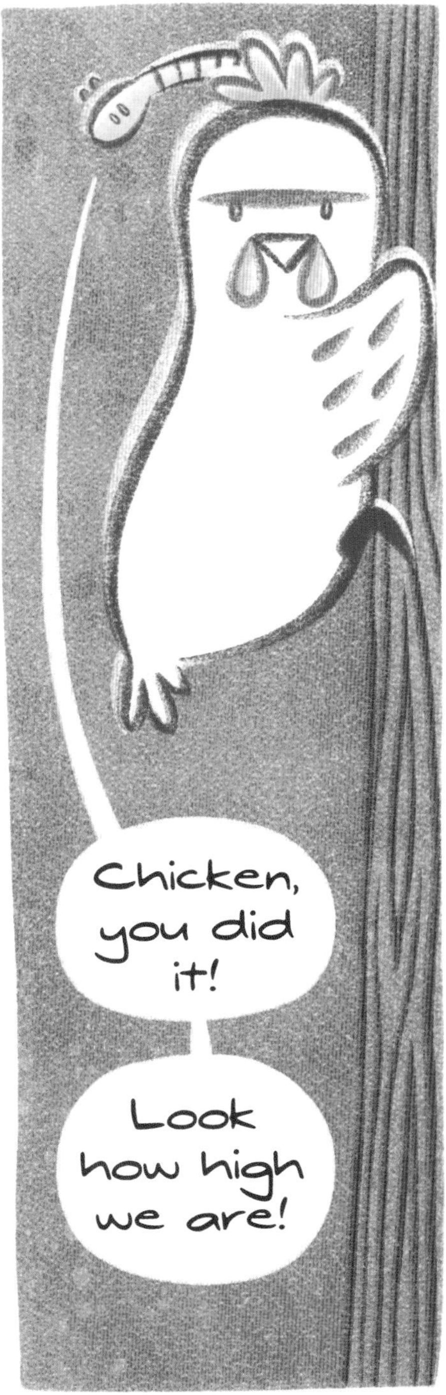
Chicken, you did it!
Look how high we are!

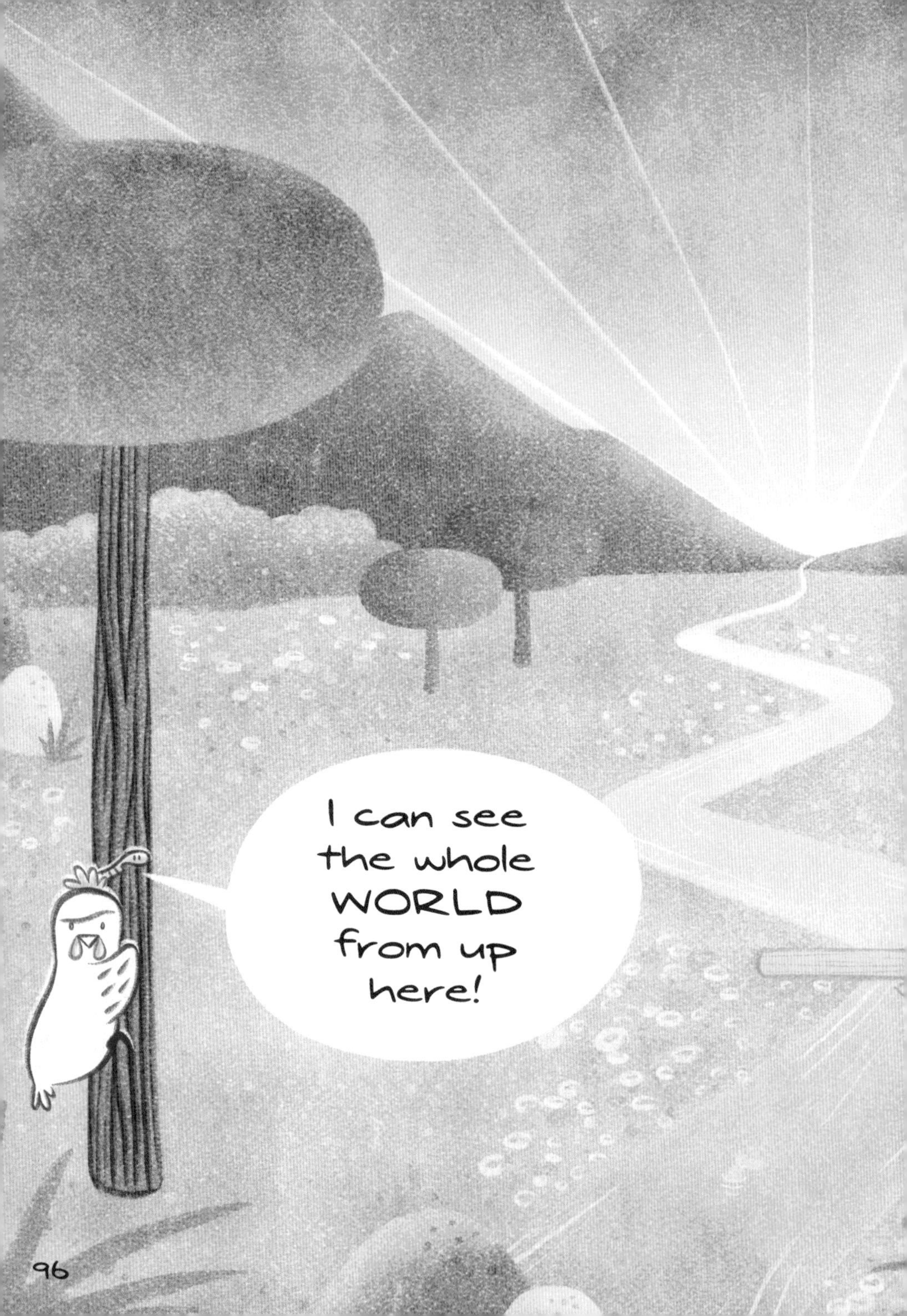
I can see the whole WORLD from up here!

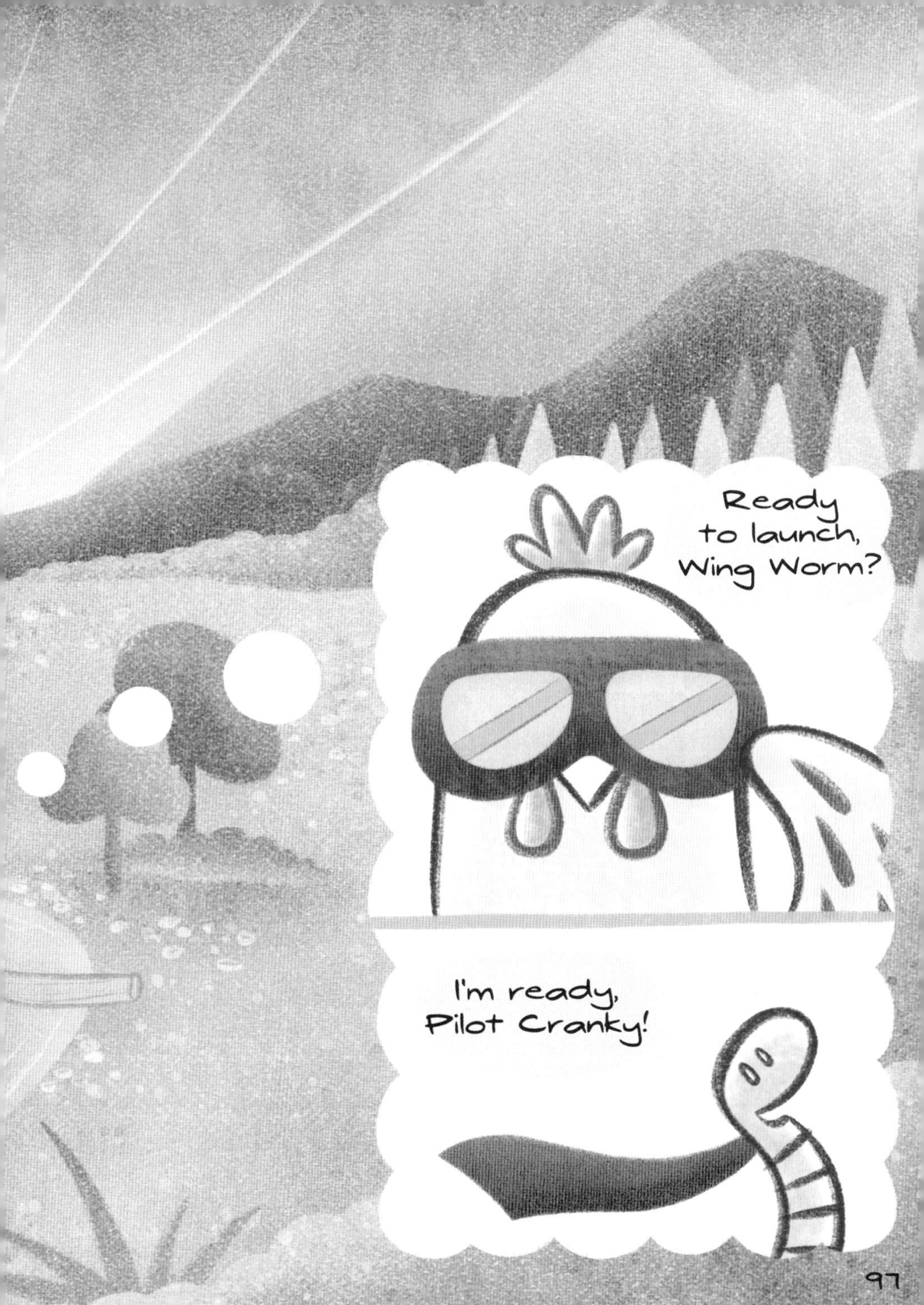
Ready to launch, Wing Worm?
I'm ready, Pilot Cranky!

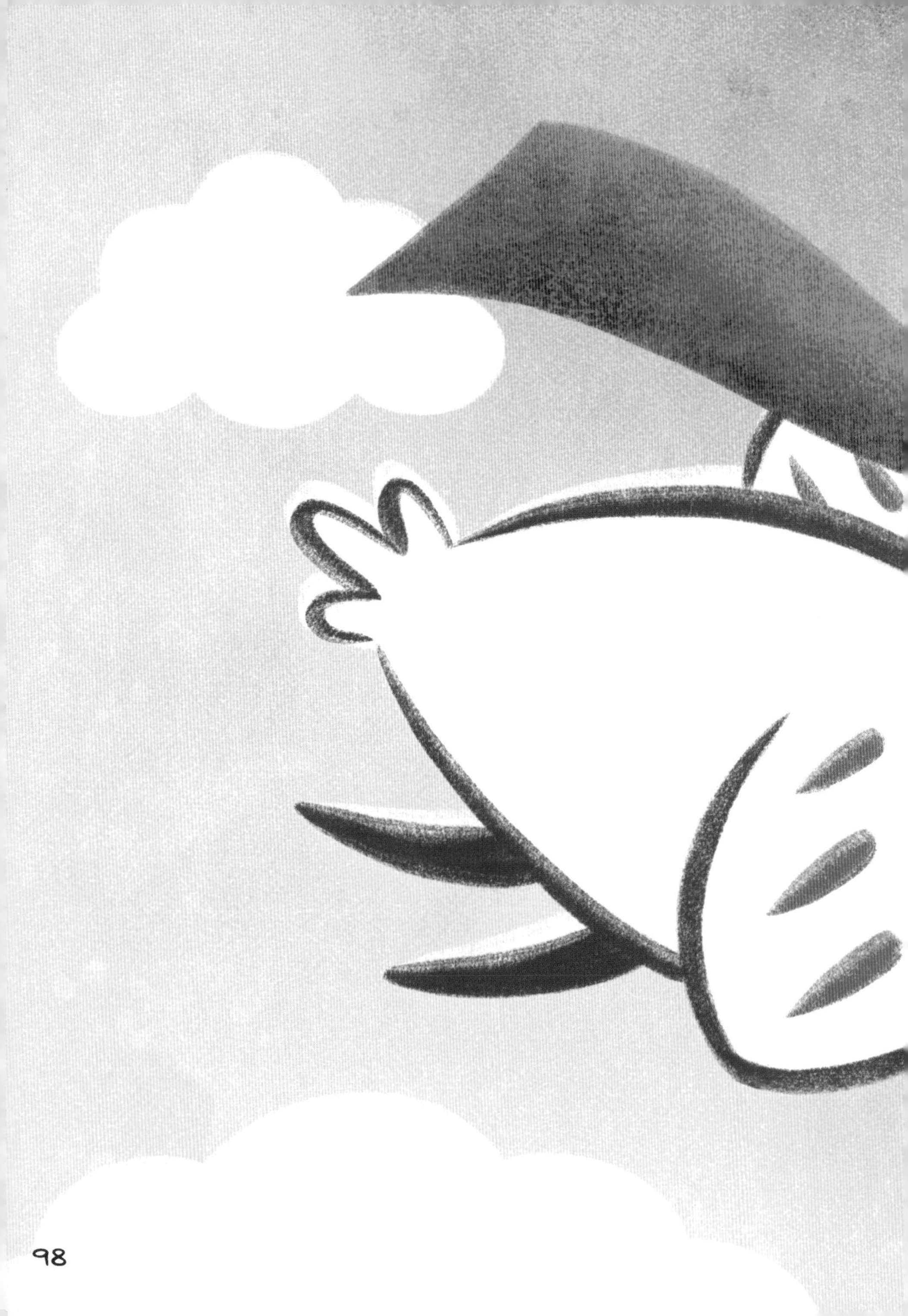

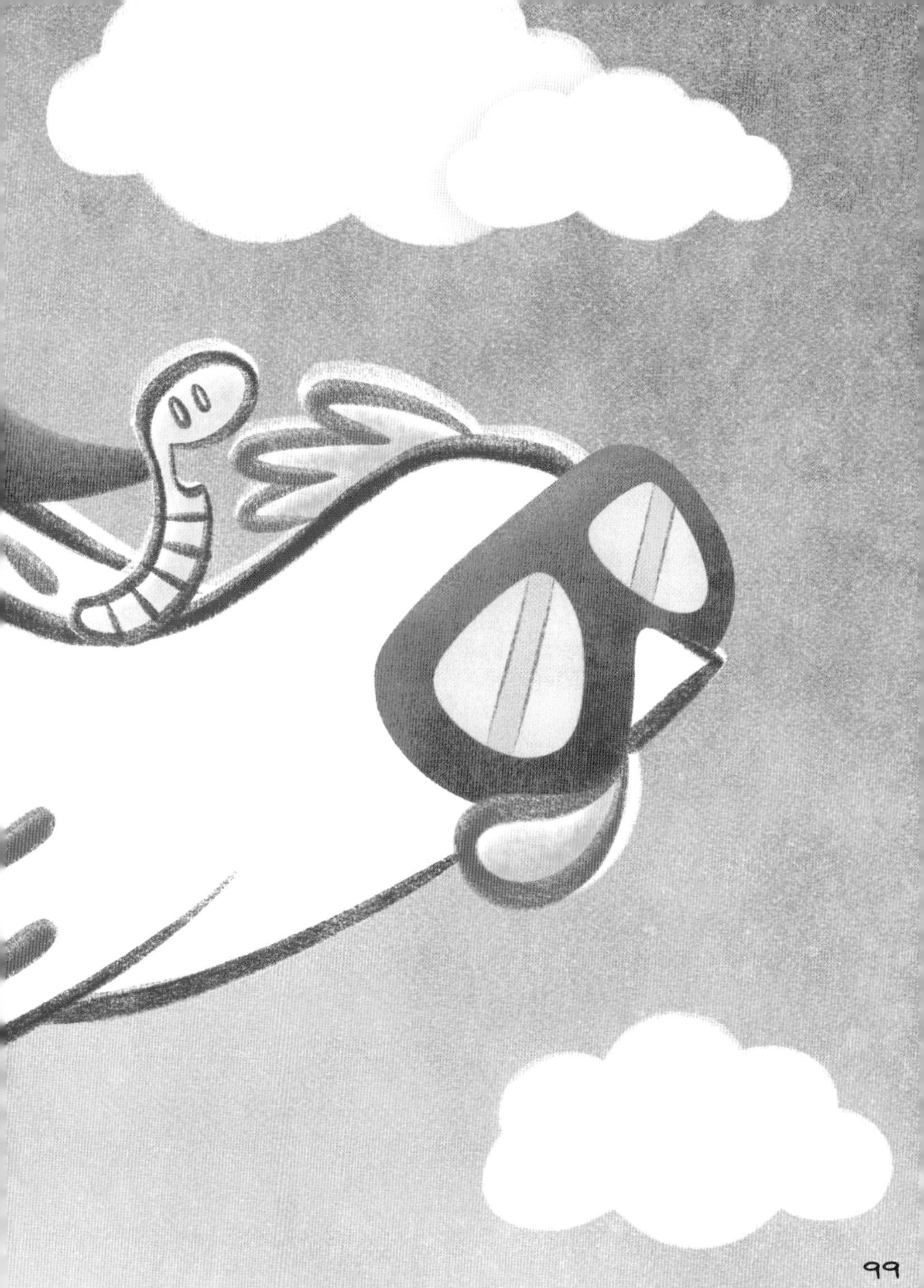

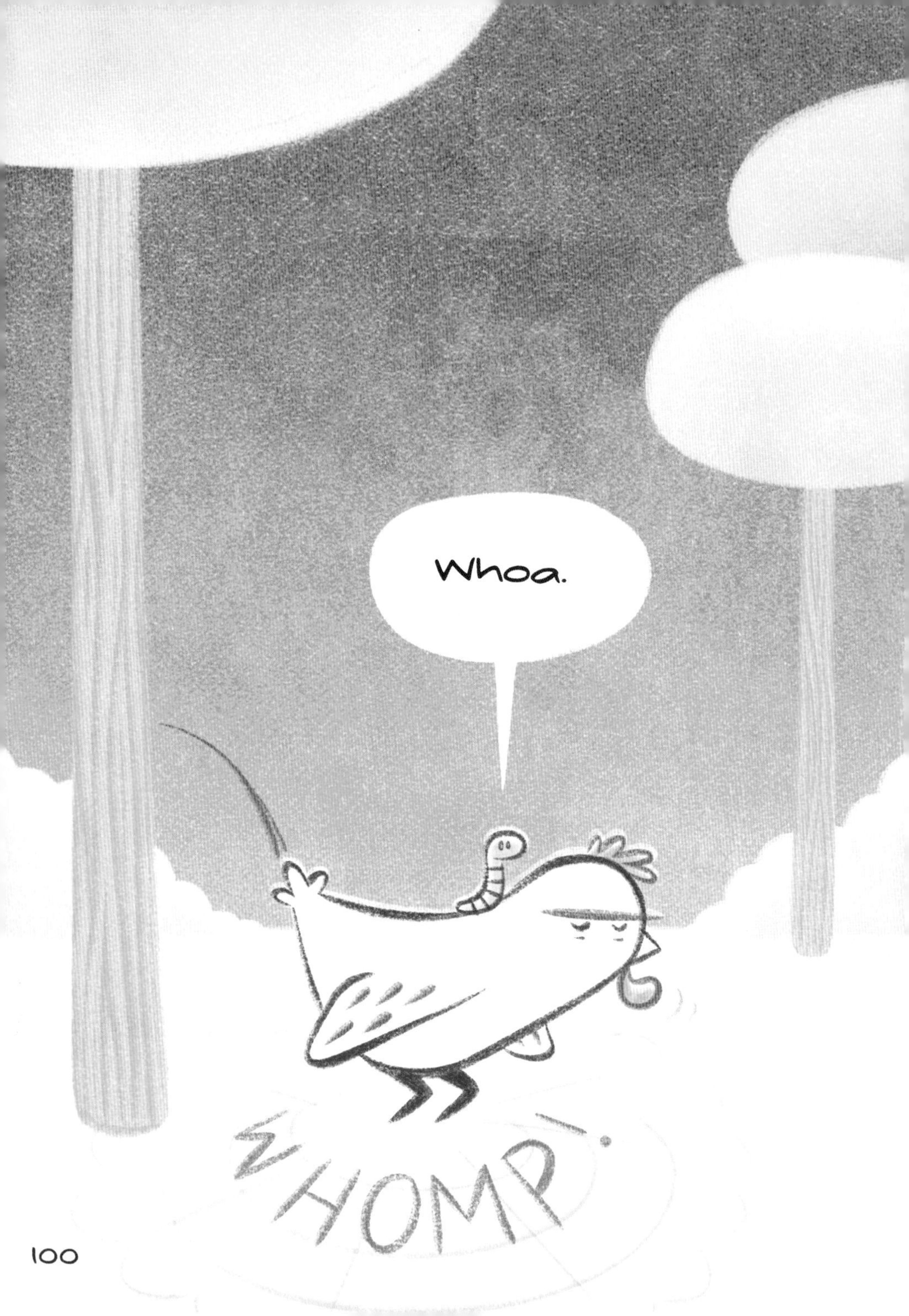
Whoa.
WHOMP!

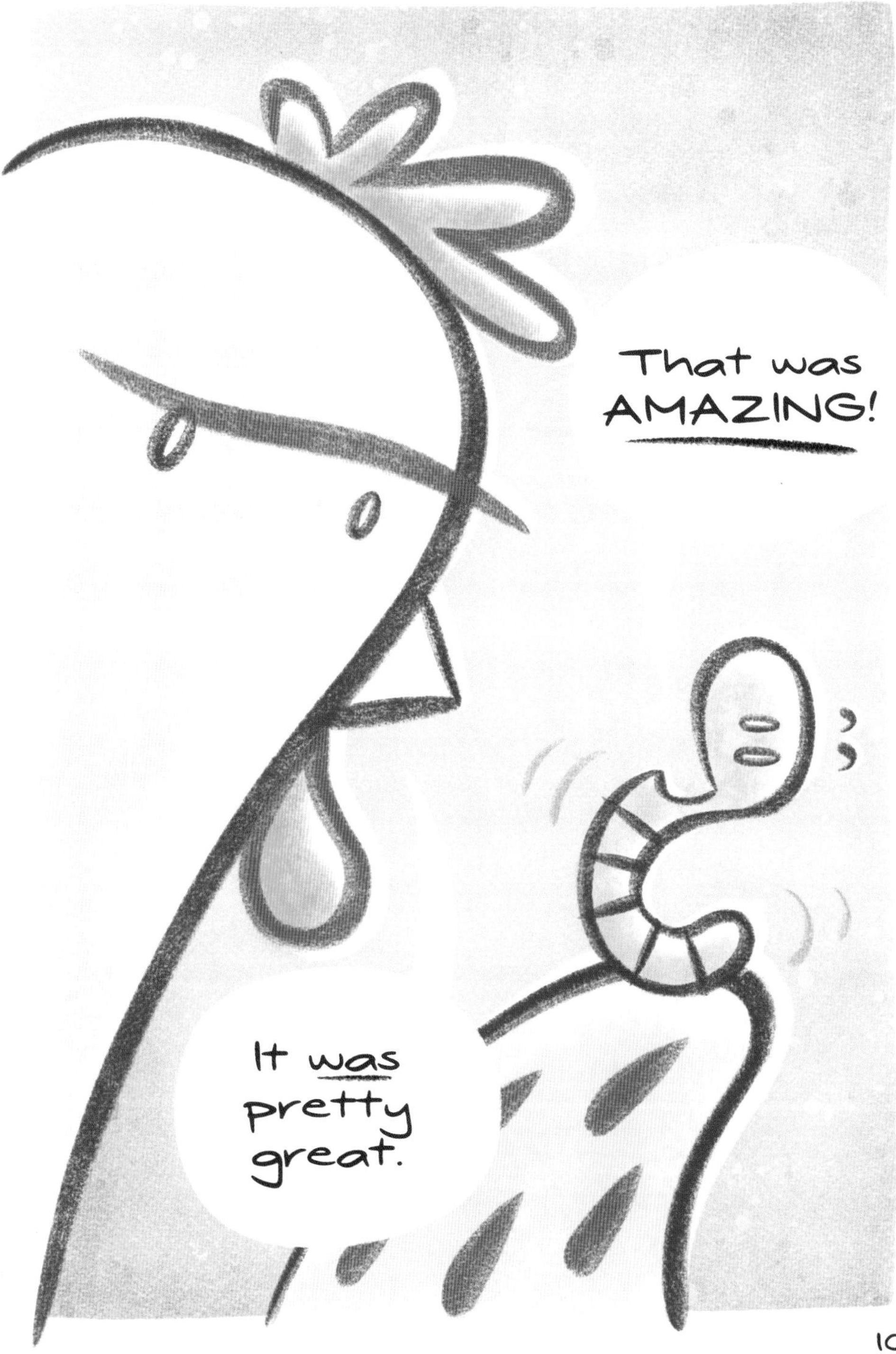
That was AMAZING!
It was pretty great.

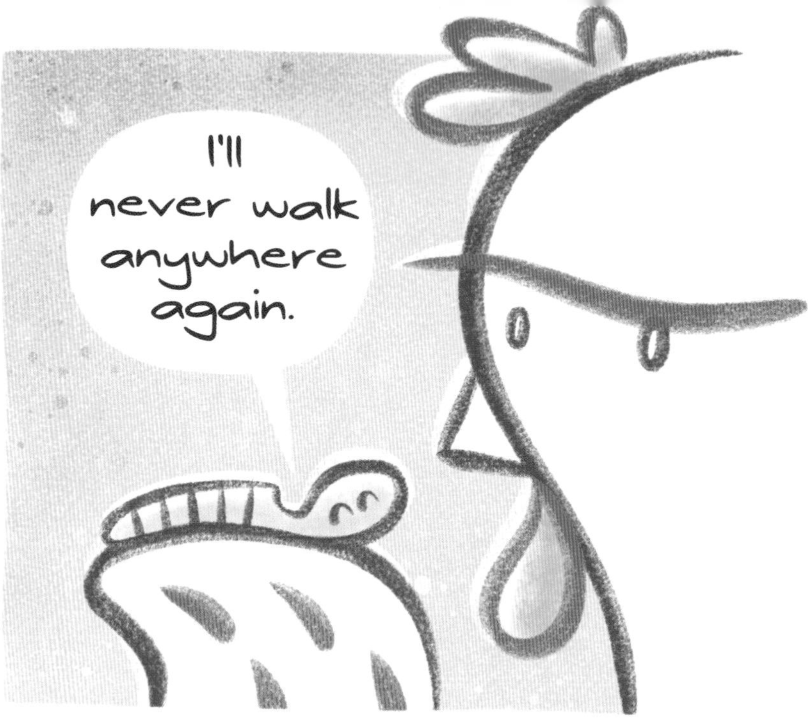
I'll never walk anywhere again.

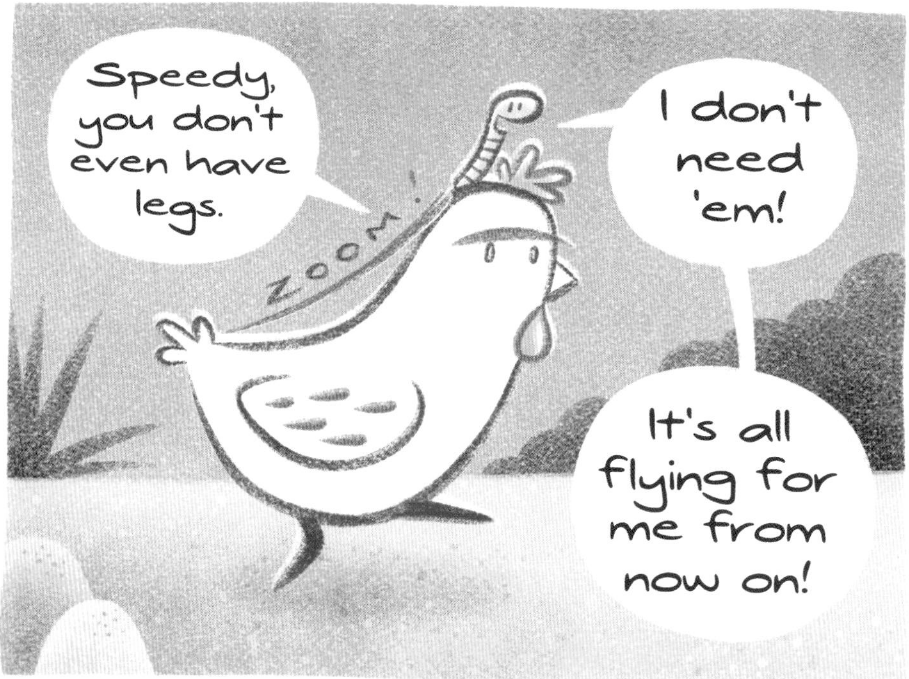
Speedy, you don't even have legs.
I don't need 'em!
ZOOM!
It's all flying for me from now on!

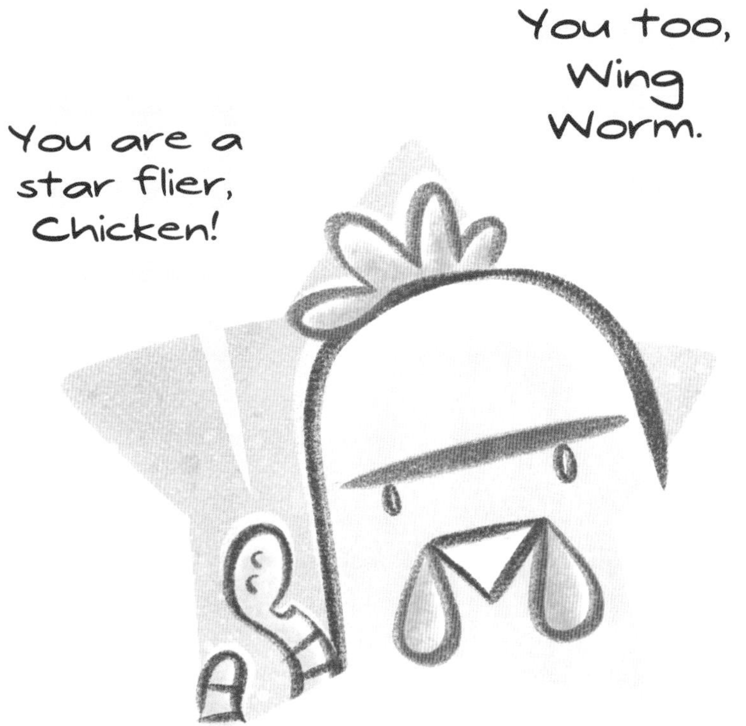
You too, Wing Worm.
You are a star flier, Chicken!

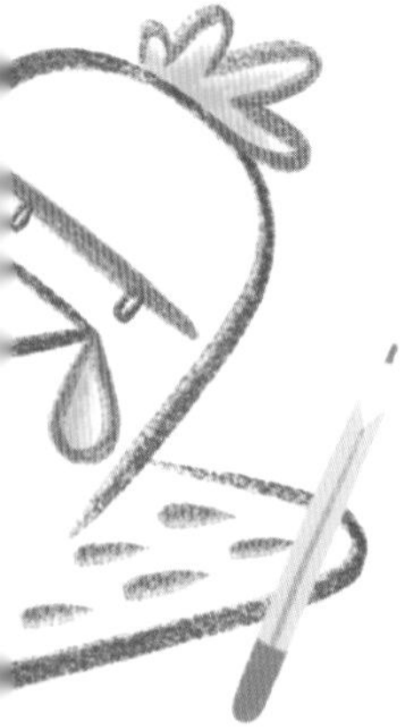

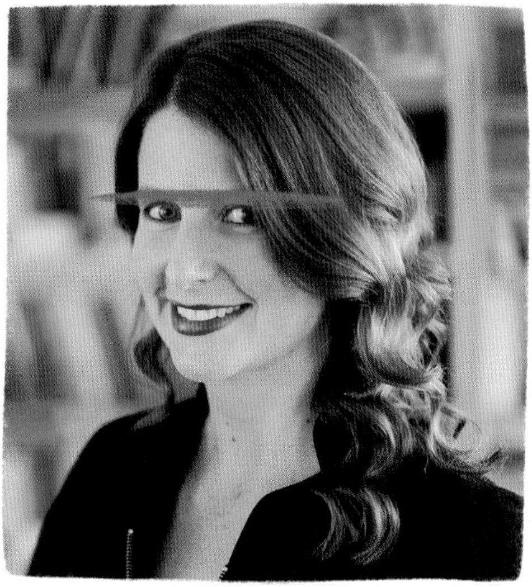

Katherine Battersby

is the critically acclaimed author and illustrator of a number of picture books, including *Perfect Pigeons* and *Squish Rabbit*, a CBC Children's Choice Book. Her books have received glowing reviews in the *New York Times* and starred reviews from *Kirkus* and have been shortlisted for numerous Australian awards. Katherine lives in Ottawa, Canada. Visit her at KatherineBattersby.com.

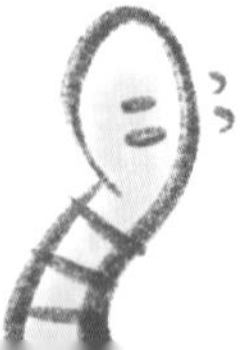

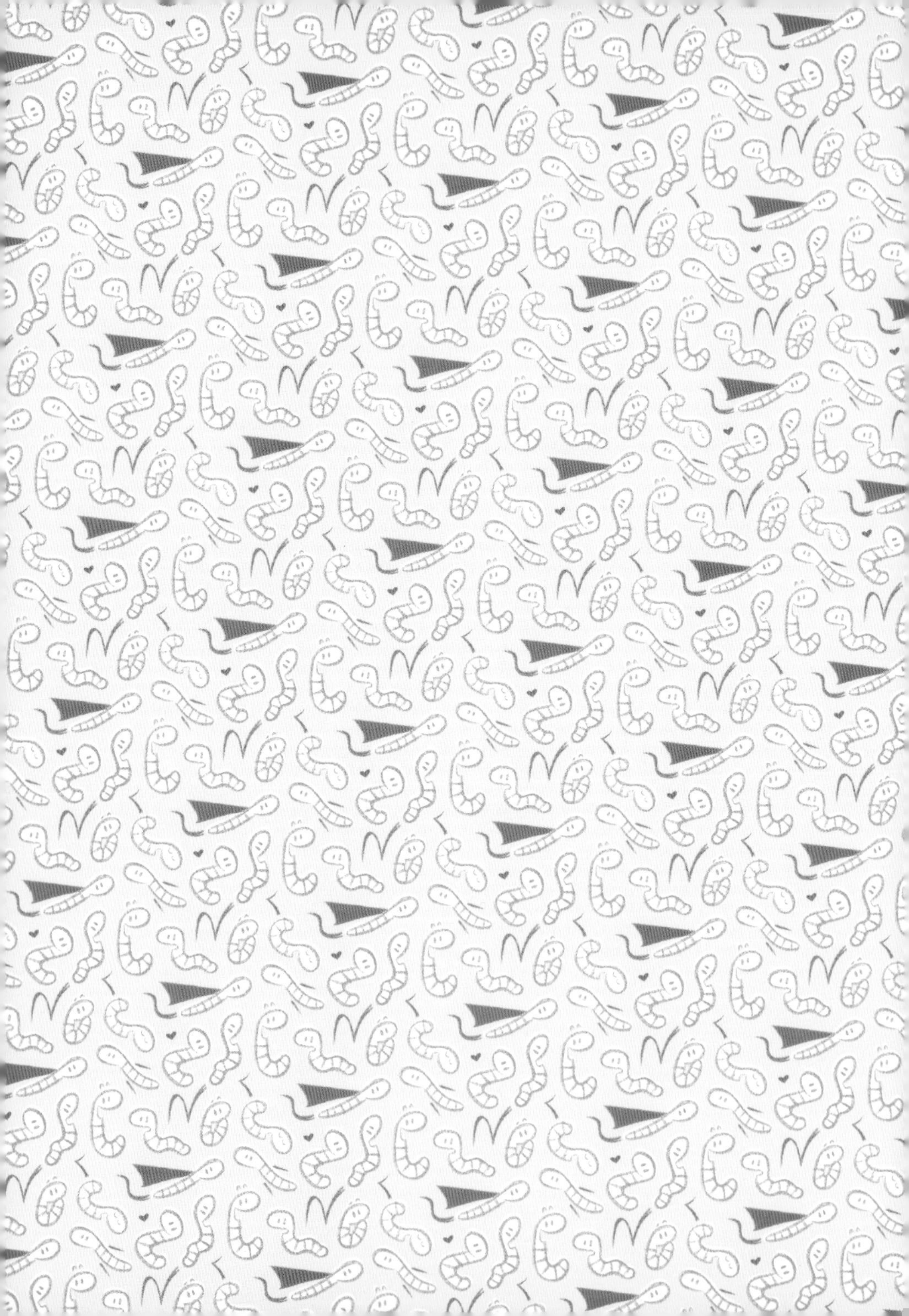

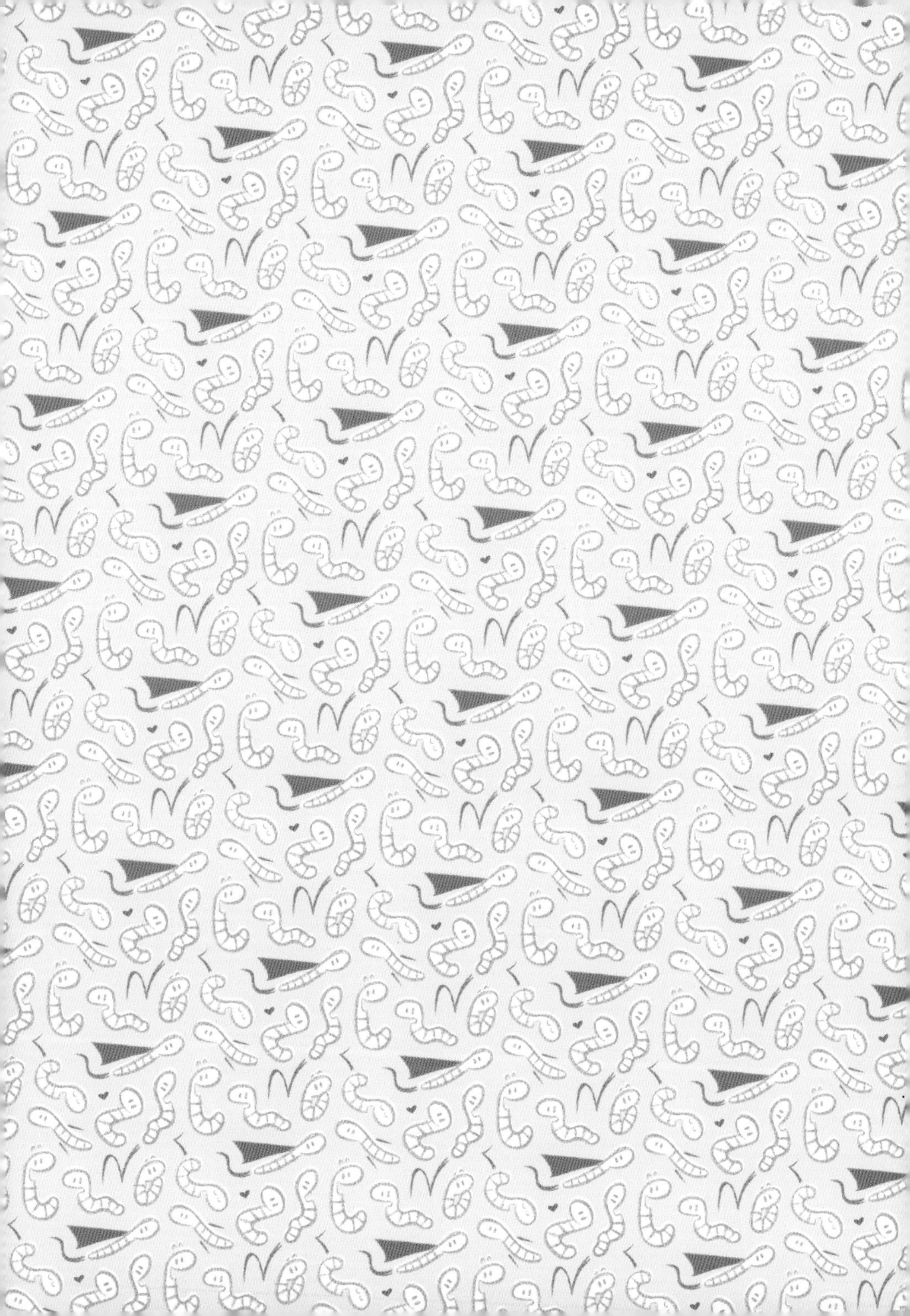